The SECRET Recipe for SECOND Chances

The SECRET Recipe for SECOND Chances

J.D. BARRETT

hachette
AUSTRALIA

hachette
AUSTRALIA

Published in Australia and New Zealand in 2016
by Hachette Australia
(an imprint of Hachette Australia Pty Limited)
Level 17, 207 Kent Street, Sydney NSW 2000
www.hachette.com.au

10 9 8 7 6 5 4 3 2 1

National Library of Australia
Cataloguing-in-Publication data

Barrett, J.D., author.
The secret recipe for second chances / JD Barrett.

ISBN 978 0 7336 3477 2 (pbk.)

Women cooks – Fiction.
Restaurateurs – Fiction.
Life change events – Fiction.
Domestic fiction.

A823 4

Cover design by Christabella Designs
Author photograph courtesy of Craig Peihopa
Text design by Bookhouse, Sydney
Typeset in 11.5/16 pt Sabon LT Pro by Bookhouse, Sydney
Printed and bound in Australia by Griffin Press, Adelaide, an Accredited ISO AS/NZS 14001:2009
Environmental Management System printer

For Charles and Eve Hughes
in honour of the meals we shared

1

Lucy

I'M NOT SURE IF THERE'S AN EXACT MEAL I COULD PINPOINT when I knew that Leith and I were done. Actually, yes I do, it was the roasted snapper stuffed with kaffir lime, ginger and lemongrass I baked in foil when we were on holiday up at Seal Rocks ... the one where we were meant to try to make up, to reconnect. He used a bone from the fish as a toothpick. Leith pretty much uses any device, accoutrement, item of clothing, menu or other inanimate object as a toothpick ... and as a result he has brilliantly healthy teeth.

Was it the fish or was it the creeping realisation that everything about his eating annoyed me: the clicking of his jaw, the loud swallowing, the way he shovelled peas on his fork? It was on that day I realised I was fantasising about raising the fork, dropping the peas over his head and slamming the prongs into the back of his hand.

I knew this wasn't yogic, wasn't kind, wasn't real, but the rush of it was what told me that there would be no reunion.

That and the fact that he had slept with three other women, two of whom were our staff.

Worse than any of these crimes is the simple truth that he doesn't believe in meal sharing. How did I marry someone – a fellow chef, of all people – who refuses to share food? To Leith it is always the competition of who ordered the better meal, salad combination or smoothie. With him, there is no harmony in a bowl of pasta, or anything else.

I don't want to take myself to the 'What was I thinking?' place – my best friend and my mother are filling that space already – because I did love him, and we were good together for a time.

We created Circa together, a restaurant that has become the go-to destination for middle-aged yuppies in search of marital distraction via the bells and whistles of the expensively printed menus and pandering service.

I wonder how many of the meals we served actually saved people's lives with their sheer ability to distract – *Stop looking at your heartbreak; the chicken is on fire on a tray and it's being carried to the table*. A fair few, I expect. Circa has also become the place cashed-up international hipsters visit for a memorable proposal; 'He proposed to her at Circa, Sydney's celebrated exclusive three-hatted restaurant' is a common sentence in the *New York Times* marriage announcements. I would say there's a sweet irony in the number of hours I have spent over the past three years baking cakes, soufflés, preparing soups and salads in which engagement rings are elegantly and expertly concealed (no swallowers yet – the dish concealing the ring is rarely eaten, everyone is too busy photographing it) while my own marriage was terminally ill.

The majority of the proposers opt for a ring passed gently across the table, a few do the entire bended-knee spiel; always just before dessert, and so the rate of consumption of perfectly prepared panna cotta, brûlée, or other creamy buttery concoction coming out of the kitchen is next to zip when this occurs. The benders always make me nervous, not just for fear of waiters tripping into or over them, but also because there's something slightly desperate, not to mention foolhardy, about getting down on bended knee in a busy restaurant. I mean, what if the answer is no?

Anyway, we – the restaurant industry – seem to be the destination for romance. Don't get me started on Valentine's Day, officially the most gruelling, disillusioning and thankless day for restaurateurs and florists globally. It is ironic, as well as painful, humiliating and just plain shitty, that together Leith and I created the beacon of love in restaurants while crippling and eventually killing our marriage.

Julia, my best friend, says her marriage to Ken is akin to her mother's roast chook: slightly dried out, not that hot, but still comforting, filling and the thing you look forward to all week. My mother has never cooked a roast – too pedestrian, and at odds with her vegetarian hippy thing. Her culinary pursuits have always involved tofu, prepared in a way that renders it inedible: microwaved tofu, Swiss-cooked tofu, and her out-and-out weirdest, tofu boobies (two slices of Golden Circle tinned pineapple topped with two small circles of fried soggy tofu and finished with a dollop of oyster sauce). My mother's cooking could make you lose the will to live, but she is nothing if not experimental. She raised me in a commune, where she was often described as a culinary rebel and an enthusiastic food anarchist. Each accolade sounds more impressive than it is. In reality it meant she rarely had to cook and I spent giant chunks of the year counting down to my holidays in the tiny coastal town of Manyana with my grandparents, who served me food – actual food; glorious, real, homemade food like savoury mince with mashed potatoes and fresh beans, fish pie with cream and fresh scallops, roasted rack of lamb with Grandad's mint sauce with mint picked fresh from the garden and slivered, mixed with vinegar, a dash of sugar and water. I would dream about Grandma's apple pie and write her letters about it; getting her to send me the recipe and practising with her during holidays so when I got back to the heat and horribleness of the commune I could re-create some sense of what I knew home should be. Mum took it as a slight.

The commune was near Casino in northern New South Wales. It was run by the superstar Guru – or Bhagwan – of the time, and everyone wore orange and various shades of pink. It was supposed to be some kind of utopia but it was hot and hellish – full of flies, spiritual junkies and academic drop-outs who thought they would find enlightenment via multiple sexual partners. Because most nights for the adults consisted of satsang followed by pot and acid and love-ins, we kids were pretty much left to our own devices. We used to steal away and hang out at a neighbouring cattle farm discussing hamburgers that we would sometimes hitch our way into town to buy and eat. Cradling the greasy paper with egg and meat fat seeping through barbecue sauce and a toasted bun, we would line up in front of the public phone and take turns calling people from the other side – that is, anyone who wasn't being subjected to life on the commune. I guess food has always been my saviour. And in some ways it's a form of rebellion against Mum, who is about to have the last laugh.

After living with Leith in a beautiful Elizabeth Bay apartment with harbour views for the past seven years, five of them married, my only option is to move in to Mum's two-bedroom dive in Glebe with no job, no savings, no property and no real prospects.

You know how they say to be careful of epiphanies? ('They' being the people who have obviously been through one and been spat out the other side.) Well, I wish one of them had got to me to warn me before I had mine.

It came after realising I wanted to stab Leith with a fork. 'Get out. Now!' screamed the voices of my ancestors through my veins. As soon as we got back from the holiday from hell I began to demonstrate the behaviours of an epiphany-reacher: relentless daydreaming, journal-writing, vision-boarding, googling properties I could never afford, and driving around looking for . . . what, exactly? Peace? Answers? So far all I know is that my only way out of this, my only salvation, will once again be food.

The drives usually end up at Harry's Café de Wheels and the answers take the form of a chilli dog eaten while I sit and watch the naval base and the colourful array of residents, staff and patrons who now live, work and play in the huge long building that was once the woolshed. Usually a part of the chilli dog ends up on my clothing, but in terms of providing answers it is helpful. From there I begin to drive around Woolloomooloo and Potts Point, perusing the streets that have managed to hang on to their bohemian roots – the streets the property developers and the yuppies haven't taken possession of, mainly due to their heritage listing.

Potts Point is a funny place – it's as if a great divide occurs at the fountain on Macleay Street where it merges into Darlinghurst Road; regardless of multiple attempts, some force larger than the street itself ensures that anything to the south of it will remain sleazy, but to the north, florists, gourmet butchers and designer shoe shops flourish, as well as dog-grooming and leash-buying temples and gourmet-cheese businesses. If you keep heading north, the age of the residents hikes, as do the incomes; gracious art-deco buildings house famous actors, obstetricians and their well-heeled PR wives, beautiful men and many an excellent coffee house. The lattes and meals around this nook are superb. The rents for restaurants are also way out of my price range, but if you keep walking back down towards Woolloomooloo (possibly the best word ever – apparently its origins lie in the Aboriginal name for 'place of plenty'), plenty of everything appears: it's a mix, which I love, of lowbrow and upmarket, scruffy public housing alongside sleek Lycra-clad cyclists who toil their red-faced way back up the hill. The side streets possess a number of abandoned terraces, still looking like they have a closer relationship to their working-class origins than to the gentrification going on just a few streets up.

And it's here that I find it. In one of the few streets without views to the sapphire harbour or the former bat-loving gardens. A tiny neglected cul-de-sac that few people would like to park in. There on the corner stands a faded, ramshackle, once-loved, free-standing single-storey terrace that long ago was painted pink but over the years has revealed its undercoat of grey with bits flaking off it like an elderly aunt's powdered nose. I park the ute, my grandad's old pride and joy, get out and look around. I apologise for sounding like a hippy – trust me, I know how irritating that is – but the place feels lonely, and an almost audible sigh falls from it as I touch the front door. I peer in through a filthy front window with panels of chipboard nailed to it; I wonder if perhaps there are squatters in residence, but instead I see a dark, long-deserted front room filled with empty tables and chairs . . . a restaurant! The chances of an out-of-work, soon-to-be-homeless, heartbroken chef finding an old abandoned restaurant are about as likely as a single straight woman over thirty living in the eastern suburbs of Sydney finding a husband.

I attempt to look further in but can't see much more than the tables and chairs, circa 1970-something, sitting unused and uncleaned. Several salt-and-pepper shakers are strewn along the tables at illogical intervals and the occasional single-bud ceramic vase is visible. I walk around the side of the building, which seems to be a collection point for urine from dogs, homeless roamers and late-night revellers on the bad side of a wrong turn. There's only one side window and it's too high for me to get a view, so I grab a nearby wheelie bin in lieu of a ladder. I am not known for my athletic prowess, but I clamber up, wobble, then stand and peer in. It's definitely a restaurant. A huge gas oven dominates the kitchen space, and appliances from the eighties remain in place from the last meals the restaurant served. Work benches, warmers, fridge.

Excitement is gathering within me when a homeless man appears and screams at me for moving the bin, then stops when he sees the carnage of the chilli dog that has fallen all over my white blouse; he reconsiders me for a moment and then asks me for a cigarette. All I have are two squares of a bar of Cadbury Dairy Milk chocolate, which I offer him and he takes suspiciously.

I ask him about the restaurant, but he merely laughs, makes a clucking sound and tells me to put the bin back where I found it – and warns me that the odds of getting a parking fine are high. I obediently replace the bin, and get back in my ute.

I begin a frenetic online search for more information on the house, then catch sight of myself in the rear-vision mirror. I look like a mad woman, my blonde hair matted and bits of tomato sauce on my face. The sun is setting and Leith will be opening our restaurant to our customers . . . I think of Julia, who would tell me to catch my breath and take a reality check. I know I won't listen to her; it's too late – you can't put an epiphany in reverse.

I drive back to the apartment I share with Leith, load my ute with my life and move into Mum's.

Chilli Dogs

Ingredients

Chilli

2 tablespoons olive oil, plus extra, for brushing
500 grams minced beef
½ teaspoon smoked paprika
1 brown onion, finely chopped
2 cloves garlic, finely chopped
2 tablespoons tomato paste
1 teaspoon Worcestershire sauce
1 red bird's-eye chilli, seeded and finely chopped, or 2 teaspoons
   chilli powder or ½ teaspoon chilli flakes
400-gram tin chopped tomatoes
salt, to season

Hot dogs

6 hot dog frankfurters
6 hot dog buns, halved
sour cream
grated cheese (I use a sharp one)

Method

To make the chilli, heat the oil in a saucepan over medium heat. Add the mince, stirring continuously with a wooden spoon to make sure it breaks up evenly. Keep going until it's flattened out and browned, releasing its juice. Add the paprika, onion and garlic, and cook, stirring until the onion starts to soften. Add the tomato paste, Worcestershire sauce and chilli, and stir to combine. Finally, add the tomatoes and simmer on a low heat, stirring occasionally, for half an hour or until the sauce is thickened. Season with salt.

Preheat a chargrill pan over medium heat. Halve the hot dogs lengthwise, not quite cutting all the way through, and brush the cut surface with a little extra oil. Cook each side until it crisps and heats through. Alternatively, boil in a saucepan of water for 5 minutes and drain.

Place the hot dogs in buns. Spoon over the chilli, sour cream and grated cheese.

Alternatively, head down to Harry's Café de Wheels at sunset, bring a bottle of champagne and numerous napkins. Order, receive – sit and enjoy.

2

I CAN'T SAY MUM IS BESIDE HERSELF TO SEE ME – BUT AT LEAST she's awake.

'I've left Leith.'

'About time.'

'He wasn't faithful.'

'Who is?' Her gaze doesn't shift from the gigantic TV screen set up in pride of place beside her other altar – her puja.

My mother isn't big on monogamy – her time at the commune ensured that – and over the past few years, after a very full romantic life and numerous hopeless boyfriends, she has decided to stick to her cat, her television shows and the 'medications' she makes me bake for her. All this from the woman who once upon a time was a debutante, admitted into several art schools, and the most beautiful woman in her hometown of Manyana. Admittedly Manyana only possessed a population of 798, but when she was young she was a stunner: olive skin, green eyes, a beautiful laugh and the power to make men want to perform all sorts of bizarre feats for her, much to my grandparents' despair. I guess Mum felt that this was her best career path – getting guys to do stuff and buy things for her. Apart from an abandoned apprenticeship in jewellery making, she's never really worked in a normal job, which is part of why I'm sceptical about the whole new-age spiritual thing. I think Mum mistook moving to a commune, smoking pot, chanting and arguing with boyfriends for a vocation. She has always wanted to write a romance novel, but then she has also always wanted to open a teahouse, start a dog-grooming business and become a guru. Right now no one is knocking down the door to offer her entrée to any of these stellar career paths, so for now it's life on the couch, with the occasional tarot stand at the markets.

The glamour of my life can never be overstated.

Mum, who's in the sunrise of her sixties, still looks cute, in an ex-'It'-girl-meets-hippy-meets-kewpie-doll kind of a way. Men still ask her out on dates, but she's not interested any more. I think she exhausted herself.

'I need to stay here,' I say.

'Fine.' ,

'I don't have any money,' I add.

Mum shrugs with her usual laissez-faire attitude to the fiscal ups and downs of our life, an approach that unfortunately I seem to have inherited.

'I'm going to open my own restaurant,' I offer with an attempt at chutzpah.

This is the point at which most sensible parents would sit you down, call their accountant, try and dissuade you. Or in the best of worlds, offer help.

Mum does at least look at me, before her eyes return to the Bondi Vet.

'Good.'

And that is that.

I carry my suitcases and boxes of badly packed bits into the spare bedroom and find a place amid the detritus of Mum's latest hobby: quilting. The room is a shrine to her hobbies of the past – macramé, card design, cross stitch, Knitwit Kwik Sew with a focus on terry-towelling tracksuits. Numerous projects, none finished, cover the bed. The walls hold framed spiritual slogans and pictures of the Bhagwan, including one that always makes me laugh: it's of Mum, resplendent in an apricot taffeta number, at the feet of the Bhagwan, who flicks her over the head with a peacock feather while checking out her cleavage. Over his throne a banner reads, 'Bhagwan Santosha World Tour 1987 – "We are living in a state of Grace".'

I make a little clearing on the springy single bed and lie down to stare up at the ceiling and count down till the phone rings. Julia always calls at 7pm, after she's put Attica to bed. The woman is a phenomenon. Not once does she miss a night; the fact I'm usually full tilt at the restaurant is not a deterrent. When Julia makes a commitment, she superglues herself (and often the rest of us) to it.

'You at Sara's?'

'Yep.'

'You know you could stay here; you're one of the few people Ken likes.'

'Thanks, but Mum's is probably better for now.'

'That makes me realise just how uninviting having a thirteen-month-old baby makes me.'

Julia's voice makes the world sane again.

'How was Leith?' she asks.

'Underwhelmed.'

'To say the least. I bet he's shitting himself he's going to lose a hat without you.'

'Maybe it's more he's shitting himself over losing me.' I know there is no substance beyond a thin and waning hope in that comment.

Julia's tone shifts gears into a warning. 'More like the *idea* of losing you.'

'I'm not sure there's that much of a difference at three in the morning.'

'Lucy . . .'

I sit up, wondering suddenly how to broach this.

'I met someone,' I manage.

Julia's breath catches, joy overwhelming her need for oxygen. I continue before she can speak. 'A restaurant.'

She exhales and makes her *hmmm, the jury's out* sound.

'It's in Potts Point.' Julia loves Potts Point.

'You'll never be able to afford it.'

'Closer to Woolloomooloo.'

'You still won't be able to afford it *and* you'll get robbed and/ or raped.'

'I feel like it sighed when I found it, like it was relieved.'

There's a pause.

'Honey, have you been eating Sara's cookies?'

'I'm serious. It's an old restaurant that looks like it's been empty for decades.'

'In Sydney that doesn't happen without good reason.'

'But—'

'Sweetie,' she interrupts, gaining momentum as she settles into *sheltered workshop instructor for the emotionally handicapped* mode. 'Just focus on getting the rest of your stuff out of the apartment, extricating yourself from Leith and getting a job. You could get a great one. Neil would always take you back . . . Are you listening to me? Lucy?'

I fidget with one of Mum's unfinished macramé hangings. Maybe I should take up macramé . . . maybe I should get off the phone and have a hot bath and a good long think.

'Yes, I'm here. Bit of a draining day . . .'

'Don't eat your mother's cookies.'

'I won't.'

'Luce, you've had enough heartbreak, now is not the time to throw yourself into opening a restaurant. You of all people know how many of them fail!'

It's true, a good twenty-five per cent of fabulous openings end in insolvency and bankruptcy. But I'm ahead of that curve – I have nothing to lose.

'Mum's calling me,' I say, even though we both know it's not true.

'No, she isn't.'

'Okay, I just need to go.'

Julia sighs, then continues in her firm voice. 'I'll pick you up at eight tomorrow morning and we'll do a drive-by.'

That's what I love about Julia: she's never averse to being completely contradictory for the sake of our friendship.

'I love you. 'Night.' I hang up and stare down at the three-month lease in my hands. How do you open a restaurant with five hundred dollars?

3

Lucy

I WAKE AND FOLLOW THE SHADOWS ON THE CEILING, WATCHING their shapes morph into a unified pattern of loss. How is it that the certainties of the day can so completely dissolve into the disorientation and aches of the 3am panic attack? Is this why the spiritual gurus pronounce it the most psychic hour to meditate? I often wonder if you looked at a cross-section of all the inhabitants in my time zone, how many others would be awake at 3am, not including the pissed ones or the night-owls who haven't been to bed yet; those of us who wake to the sudden apprehension of our own mortality, the waking from the dreams of the everyday. The muffled ambience of sound bites mutating into the sharp relief of panic, pain and loss. I guess this is why comments on blogs and chat rooms are popular at this hour – cyberspace is a good place to convene and fool yourself that you're not actually alone.

But really, aside from Mum's steady snore in the next room, there's nothing. No messages from Leith, no lightning bolts of brilliance showing me how to make a three-month pop-up restaurant work with no money. Julia's right, I make life so much harder for myself. Why?

I do not want to be here. The only place I really want to be is . . .

I pull up outside the heaving home of my hopes. The bum stands outside raving to the front window. He spots me and shakes his head, then waves and moves off.

I have the keys in my hand. I was going to wait for Julia tomorrow. Right now I'm shaking and I'm sure I'm about to be mugged/raped/killed – thanks, Jules.

As I put the key into the lock I hear the almost-sigh again. I turn it, and miraculously it opens, although I'm not sure why I think that's miraculous – I did, after all, find the real estate agent, sign a short-term lease, hand over money. I guess I'm just not used to things working out. The real estate agent seemed surprised that I wanted to use the space as a pop-up. He made a few calls out of my earshot and returned very keen for me to sign, from which I surmised that he was taking me for a ride in some way. Yet I did it anyway.

Of course the electricity isn't on, so I use my phone to light the way. All is still, dusty, filthy from years of neglect. It can seat fifty at the most. Oh god, I'm sure there's mice, though the real estate guy said it had been pest-sprayed recently; I'm guessing five years ago. Still, there's warmth to the room, the echoes of many a wonderful meal . . . someone loved this place once. I move into the kitchen. All is in place – from 1982. That's apparently when the restaurant shut down. It was called 'Fortune'. Obviously there's an irony there.

A Kenwood mix-master like my grandma's stands tall and proud alongside an archaic processor, and the cooking knives are still in place. I move to the oven, a huge eight-burner gas monstrosity that tells me the guy who owned this place was definitely serious about heat.

I cross to the drawers, each laden with things I can use and one full of cookbooks and *Vogue Entertaining*, *Gourmet Traveller* and other foodie magazines of the day. I feel like I have opened

Pandora's box as I see hundreds of recipes for dishes no longer in our collective psyche – bar a few urbane hipster chef re-imaginings. I'm in heaven, but my phone is about to die. And then I find it. Tucked inside an issue of *Gourmet Traveller* from December 1981 – a little red book. It is filled with recipes written in a distinctive hand; beautiful, bold recipes created with devotion and style. Food of the era of my childhood, dishes I imagined happy families and sophisticated couples eating: Lobster Thermidor, Beef Wellington . . . I am starving. Most recipes have scrawled annotations and a list of dates, possibly of different times said meal was cooked. I turn to French Onion Soup and see only one date, my birthday. That is, my actual day of birth – 11 July 1980. Perhaps the soup wasn't good and he never made it again? But it's such a beautifully crafted recipe: the quantity of onions, the sweating technique, the slicing of the baguettes and their toasting with gruyère. There's only one comment beside it: *Perfection.*

I'm snatched back from the daydream of cheesy utopia by my phone buzzing. Leith. His photo creates its own shadow as I stare at him on the screen. I will not answer, I will not answer; oh god, he's obviously as lonely and messed-up as I am. I am about to answer but a door slams and the phone dies. Thank you, universe. Now I have to find my way out of here in pitch darkness.

Where is my life?

4

Lucy

JULIA'S HORN SOUNDS AND MUM ROLLS HER EYES. THEY ENJOY a relationship of mutual disdain. Though they agree on which parts of my life need improvement and have been known to bond over it . . . that, and hating Leith.

'Tell her to just come in.'

'Can't, we're late. Do you want to come?'

Mum sports her scarlet velour house-gown and has her feet up on the Jason recliner. Crumbs from a brownie outline her mouth.

'My arthritis is playing up, and Sandy is coming by to do some reiki later.'

The mention of Sandy and reiki, particularly when they're combined in a sentence, makes me even keener to get out the front door.

'Okay.'

'You'll be fine.'

'I think it has rats.'

'It's your destiny.'

I kiss Mum's head, her steadfast weirdness a comfort. The horn blows again.

'Oh shut up, Julia.' Mum accompanies this with an unfathomable gesture – somewhere between flipping the bird and waving her remote control like a fairy wand.

I head out to my destiny in the form of Julia in her gargantuan city-bound SUV. Julia looks and drives like a woman whose life is comprehensively insured. A little child seat complete with little child is rigged up with military precision in the back. The largesse of Julia and her car makes Attica, sporting gender-neutral designer overalls, and me look like two Tom Thumbs visiting the land of the big people.

I climb up and in and kiss both Julia and her mini version on the cheek.

'I cannot believe you signed a lease without showing me the place first.'

'Good morning. I'm going to show you now,' I reply, teenage defiance resurfacing.

Julia groans, delivering the parental discipline that has always been lacking in Mum. Considering I'm in my mid thirties it's something you'd think I'd be over by now, but then do stupid decisions have an age limit?

I sulk and we drive on in silence punctuated by toddler gibberish for a while.

'Leith called,' I say.

'Has he offered you a legal partnership at Circa yet?'

'I don't know, my phone died.'

'Good,' she replies.

She turns and merges into the left lane as we pass Macquarie Street professionals making their way to their professional jobs and professional appointments. They all seem so grown-up and together against the backdrop of Sydney's jumble of mirrored high-rises and sandstone relics. Even Attica with her unblinking stare seems to have it over me in the maturity stakes. Julia is going to hate the restaurant.

'So, I googled the address. It's a terrible street and the restaurant hasn't operated since nineteen eighty-two.'

'Hmm.' I should have come alone.

'A restaurant isn't empty for that long without good reason.'

'Thanks, Confucius.'

'Someone obviously hasn't had their latte this morning.'

'Mum doesn't do caffeine . . . just hash.'

We drive past the park and the wharf, glittering in the sunshine of another picture-perfect day that will be forgotten by most. Julia toots her horn and instructs drivers who can't hear her as irritating music sung by Smurfs sounds through the car's speakers.

I am feeling sick. Even after our coffee stop. I know Julia needs to see the restaurant but I also know she is the reality check who is going to make my excursion into insanity official.

We stop outside the restaurant. The homeless guy squats at the front cleaning his nails with a matchstick. He shrugs when I wave. Julia makes her swallowing sound of trying not to judge . . . yet judging.

'He comes with the restaurant, then?'

Julia double parks, then we disembark and she triple locks.

'Jules, what about Attica?'

'Shit.' She beelines it to her bub. 'Every now and then I forget I have her.'

It's nice to see that Jules is in fact human and fallible; I think sometimes we both forget that fact.

We enter, mops, buckets and bleach in tow. Our mission, once Julia is done lecturing me, is to remove the first of the little restaurant's many layers of grime.

Attica begins exploring power sockets and is swiftly scooped up by the mother ship. Julia takes two steps into the centre of the room, tightens her grip on Attica and looks around.

'*What a dump.*'

'Thanks, Jules.'

'Bette Davis, *Beyond the Forest.*'

I happily encourage Julia's love of old movies; it brings out her romantic streak. 'Yes?' I say with a smile.

'And if the line fits . . . Oh Lucy, what have you done?'

On cue, Julia is echoing my thoughts. By the light of day the derelict condition of the tiny space is amplified.

'Doesn't smell bad though – that's weird.' She satisfies herself with a sniffing inspection.

'Years of cooking have probably permeated the walls.'

'Baked potatoes.' She responds to a silent quiz question.

She's right; the space smells like Sunday roasts at my grand-parents' house.

Sounds of rustling. Julia backsteps. 'Oh my god, there's a bird's nest in the corner.'

We look to each other and then up to the nest with accompanying sparrow.

'At least it's not a pigeon. Or a rat.' I am Pollyanna clinging to the outskirts of positivity.

Julia takes my hand, eyeballs me and speaks slowly, the way you do to people who have lost the plot. 'Honey, if we head back to the real estate agent now I can play the lawyer card and we can try to get your bond back.'

If Julia had met the real estate agent she would know how unlikely that is.

'No. I . . . I'm committed to giving it a whirl.'

I nod. She stares. I nod more fervently and throw in a slightly manic smile and raised eyebrows. She inhales. So do I. She sniffs. I do too. She releases a long sigh. I nod some more . . . backup nods, you could say. Julia gives in.

'So, you have a three-month lease. When do you want to open?'

I pause, attempting to look like I am considering a large array of potential dates. 'Thursday.'

Julia shoots me another look that says, *You really have lost it.* 'Next Thursday?' she asks.

'No, silly, as if.'

Julia does the stare-down. 'When?'

'Three Thursdays away.' I keep focused on not blinking; I will win the Julia stare-off.

'Including or excluding the one that happened yesterday?'

Julia knows I don't do dates well. I blink.

'Including.'

I know what she's going to say next – she's going to make 'right' a two-syllable word.

'Riiiight.'

Bingo.

'So, you have just over two weeks. To create a restaurant.' She emphasises 'create' with a nuance that makes it seem I will need to be able to spin gold from straw while locked in a cell.

'That's the whole concept of the pop-up, otherwise it wouldn't just be . . . popping up . . .' I fade out.

'How? Who? I mean, who besides me is helping you?'

'Well, I spoke to Maia and Hugo, they're both keen.'

'Do you have the money to pay their wages?'

'Not yet.'

Julia narrows her baby-blue and far too clever lawyer's eyes. 'How much money do you have, Luce?'

'A bit . . . I told Maia she could be a part-partner.'

'Of all this?' Julia makes a slow turn around, her gaze taking in the peeling paint, the chipped skirting boards, the literal and figurative crap strewn over the floor. 'I bet she was beside herself.' She turns back to continue her cross-examination. 'So, Leith knows?'

'Not exactly.'

'Honey, if you told two of his key employees and tried to poach them, he's going to know – and he's not going to like it. I have no personal issue with that, but still, you know what a shit he can be, and you *have* pretty much dumped him, moved out of your home and decided to open a wacky pop-up restaurant all in the space of twenty-four hours.'

Oh god, I am insane.

'You're definitely not going back?'

Another stare-down has commenced when a door slams. It must be the one out to the loos that slammed last night.

'We've been separated for a month, you know that. It's just I officially moved out last night.'

'Uh-huh. Let's get started. I have to get Attica to her music lesson by two.'

Julia grabs a broom and sets sail. Attica busies herself with a pile of paper she industriously places inside a bucket before emptying it back out on the floor and laughing. I head to the kitchen and set to work. The homeless guy sings as he pisses against the side of the building. We're just one big happy . . .

5

Lucy

I HAVE CLEANED MY WAY TO THE MIDDLE SHELF OF THE FRIDGE when the electricity is reactivated and Julia screams. The lights brighten and dim. I rush out to the dining room.

'What?'

'The lights are working.'

She looks up and points to the holy grail of an old, filthy chandelier that buzzes and attempts to shine.

'I know.'

'So, I just got a hundred-watt close-up into what a shithole this place is.'

The lights brighten and dim again. A crashing sound turns us both around in time to view a possum appearing out of the bottom of the ancient fireplace.

We both scream. Julia grabs Attica, who remains unperturbed and gurgles. I have to hand it to the kid, she has been awesome all morning, entertained by her mother's cleaning antics.

'Catch it!' Julia shrieks.

'What with?'

'Him!' She jerks her head at the muscular, handsome form that has appeared at the door.

'Delivery. The service door was shut.'

I can't help but smile at Henry. The nephew of our delivery man from Circa, he's just started his own business; he's closely enough related for me to trust his sources, but distant enough not to be in Leith's immediate sphere. He holds a load of produce, akin to the promised land, kitchen staples I ordered late last night – rice, oils, fats, vinegars.

'Can you catch possums?' Julia screeches.

Henry looks slightly scared, but clearly decides that between the possum and Julia, the possum is the better bet. 'I'll give it a shot, but I think there's someone we can call.'

'She hasn't got any money,' Julia replies, now jerking her head in my direction. 'You'll have to do it.'

Henry shoots me an apologetic smile and is soon able to liberate the possum and the sparrow back into the wider world. Later, he eyes off the tiny lopsided dining room.

'This is an interesting space.' His voice is thin.

'You're being facetious?'

'Are you fine to pay cash for all of this?' Henry provides me with a sideways glance, wriggling with discomfort.

'Give him your credit card,' Julia instructs.

Here's the moment I've been waiting for . . . another one. I can't even pretend to be up to another stare-off.

'My card's connected to Leith's.'

'So?'

'So, I took myself off it last week, and Leith froze our other accounts this morning.'

A groan from Julia.

'Will you take a cheque?' I offer.

Henry adds a shuffle to his wriggle. 'Ah, it kind of has to be cash.'

'Why?' Julia is back in prosecutor mode.

'Well, it's just . . . so, I guess Leith warned Uncle Les, who told Dad that you were having money problems.'

'He did?'

'Yeah, in the email.'

'What email?' Julia's eyes narrow. I sense incoming calamity.

'The one he sent out to all your suppliers last night. He said he wanted to give a heads-up that you two had split and you were having some . . . issues.'

'What kind of *issues* did he say she was having?'

'Like, a nervous breakdown kind of issues . . . and you're bankrupt . . . I mean, broke.'

'She's not bankrupt. She hasn't got enough possessions or debts to declare bankruptcy.'

'I'm not having a nervous breakdown!' Am I? I look around again . . . I probably am.

Henry nods sweetly and somewhat unconvincingly. 'Sure.'

'This is Leith sabotaging me.'

Henry nods again, his smile growing slightly less nervous. 'I get breakups. Me and my girlfriend, we've had our moments.'

'You're nineteen. You don't get to have *moments* until you're at least twenty-five.' Julia is always equating psychological depth with specific ages.

A fit of righteous indignation heats my face as I grab my wallet and hand over two hundred and eighty dollars.

'I have money.'

'Obviously swimming in it.' Julia is now shaking her head at me, her eyebrows rising.

'Great, thanks,' says a clearly relieved Henry. 'And hey, I bet this place will rock.' His voice wavers only slightly as he speaks.

The lights dim and brighten again.

Julia's eyebrows remain raised as I escort Henry and his box of staples to the kitchen. After he leaves she appears holding Attica, who, desperate to walk, waves all her limbs about, making Julia look like a six-armed nameless Scottish monster from the deep.

'How much money do you have exactly?'

I shrug.

'Exactly?'

I sigh. 'Nine hundred and seventy-two dollars, minus petrol.'

The reality of the numbers crashes to the ground and reverberates in a tuneless cacophony of disaster.

'Does that include council permits, insurance?'

'Pretty much.'

It doesn't.

'I will loan you some.'

'No,' I reply immediately, and firmly. 'I may not be able to pay you back, and then I will feel bad and avoid you and it will ruin our friendship.'

'So, you've already thought that one through.'

I have.

'I will donate five grand,' she says, topping my firm tone with a finality that makes both Attica and me stop still. 'I can write it off as charity, and you can at least buy some paint. And I'll get onto insurance, you do the council permit. Wait, are you *crying*?'

'No.' I am. 'Maybe a bit. I don't want charity.'

'Oh please, be proud later, after you've opened. I have to get Attica home.' Julia envelops me in a motherly hug that momentarily puts the world right-side up.

'Now, stop bawling. I'll call you tonight.' She heads out with a Queen of Sheba spring in her step. And reappears moments later to grab her nappy bag. Then drives off into the sunset, my hero Julia.

I hate feeling self-indulgent and figure I should do something productive . . . so, I sob.

After a while I take the little red book I have been carrying around with me and flick through the well-loved recipes, searching for some kind of universal sign, the domain of the tarot readers and feng shui consultants I have repeatedly sworn off. French Onion Soup re-appears. I am starving, I have onions and most of the basic requirements, and I need to get acquainted with my new kitchen by putting it to work. And so in the search for self-soothing, I begin to chop onions, wailing freely.

6

Lucy

CHOPPING, SOBBING, SNIFFING, WAILING . . . IT REALLY IS A PRETTY
recipe . . . I hate Leith . . . but it's not all his fault . . . or maybe
it is . . . if he'd kept it in his pants . . . but if I'm honest there's
always been something missing between us . . . and then there's
the chewing thing . . . but who has it all? Who gets it all right?
I'm no vision of perfection – I'm moody and hypersensitive, I'm
a food snob . . . except for the chilli dogs . . . I blush too readily,
stumble over words and my brain has a tendency to freeze when
I'm put on the spot . . . I still haven't mastered risotto; how can
any self-respecting chef not have mastered risotto? I get horrible
PMT . . . I like putting my cold feet on warm limbs, even when it
wakes him up . . . I have trouble saying no . . . I run from situations
I don't like instead of facing them . . . I have a high-pitched sneeze
when I'm nervous . . . oh my god, I am basically my mother but
with blonde hair. Shit . . . bugger . . . bum.

An onion is passed to me. I mumble thanks and continue
chopping. Then I remember: I'm alone.

I hear the words, 'You're welcome.' They are deep and
rumbling, spoken by a voice that doesn't belong to Leith . . . or
to anyone else I know.

You know that feeling you get when you realise you have
dissociated to the point of being outside your body and looking

in? Probably not, you're probably sane and married to your first boyfriend and living in the house you bought from your grand-parents just around the corner from the one your parents live in. You probably start planning Christmas in May and have the contact numbers of the police, fire, ambulance and your top five friends printed and stuck onto a corkboard near the phone in your kitchen. I wish I was like you, but I'm not and consequently I venture to look far enough to see that the hand that passed me the onion has an arm attached. It's hairy and masculine. The arm wears a sleeve that looks like . . . okay, there's a kaftan-wearing, fairly hairy, not unattractive man sitting on my bench. He smells good, so he isn't one of my homeless friend's clan; he smells like the restaurant smells – of roast dinners and strength. I swallow, realising this will be the last time I swallow my own saliva because I am about to be killed by a hairy, nice-smelling, slightly gorgeous psycho killer. My mind suddenly reminds me that I once read somewhere that if you look straight into the eyes of your killer it makes it harder for them to perform the deed. So, I look up into the face of the kaftan-wearing murderer-in-waiting and see the most beautifully sculpted lips, nose, eyes; eyes that are two endless pools of mossy green that spell mischief and brilliance – and that are staring directly and curiously into mine.

'So, you can see me?' That voice again. Do all would-be killers sound like this?

'Yes . . .'

'And hear me too . . . good, good.' His lips break into a smile that has the hypnotic effect of making you believe the universe was created just for this moment. What the frig is happening?

I sneeze.

'Gesundheit!'

That voice I know, and it comes from behind me. I turn to see Leith. Thank god. He can get killed with me. Or maybe instead of me.

I look back to see that onion man isn't there. Wait. Onion man isn't there? I have wholly lost my shit.

'What, why, you, here?' It's as much as I can articulate, which isn't bad considering I am sure to be walked out in a straitjacket in a matter of minutes.

'What kind of welcome is that?' Leith moves in to kiss me. I still have the knife in my hand; he moves back. He stands in what I know he believes to be a 'favourable posture', which means one that shows off his biceps, his height and, at particularly cocky moments, his crotch.

'What are you so nervous about?'

'What? Huh, nothing, no. Why are you here?' I look around again. There's nothing, no one . . . hello?

'If the mountain won't come to Muhammad . . .'

Back to the wastelands of Leith.

'Can we not talk in platitudes for at least five minutes?'

Leith shrugs, picking up the little red recipe book. 'Cute.'

I grab it off him. I have always hated the way Leith assumes he owns everything, particularly me.

I hold the book to my chest as I search the bench where the hot man had sat. At least my hallucination had the manners to be unbelievably handsome, and masculine, like something out of an Old Spice ad – not in a gold-chain-wearing way but, oh—

'Are you all right, LiLi?'

I also hate the way Leith insists on calling me LiLi in a baby voice, and the way he signs it as my name on cards; and the fact that *he* signs *my* name on cards for fear I might write something more memorable than he could for a seven-year-old's birthday irks me. Leith irks me all round. That's what guys who break your heart do. Bastard.

'You keep making your weirdo face.'

'It's been a big week.'

'When are you coming home?' He glides his perfect hands (another feature he knows how to show off) over the kitchen equipment, making it and me look ridiculously ramshackle by contrast. His very presence is sucking oxygen out of my lungs.

'I told you on the way back from Seal Rocks that it's over. I need space.'

'Not moving-out space.'

'What other kind is there?'

He watches me, clearly unsure how to answer that. 'Why are you looking around like that – is there someone else here?'

'Is there?' I try to make this sound cavalier, but realise I'm not making sense.

Leith appraises me, a glazed-eyed and crazy woman in front of him.

'Maybe you should come back home and have a rest,' he says finally.

Leith wants to have sex. I do not want to have sex with Leith.

He puts his arms around me and pulls me in. 'I know I pushed it with the holiday. It was too soon, I just wanted everything to be okay again.'

He keeps hold of me, and I slowly begin to melt. Oh god, I hate myself.

'Come home and have a nap, and then you'll be all fresh for tonight.'

And there it is, the Leith agenda. He doesn't want me to miss a Friday night at work.

I pull back. 'I need you to go.'

'Why?' Getting turned down, in any way, shape or form remains outside of Leith's ego-endorsed orbit.

'Because I can't have space if you're in it.'

'And *you* decided *this* was a good idea?' His rage surfaces instantly. 'Who says they need a "trial separation" and then cancels credit cards and rents out a space that isn't fit to be a soup kitchen?'

The lights dim and rise.

'Even the electrics are shoddy. You've punished me enough, now come home.'

How is it that men think they are being punished when a woman gets upset that they're not being faithful? How is that too our fault? They fuck you over and then they blame you for it.

'This restaurant isn't about you,' I say.

'And you say *I* speak in platitudes. I never have a clue what's going on with you; you withdraw into god-knows-where.'

Something in me snaps. I could say a force greater than me erupts but that would be me finding an excuse. All the frustration of the past years, especially the last months, is released, some kind of evil genie within me escapes.

I roar. 'I want you to go, that's what's *going on*. I want you to stop taking credit for my menus, stop sleeping with our staff, and get far, far away from me – go and fuck yourself sideways till next Tuesday.'

Leith, like me, looks shocked. I have never spoken to him – to anyone – like this. What a freaking relief it is.

'You're unhinged.'

'And you're an arsehole.'

He looks me up and down. I know what's coming.

'Whatever.'

My least favourite expression he picked up from a hipster bartender a few years back and has been perfecting ever since.

He leaves. I look around. There's no one else here.

French Onion Soup

Ingredients
120 grams butter
5 medium brown onions, peeled and sliced in rings
100 millilitres red wine
1 teaspoon Dijon mustard
leaves from 4 sprigs of thyme
4 bay leaves
150 millilitres beef stock
1 baguette
100 grams grated gruyère cheese
50 grams grated parmesan cheese
ground black pepper, to taste

Method
Heat the butter in a large, deep, heavy-based saucepan (Le Creuset is ideal). With the lid on the saucepan, gently sweat the onions for about 15 minutes or until tender. Remove lid and increase heat till onions are brown and lightly caramelised. Be careful not to let them fry to crisps.

Add the wine (and if in the mood, pour yourself a glass), mustard, thyme and bay leaves. Bring to the boil until alcohol has evaporated, then add stock, reduce the heat and simmer very gently for around 30 minutes, stirring from time to time.

Cut the baguette into 2-centimetre slices and lightly toast it on both sides.

Ladle the soup into ovenproof bowls and inhale aroma deeply. Place 1 or 2 pieces of baguette on top and sprinkle generously with the grated cheeses and a pinch of black pepper. Put the bowls under the hot grill in the oven. When the cheese is golden and bubbling, remove from the oven and serve immediately to someone worthy of your time and flavours.

7

Frankie

SHE'S SPIRITED, I'LL GIVE HER THAT. AND WHAT'S MORE, SHE HAS gumption. After that joke of a husband left she stayed and finished the soup. And by god the woman can cook. Of course, she cried the entire time, but by my estimation the tears would have seasoned it perfectly.

I let her be but watched everything.

She gave Bill a bowl before heading out. He devoured it. Clever girl. She just needs to quit the sobs and keep focused and she could do well. She's not as good as I was, though she swears nearly as much. Oh, how I would love to taste that soup again. She left none here, packed it up in Tupperware and took it home, via a bottle shop if she has any sense.

She's gone again. But she will be back, and she will be the key. Of that I am certain.

Already, she can almost hear the words rattled off between patrons, almost see their faces filled with anticipation. She feels the warmth of this place because it's always bloody full. A plethora of customers in the afterlife are still here, eating their meal, the one that made them rethink the divorce or start the affair. The one that changed their life.

The building is alive with the chatter of the dead who dine light years from the dining dead who fill the hours of their marriage with pork pot pies of waste. These people lived to eat, and damn it all, I love them for it. No matter their bank balance, they would find their way to me, saving for a year if need be, to have me sate their palate. And I remain at their service. I lived to feed others, to make love through their tastebuds.

The tables are full. The Denisons, wistful with a prawn cocktail. Marie with her chocolate mousse and her uptight daughter who could do with a few bowls of pasta; she insists on following her mother everywhere – sometimes you can't shake family, not even in death. My beautiful Tiffany laughs elegantly, watching the room, waiting for her girl. Awful, crooked Mickey the lawyer who got so many crims a shorter sentence – all he wants is an Irish stew like his mother's, except he likes mine more. Clancy blows out ten candles on the ice-cream cake his aunt convinced me to make. Tom placates his drunk father and offers a toast.

She will get to see, she must. She isn't alone.

Viola pushes Ted's face into the meringue; she does it every time. Reliving the highlights is our sport. And it's right that they come here – nothing can renew your will to live like a good meal, even after you're dead.

8

Lucy

I ARRIVE HOME TO MUM AND SANDY WATCHING A QUILTING show, each with their handiwork on their lap, staring and stitching. Mum got Sandy involved in both quilting and *The Bold and the Beautiful* and Sandy is still reaping the rewards.

Sandy is a faded reiki master who has an obsession with alpacas and a gay son who bemoans her lack of flair in fashion, food and art. Sandy has proudly renounced fashion and leather and hair maintenance. I think she has a crush on Mum, or some type of groupie thing going on, anyway.

Mum's tarot cards sit on an abandoned coffee table. I take them as subtly as possible, pour myself a glass of the chenin blanc I picked up from my favourite bottle shop and make a beeline for my room.

Once there I attempt to stop myself doing a spread. As the child of possibly the most committed hugably-boogaly woman I know, I am nothing short of ashamed to find myself here, performing a Celtic cross tarot spread – but seeing a man in a kaftan appear and disappear on your kitchen bench can push you to undesirable places.

I don't believe in ghosts. Actually, that's not true, I do believe in them – I just wish I didn't. I believe that the ghosts of disappointment and failed relationships can haunt you for a lifetime.

And failure in itself is a ghost with a vicious presence. But an actual ghost, an apparition? I'm not even sure I believe in god or an afterlife. I believe in feelings between people that have a life of their own, and memories, but to believe in a ghost means believing in a spirit that has some type of deceased existence, and that, by all indicators, is whacked. Then again, my experiences, thanks mainly to Mum, are of remnants of people's lives and personalities that hang around and haunt. I cannot explain it, but I can feel them from time to time. Not in any psychic bizarre way, just inklings that someone laughed here or cried there and that memory means something to more than one person and so it lingers. Is that a ghost?

But a man appearing and disappearing from my kitchen? Who is he and why was he there? And why did I see him when Leith obviously couldn't? And why is he so handsome? He didn't smell like an axe murderer, and he looked at me with something like amusement. A man with twinkling eyes is trouble. A dead man with twinkling eyes would be even worse.

The only ghosts I have ever really sought are those of my grandparents. While they were alive they were my sanity-keepers and the reason I am any type of functional in this world. But there have been no sightings of either of them. They were both content with their life – though of course they were always concerned about Mum and me. When they left, they were resolved; it was time to hand over. I re-create them when I cook their favourite dishes, they are on my mind most mornings when I wake – but it's peaceful. I miss them terribly, but the only thought I have towards them is, *thank you*.

Was he really a ghost? I know that when people lose it they can have aural hallucinations – and really, why wouldn't I hallucinate about a hot young guy helping me with the cooking? My life is in the toilet, so he could be the fairy godfather of my imagination.

But . . . he *was* there. He was there and then he was gone, and that adds up to either: A) I'm completely delusional (possible); B) he is a ghost (improbable); or C) this is a stunt set up by Leith. Though really, Leith lacks the imagination for such an enterprise; his mode of dealing with not getting what he wants is via manipulation and bullying shabbily hidden as charm.

Leith and I have become ghosts to each other. Beyond the irritation, the betrayals, the humiliation, you know it's over when each conversation is a revisitation and a colourless re-creation of what came before; like you're speaking from a script. When the touch of each other is like a memory while you're still there; somehow it doesn't connect. Like watching someone wave their arms when you know you've already drowned. The timing is a beat behind, the laughter a moment off cue. When you no longer believe in them. When their love has proved false and retreats into the shadows – you know it's a ghost. What no one tells you, though, is how being haunted by a dead relationship can hurt like hell.

This is what my life has come to – a Celtic cross tarot spread on my mother's spare bed. Why don't I just go back and write this entire 'unfortunate episode' off as a pre mid-life crisis? Go back to Leith: suck it up, cook, buy a dog, have a kid. Shit, have I created this entire situation because I really wanted babies? A hairy man in a kaftan at a rundown restaurant – what would Freud say? Jung would say *I* am the guy in the kaftan; Freud would be more imaginative and say I wanted Leith's penis.

Just as I've laid out the last of the cards and am getting to work with the introduction booklet, Mum, with her impeccable timing, appears at the doorway.

'Don't say anything,' I almost beg.

Mum shrugs, and moves into the cards. When I say that, I mean it literally; she pretty much merges with them as she scans and taps them, nodding and mumbling to herself.

'The hanged man, good.'

'Really? Good how?'

'What a brilliant reading.'

I have heard my mother say this too many times over the years, mainly to girlfriends with a broken heart, reprobate children or a lump in their breast.

'How so?' I challenge with a tone of doubt that is the norm between us.

'You have a new beginning with the tower, you had to sacrifice something – I guess it's the restaurant, because if you ask me leaving Leith is hardly a sacrifice.'

'Thanks, Mum.'

'You are poor . . .'

'Does it get better?'

'There's a man.'

I sit up. 'Who?'

'He's unorthodox – a bit of a trickster, a magician. I like him, he's great for you. 'Bout bloody time you met someone who challenged you.'

I hover for a moment and then . . . 'Is he alive?'

Most people would question my asking this, but not Mum. She merely pauses to consider her answer.

'Depends what you define as "alive". He's *lively*. You're going to help each other. Two of cups, soulmates. Let's hope you have a baby with him.'

'Hardly,' I scoff. Then I look at her. 'Is that in the reading?'

'No, but I'd like to be a grandmother.'

So typical of Mum – even my tarot readings are about her.

'You have some challenges ahead, but you . . . There – nine of pentacles – you have your own garden . . . you never could with Leith. Where is this restaurant?'

'I told you, it's in Woolloomooloo, on the corner of Myrtle and Webster.'

'Oh . . . you mean Frankie's old place.'

I feel the brakes go on my oxygen intake. 'Who?'

'Frankie Summers. He owned and ran it.'

'You knew him?'

Mum looks at me as if I haven't heard that man has walked on the moon. 'Everyone in Sydney in the seventies knew Frankie. What a dish!'

A sinking feeling. 'Mum, did you . . .'

'Don't be silly! I had my hands full with your father.'

'Which one?'

'Who cares, they were all no good.'

That's the sort of thing Mum says whenever I ask about my dad (whoever he is), which hasn't been often . . . I've spent most of my life just trying to make sense of and keep up with her. Any curiosity about my paternal lineage has been eclipsed by my attempts to comprehend and survive my maternal one.

We're interrupted by Julia's personalised ringtone on my phone.

'My program's starting anyway,' says Mum. 'Make sure you get a sage stick into that restaurant. When I think of what we got up to there—'

Mum's voice is overlapped by Julia's.

'I'm on my way to get you.' She has sirens in her voice.

'Why?'

'So you can tell Leith off in person.'

'Why would—'

'That's the problem with social media,' she powers on, 'too easy to completely assassinate someone's character.'

I have no idea what she's referring to; maybe she's watched one too many episodes of *Peppa Pig* with Attica and it's pushed her over the edge . . .

'Julia?'

'He went to town, saying you've been derailed for months but now this new restaurant has sent you to crazytown and you pushed him away so . . .'

Twenty minutes later I'm in the SUV of security, though sadly it isn't protecting me from the Tweets or the Facebook uploads. My mouth is dry and my stomach has taken on the role of translator, audibly growling my resentment.

'I mean, really, he reads like a case study for a narcissistic arsehole.'

'Yeah, but I sound like a mad woman! And people *expect* chefs to be narcissistic arseholes, helps them trust their food . . . particularly famous ones with several books published and their own YouTube station . . . channel . . . thing.'

'He's a recipe-thieving publicity whore – and his teeth are too straight.'

'Can we print that on a t-shirt and make it the staff uniform at my place?'

'Sure.'

We pull up outside Circa, the one-time home of my culinary hopes. The aftermath of sunset leaks a soft crimson into the backdrop of what remains one of the city's most stylish restaurants. I'm still reading his Tweets and posts as I disembark.

'I can't believe he's given the date for the restaurant opening! *I* barely even know when I'm opening.'

'Well, consider it a favour. You work well with deadlines.'

I enter the golden doors of Circa to find that all is buzzing away and a full first seating is in the throes of entrées and mains. No one looks like they're missing my cooking. All is perfectly fine. The terrines. The pâtés. The lobster gazpacho I came up with last summer after our trip to Flinders Island. God, the sight of happy people enjoying food can make you feel lonelier than ice when you're on your own. I perform a few customary greetings, and note the look of bemusement in several of my regulars' eyes. Am I back? Not quite.

I head to the kitchen. Everything hums merrily under the steely control of Leith. He knows how to run a kitchen, I'll grant him that . . . bastard. Maia shoots me a weird half-smile and seems to shrink a bit. I love Maia, she's been my assistant for the past two years and is a brilliant cook in her own right. She has seen Leith devastate and steal from me, which is why I asked her to come and be my sous chef at the pop-up. And she accepted, I think. God, I hope we make enough for me to be able to pay her. How am I going to—

My cyclone of thought is interrupted by the sight of Leith, torching brûlée. I grab a nearby colander of fusilli – not too hot, not too cold – and fling the contents at him.

Sadly, he ducks. Life's like that.

Of course he chooses the sentence that will infuriate me the most: 'Good to see you back.'

Arsehole.

'What are you trying to prove?' I shout over the noise of the new processor I bought us. 'You already have the apartment, the restaurant, the clientele. Why would you do this?'

'Do what?' He plays oblivious badly, waving the sceptre of his blowtorch around, fuelling it now and then for some extra drama.

I wave my iPhone at him in response.

'Well, sweetie,' he says, 'I hate to say it, but is anything I put there actually untrue?'

'Why don't you just stick to your own life and your sexual conquests?'

'I don't appreciate you trying to poach my staff.' He reflames the blowtorch one last time, then blows on it as if it's a gun and he's John-fucking-Wayne. Seriously, the man is insufferable.

'Poach your— It's Maia!' Maia is chopping stoically, pretending she can't hear. 'She hates you nearly as much as I do. She's already tried to resign three times. And Hugo wouldn't even be your maître d' if it wasn't for me. He was mine from the start.'

'Maybe so, but what kind of work can you really offer them, what kind of wage?'

'Why don't you unfreeze our bank accounts so I can give them something?' I fire back.

'No can do, sorry. You started it by cancelling our joint credit cards.'

'That was to stop you from blaming me for any expenditure. Just leave me alone. Leave my business, my friends, my pop-up, my tits, my heart alone.'

Leith smiles stupidly at this. All he's now thinking about is my tits.

I turn to Maia. 'Do you want to come with me now? You don't have to stay here.'

Before she can respond, Leith sidles up to her.

'You should tell her, bubkins.'

I look from one to the other. That sick feeling you get when someone tells you they need to 'talk', or the wedding you've arrived at was actually held yesterday, resonates through my digestive tract.

'No.'

Maia attempts three different sentences but settles on, 'He gave me a raise.'

Thud. I think I'm going to throw up.

'I'll bet,' I say. Hoping to sound wry but failing. 'You're my friend.'

She blinks stupidly. I know that look, I had it once: she's falling for him.

Rage spirals up my spine. 'When? When did this happen? And how?'

No response.

'He won't be loyal to you either, you know. You'll think the sex is so amazing he won't need to go elsewhere, but he will. And, that thing with his tongue? He drops it after the first three months.'

Maia's eyes refuse to meet mine. I wait a moment. Leith smirks.

As I march out I hear Julia, who till now has kept in the background watching, making some kind of lawyerly threat about character-slaying and AVOs, but really it's snowing a blizzard in my ears . . . until I hear the sound of my own voice in the centre of the dining room: 'Hi everyone. I hope you're having a lovely evening and that the person sitting beside you is someone you love, or at least esteem, and not a cheating arsehole like the guy who runs this place. I'm Lucy Muir. I am – I was the sous chef here. I'm the woman who was silly enough to fall for, and marry, a philandering creep, but now I'm leaving and I'm opening my own restaurant just down the road, and while it may not be on *Good Living*'s best-restaurants list yet, it won't be long. It's going to be great, excellent, big and I would like it very much if you would all come to my opening night. Bring someone nice with you – no arseholes allowed. Oh, and Leith adds an extra fifteen per cent on for cake-age because he's a dick. It was never my idea. Enjoy your meals.'

I leave to whispers and upheld phones, Julia by my side.

'You're really not doing much to derail the rumours.' There's a certain pride in her voice.

'Fuck the rumours! I'm going to make my place brilliant.' And for a moment I know it's true.

'Thatta girl. Have you thought of a name?'

'I'm sticking with Fortune.'

'Can we place a "good" before it?'

'It will tell me what it wants to be called.'

'Sometimes you really are your mother's daughter, Ms Restaurant Whisperer.'

Julia drops me off and I head in to another sleepless night on the single bed. Good times . . .

Lobster Gazpacho

Ingredients

8 medium-sized tomatoes, chopped and finely diced
1½ red capsicums, chopped and finely diced
1½ green capsicums, chopped and finely diced
2 English cucumbers, chopped and finely diced
1 medium red onion, chopped and finely diced
½ cup olive oil
1 teaspon balsamic vinegar
juice of 1 lemon
½ cup lobster stock (cooled)
¼ cup chopped coriander
½ cup seeded and diced jalapeño chilli
1 teaspoon salt
½ teaspoon ground black pepper
fresh cooked lobster meat from 2 medium lobsters, finely chopped.
Best if you do it yourself – kill humanely by freezing before cooking

Method

Mix the tomatoes, capsicum, cucumber, onion, olive oil, vinegar, lemon juice and stock.

Transfer to a non-reactive bowl and stir in the coriander, jalapeño, salt and pepper. Cover and chill for 4 hours, allowing flavours to acquaint and connect.

When you are ready to serve, fill pre-chilled bowls with the soup, and garnish with the lobster meat. Devour according to temperament.

Note: Of course, you can use a food processor to quicken the process – but I remain old school with my chopping – and you don't want it too mulchy!

9

Frankie

I KEPT THE SAME TABLE FOR THEM EVERY TUESDAY FOR TWELVE years. They used to bring him, their pride and joy – and then one day another customer told me of a skiing accident, a fall, and from that day the party was for two. He was eighteen. How do you get through that? Answer: you don't. You stop talking to people in anything other than sound bites because anything else is too excruciating. You stop caring if your boots aren't polished, your fingernails aren't clean or a car is heading towards you as you cross the road. Nothing is of consequence. Each meal is an anniversary of life without their son. When they are alone together they don't bother with small talk, when they are alone together their wounds ooze regret. He usually starts off okay: a small exchange with Serge. She remains elegant and reserved. They both look to the sanctuary of the menu for a moment of respite from the alarms of loss that sound. But then, between courses, after the first bites and a tender exchange, he sinks into the heaviness of his grief; resentment of young lovers and grandchildren he will never see. She attempts to focus on the food and the other diners. Tries to make the heavy silence between them soften into a song, but he stares at his meal. If only he knew, as I do now, that all the while their son was sitting there, watching with sadness at his parents' refusal to move through the pain, heal, and yield to a future. Every week he sat there, invisible. Wanting his father to try new dishes and his mother to look forward, not down into his father's despair. The dead want you to live and eat life, not starve on their memory.

10

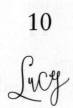

I CAN'T SLEEP. WHAT WAS THAT? *WHO* **WAS THAT?**

11

Frankie

I WOULD LIKE TO PAY HOMAGE TO THE HUMBLE EGG. IT HAS saved my life on several occasions. From its modest beginnings in one's diet as a boiled goog with toast soldiers, to the heady heights of the soufflé, the egg is the soul of French and English cuisine. What would life be without hollandaise or béarnaise sauce, without pancakes, without quiche? God knows you need sufficient custard in your life to be eligible to curdle it. Little else satisfies like a scrambled egg, or a crab-and-tarragon omelette to welcome your new lover to her day. How empty life would be if not for mousse. And as for meringue, though it was the bane of my worldly existence, one of the few dishes I never mastered, I remain a servant to her strong white peaks, her style and her delicacy. And where would bacon be without his majestic wife, fried, frilled with white and oozing sunshine goodness – the perfect balm for bad weather and a hangover. I salute *l'oeuf*. God knows I've worn it on my face often enough to feel intimate with it.

Where is that girl? She has something. Why she was crying over that joker is beyond me. Still, it's what nice girls do: cry and sigh over moronic men. I should know, my achievements in the field of moron have been outstanding. No. The girl can do better than him.

Where *is* she?

12

Lucy

IT'S 3AM, WHEN EVEN THE GHOSTS ARE NAPPING AND IT SEEMS there will never be company in its purest sense again. Moments like these you hope no one else has to endure because they feel infinite and insurmountable. Because they are full of pain and nihilistic lost seconds.

And it's in these moments when I reach out. Not for porn, or tarot, but for that little red book. I flick through the recipes. Are they his? Earlier in the evening I convinced myself I have fabricated the whole thing, but at this hour logic matters little and I feel as though the only form of comfort possible is via those handwritten recipes. My prayerbook for a miserable night. Twice-baked gruyère soufflé, oh I could do with that. Soufflés, aside from being a bit show-offy, are such an elegant starter to a meal; not too filling but not vacuous either, they are the perfect marriage of style and substance. Add to this the juicy, salty undertones of the cheese and you have something homely within something that knows its way around a swish table. I am also starving. Breakups are good for weight loss, but Mum's pitiful fridge is even better. Surely she has eggs, though.

Wrong. My stomach is rumbling, and there are far too many hours before the sun rises to fill them with hunger and sadness. I head out.

Thanks to Henry's delivery, there are eggs are in the Fortune fridge, and I'm soon whisking. If only there were a room above and I could live here . . . me and the ghost. The more I think about it, the more convinced I become that I made the whole thing up, with help from Freud, or Jung. Now it's just me and the sounds of the Bamix saluting the earliest of mornings. The homeless guy taps on the window and tips his hat as I begin to fold the egg whites into the soufflé – at least he'll have a good breakfast.

The restaurant is so far from ready, but still welcoming in her haphazard way.

Maia. How did he toady his way into her heart and her bed? Seriously, she hated him. I am such an idiot. Why does it seem I am among the few who believe that sleeping with your boss and your friend's husband is not cool? In some weird way I can imagine them together; she has no imagination for recipe design either, though she's a beautiful cook. She will be bedazzled by his bullshit, his stories of his training at the Culinary Institute of America, his run-ins with Gordon Ramsay, his invitation to become Madonna's private chef. Before long they will be dressing alike, planning special events at the restaurant, schmoozing the editors of the important food mags, heading to late-night dinners all over town. He'll take her to Golden Century at 2am for chilli crab and she'll think she's landed on the moon. He'll promise her everything while they make love and have her so disorientated by the stamina of his cock that she will forget her sister's birthday, her appointment at the hairdresser and the dreams she had for her own life. Serving him will become her mission. Buoying Leith, helping him keep his clothes laundered and his profile sharp. In so many ways he has chosen well: she may thrive on all of it in a way I couldn't. Oh shit, I think I've overfolded the eggs.

'Better stop folding and put them in the oven before it becomes frittata.'

Double shit. He's back. As in a form, not a presence, not an outline but a real person. It's him – kaftan man. This time he's in chef's whites. Still hot, hotter even – how did I make that happen? I freeze.

'Well?'

I make a strange wheezing sound that's equal parts terror, excitement and confusion as I quickly pour the soufflé mix into the ramekins and place them in the oven without looking back. I just have to get my breathing under control, stop shaking. He's just my imagination, he's my subconscious alter ego, he's—

'Nicely done.'

Oh fuck. I freeze again, now in front of the oven.

'Yes, I'm still here. You can turn around.' His voice is grounded, warm with a playful tease. It's a voice that belongs to someone who knows themselves – at least, it would be if it were attached to a living person, not the creation of my deranged imagination.

I can't turn around. If I turn around and there's no one there I will cry and have to take myself to a psychiatrist and be scheduled. If I turn around and there *is* someone there I will die, probably a long slow death involving a carving knife, and it will be days before my body, or something even worse, is found.

In any case I know in my bones that if I turn around my entire life is going to change.

I turn.

The hunky man in chef's whites holds the recipe book.

'You followed it with great respect, except what's with the two extra egg yolks?'

I switch to autopilot. 'The eggs were small and it didn't have quite the volume.'

'Fair enough.'

'You were watching me?'

'You have a good hand with your whisking, though you could add more salt.'

Just like that, just like we're catching up over a latte on a Saturday morning, this handsome apparition chats away.

Splinters of sanity find their way to my voice-box.

'Who *are* you?'

'Francis Summers.' He bows his head by way of more formal introduction. 'Frankie is what most people call me. And you are?'

'Lucy Muir.'

'Lucy, Lucia . . . Lucille – yes, you look like a Lucille.'

He's so relaxed, I must have gotten it all wrong, tangled. He must be – what? I draw another blank and wheeze again. He seems to be waiting for me to speak.

'I've rented out this place.'

'So I see.'

'You have too?'

'I don't need to, I own it. I live here . . . for want of a better phrase.'

'You're the landlord?'

'Of sorts, yes.'

He smiles again, a cheeky, sexy, manly smile with a charge that has the promise of long dinners and salty kisses.

'You're a chef.'

'Evidently.'

'So, you don't agree with the real estate guy leasing it to me? It's only for three months.'

'I do approve. That's my book, by the way.'

'You want it back?'

'Not yet. I've retired, for now. And I'm pleased you're here.'

I'm falling through myself, roaring waves fill my ears. Ask him . . . ask him . . .

'You're very young to retire.'

He smiles and nods. Gives me nothing.

I venture on. 'Are you the son of the man who ran this place back in the seventies and eighties?'

Oh god, I know the answer before I ask it. *Please don't tell me, please evaporate or melt or, just don't tell me.*

'I *am* the man who ran this place, and there has been no one since me. I do have a son, but I wouldn't know if he can boil a kettle.'

'So, you are, you are . . . um . . .'

'We've been through this, Lucille. I'm Frankie.'

Oh no, oh dear, oh shit . . . I knew it, I knew it, oh no . . .

'You are—'

'Pleased to meet you, Lucille.'

I begin to back away. 'No, I mean you are . . . you are . . . as in, you're . . .'

He follows me, looking amused, smelling nice. Twinkling.

'You are . . . oh god, you're dead.'

Clunk. We both stop in our tracks.

'Must you use such a limiting term? I'd prefer to say I'm resting, though lord knows I haven't had a decent night's sleep in over thirty years. Although, sleep *is* often overrated – that, or my conscience was rarely clear enough to allow me a good one.'

'If you're dead—'

'*Resting.*'

'Resting. Then . . . you're a ghost?'

'Boo!' He makes a silly gesture and laughs. His laugh holds heart, depth and a strong magnetic force.

He heads to the cutlery drawer and grabs two forks. 'They won't need much longer. You don't need to twice-bake them, they'll be lighter like this.'

'You're a dead ghost who can eat and lift things. Oh god, why me?'

'Oh, we chose each other, Lucille.'

'We did?'

'Who else would be brave enough to re-open Fortune? Only a woman who has the backbone to see past the obvious.'

'Past reality, you mean.'

'Please, spare us both a twenty-minute discussion of whether or not I am really here. Allow me to assist. I am technically, as you say, "dead", but you are not imagining me, which leads us both to the correct though unlikely conclusion that I am a ghost, or one of the in-betweeners, the left-behinders, the living dead. I can use most of my senses but not all, and not all at the same time. No, I don't know why that is; I feel it's something still being refined by the afterlife. For now I cannot go beyond the walls of this dilapidated, ramshackle terrace. This may have something to do with why it has not been leased earlier. I am, as I am sure you have heard, the best chef in this city, pretty much on this continent – or I was until I was slayed before my time. Your soufflés are ready.'

At that moment the oven bell chimes.

I move to grab the tray of mini soufflés, which look and smell delectable. Frankie the ghost man appears to think so too.

'Look at the rise on those, and steamed to perfection. Well done, Lucille.'

'No one calls me Lucille.'

'No one? But it's a superb name: sophisticated, feminine with a hint of mischief. Were you named after the queen of comedy?'

'No – maybe . . . it was just one of my mum's whims.'

He studies me with a disconcerting intensity, like I'm a recipe whose measurements he's questioning.

'Do you like your name, Lucille?'

'My grandfather was the only one who was ever able to pull it off.'

'How am I faring?'

'You're a ghost. You don't count.'

'I always finish with a faint dusting of cayenne pepper, just to reawaken the palate.'

'Same,' I reply, already reaching for the cayenne pepper.

'We can help each other, you and I,' Frankie says, gesturing towards the dining room.

I follow with the ramekins and watch as he hovers and glares for a few moments until a tea-light bursts into flame. He turns, grinning proudly. 'Just a little something.'

We sit, and the old bum outside presses his nose against the front window.

'G'day, Bill.' Frankie waves.

'You know him?'

'Indeed.'

'Can he see you too?'

'Depending on what he's been drinking and for how long, yes.'

On cue, Bill holds up his flagon in salute to Frankie. 'Cheers, big ears.' The old homeless man gives a toothless smile, then turns and moves away.

'He's remembering August nineteen seventy-eight – I served this very soufflé at an anniversary dinner he had with his wife.'

'You read people's minds?'

'No, just an educated guess. Be good to him and he will watch out for you. He is a very good contact for you.'

'Obviously very powerful.'

Frankie the dead man with the hot lips eyes me critically. 'I imagine you would know better than to underestimate anyone, Lucille.'

Shame heats my face.

'*Bon appétit.*' Frankie places his fork into the soufflé. He inspects it, then raises it to his lips, where it remains. 'Perfect consistency, an elegant re-creation.' Still he doesn't taste it.

'You can't eat?'

'No. It's another blighter. Perhaps the cruellest. I can taste from memories but not from now. You know, I once travelled through Burgundy for four months with an impossible redhead just to convince her mother to give me that recipe.'

'I think maybe it was worth it.' I mean it, the soufflé is close to divine. I attempt, poorly, to elevate the conversation. 'From what I can see, all your recipes are good.'

'None of my recipes are *good*. Some are brilliant, others diabolical, but I don't do *good*.'

'Okay.'

'Okay.' He reflects for a moment before recalling something else from which to take offence and his face animates with a wretched light of accusation that makes me want to hide under the table. It's clear the man is used to having his own way. All the time.

'The word "yum" is a pox that reduces hours and hours of inspiration, skill and sweat into a three-lettered prosaic leper that belongs in an outlet mall. Don't use it to describe my recipes. Ever.'

'You've obviously thought this through.'

'I've had time.'

'I agree with you, it is a bit of a cop-out. Um, Frankie?'

'Hmm?'

'Are we really talking, or is Leith right?'

'Leith belongs in an airport lounge serving salted cashew nuts.'

I guess I smile at that. Frankie studies me for a while with a possibly-interested-but-potentially-bored expression, three beats behind curiosity. It's a look that makes me straighten in my chair and hope I haven't got cheese on my chin.

'You know, you're really quite beautiful when you smile,' he says after minutes of silence.

I produce a full-bloom blush in response to his compliment, but before there can be any type of shared moment he's off and running with his next thought.

'Let's get down to business. You're in my restaurant.'

'I didn't know it was owner-occupied when I took the lease.'

'Why did you think it had been empty so long?'

'Bad timing?'

It's half a joke, and half what I really believe. He's not falling for any glib outlets in the conversation, though.

'We need each other, Lucille.'

I perform a goldfish sequence of mouth opening and closing gestures. How can I need a ghost? And, more to the point, how can a ghost possibly need me?

'I don't think so,' I manage finally.

'Look at yourself. You're a mess.'

That does it: enough with the experts on my life – living and otherwise. 'I left Leith because I was sick of being controlled!'

'I'm trying to help you, not control you.'

'A minute ago you said I was beautiful.'

'And so you are: a beautiful, glorious mess. I don't mean to pry, but since you arrived you have been either bursting into fitful sobs and sniffles or on the brink of them.'

'I'm sensitive,' I say in a shabby attempt at self-justification.

'True, but that's not it.'

What does this dead chef man want? An entry from my journal?

'I'm sad, okay? My marriage was a farce, it's over. I'm broke and obviously mad, so give me one reason why I wouldn't be fucking sad.'

'Point taken. What did he do, the monkey-minded ex?'

'He cheated.'

Frankie's bored look returns. 'And?'

'Not just once, he cheated repeatedly. Isn't that bad enough?'

Frankie pauses, lining up his words. 'It doesn't bode well if you're in a monogamous relationship. But two chefs, what did you expect?'

'Um, let's see – fidelity?'

'But not chastity.'

'We had sex lots. Good sex.'

'I doubt that,' he says dismissively. 'There isn't enough of him to really meet with you. There's something else. An ingredient is missing.'

There's silence as he eyes me, trying to provoke a response. I finish off the soufflé.

Bugger it, what point is there in hiding the truth from a non-existent being? 'He stole from me,' I say. 'My recipes. He's taken credit for them for the past five years. And he used my hair as dental floss.'

Frankie's lips twist into an amused smile. 'Now that *is* unforgivable. The fool hasn't got an ounce of creativity in him; no wonder he's in a blind fury to get you back.'

I'm on a roll now. 'And he published a cookbook of my recipes last Christmas. He acknowledged me like I was an intern who'd helped him butter a slice of toast he never ate, then he expected me to pose for a photo with him looking like the perfect, untalented, devoted wife.'

'Did you do it?'

I can't answer.

'Oh, Lucille.'

'He's going to sabotage this place and make sure it fails and I never work again.'

'Don't let him.'

'How do I stop him?'

'Lucille, I can help you make this place sing.'

'Another man telling me what to do – albeit a dead one – is not what I need.'

'I need you to find out who killed me,' he says abruptly. This stops me in my tracks.

'Um, shouldn't you know that already . . . being a *ghost*?'

'I was caught off guard.'

'Google says you suicided.'

Frankie's temper erupts once more. 'It wasn't suicide! I was set up. And what would Google know, anyway? Who is she? Some half-witted journalist on the take?'

I'm not sure how to answer that; I'm having enough trouble comprehending that there's a dead man asking me to become Miss Marple.

'I was murdered,' he says savagely, 'and I am stuck here in my restaurant of eternity until I sort it out.'

'But – you've been dead thirty-three years.'

'So?'

'That's a cold case, isn't it?'

'Do I look cold to you?'

'You don't even exist,' I try. 'I made you up, so of course you don't look cold to me.'

I blush again, ugh.

Frankie leans in. Oh, what a charmer he is. 'I *am* here and I *am* real, death aside. There have been quite a few aspiring restaurateurs and property developers here over the years but none have been right. None of them would I trust to help me. But then came you.'

Great, now I'm supposed to save the dead guy. 'Oh no.'

'You're the one, Lucille, the one who will set things right.'

I concentrate on picking at a piece of cheesy crust from my ramekin before grabbing his to clear the table. 'Frankie, I'm in the middle of a separation, staring at poverty – not to mention impending insanity – and opening up what is bound to be a doomed pop-up restaurant. I'm a little busy right now.'

'Nonsense. Say you'll do it. Let's shake on it.'

'No. Besides, ghosts can't shake hands.'

'You have the rule book, do you?'

'I'm not doing it.'

'Oh, stop behaving like a spoilt private-school girl.'

'I'm sorry. I can't.'

The lights brighten and dim, the tea-light is extinguished.

'For god's sake, woman, you've got to help me.'

I'm not sure if it's a plea or a demand, or both, but I want out. 'Why? Why *on earth* would I spend all my time taking orders from you, trying to find out who killed you instead of getting on with my own life? I've had enough of being used. No. No. *No.*'

I feel liberated for about five seconds until chairs begin to fall to the floor, doors open and slam, and Frankie disappears. As in, poof – he's gone. I stand up. I will not be bossed around by an arrogant, dead chef.

'Is that all you've got?' I shout. 'I grew up on a commune, I've been bullied by the best of them, so you're going to have to do better than that.'

'That is *not* the way to speak to a ghost.' His voice envelopes me in its surround-sound ferocity. I still can't see him.

'Really? I think it's *exactly* the way to speak to one.'

Frankie's voice reverberates through the space. 'Fine. You asked for it.'

And then I see them: the diners of his world, a mix of eras, congregating over meals shared long ago. Tables full of customers, some laughing, others crying. A woman with a dead fox around her neck toasts me. Two teenage girls in disco pants and roller skates race past sticking their tongues out at me. A middle-aged man sporting a cycling unitard with a long black coat thrown over, still drunk in his afterworld, shakes his fist at me. They all swirl and sing in the indecipherable din of Frankie's temper. His voice rises above them all. 'How's that?'

'That's better,' I say as casually as I can. I watched *Ghostbusters* in primary school – I know this spiel . . . kind of. 'But I bet you have more. Why stop now, why not go for the full-scale tantrum?'

My heart is hammering and my throat is beginning to close over. I saw *Poltergeist* too. I know what happens. I am not going to get out of here alive.

'You want more?'

I can't answer, my voice has gone. I attempt to look brave and defiant and hide my quivering lip.

'Please, Lucille. You're the only one who can really see me. Help me.'

I still can't answer, but the whirlwind of activity around me subsides. I look down at my hands and my wedding ring, which I need to take off . . . possibly sell.

He appears back at his chair, sitting demurely, looking chastened.

'No more weird stuff,' I utter, trying to maintain the appearance of the upper hand.

'Considering our situation, I'd say what qualifies as weird is relative, no?'

He's trying to make me smile. But I need to play hardball.

'What happens when – if – we find out who killed you?'

Frankie considers. 'On an existential level I'm not sure, but I know I will let go and no longer be here.'

'You promise?'

'One thing I keep is my word.'

'And in the meantime?'

'I will help you make Fortune the best restaurant in Sydney.'

'*You* will help *me*,' I say firmly. 'I will not be your sous chef. You will not be my boss. You will not throw tantrums and scare customers away because you don't approve of their palates.'

Frankie looks at me, surprised. 'Of course not. Whatever makes you think I would do that?'

'I have no idea,' I say wryly.

'No. We will work together as a team. Consider me your invisible partner.'

'Where do we start?'

'Staff. Who do you have?'

'I *did* have Maia lined up as my sous chef, but she is now sleeping with Leith. And I also had Hugo sorted to run front of house, but last night Leith got to him as well and threatened to sue him if he left.'

'You need Serge,' Frankie announces. When he sees my blank expression he adds, 'My old sous chef.'

'How do you know he's still alive?'

'He's not *that* old.'

'Youth didn't stop *you* from being bumped off. Anyway, how do you know he still lives in Sydney or that he'd want to come and work for me unpaid?'

Frankie waves his hand in blithe dismissal. 'The money will come. Serge is not motivated by money. No, he is a purist. If you say I have recommended him – via, say, a mention in this recipe book – he will come, I guarantee.'

'Is he a suspect?' I ask suddenly.

'Hardly. He is – was – my best friend.'

Twice-Baked Gruyère Soufflé

Ingredients

80 grams butter, coarsely chopped
75 grams plain flour
½ teaspoon freshly ground nutmeg
380 millilitres warm milk
175 grams finely grated gruyère
1 teaspoon English mustard (optional for extra kick)
4 eggs, separated (5 if they're on the small side)
salt and pepper, to season
1½ cups thickened cream

Method

Preheat oven to 180°C. Grease 6 ramekins or dariole moulds (200 millilitres each). Melt the butter in a saucepan over medium–high heat, then add the flour and nutmeg and stir continuously until sandy mixture begins to foam.

Gradually add the milk, beating continuously to avoid hideous lumps. Keep going until smooth, then stir on until thick (5 minutes).

Sprinkle in 80 grams of the gruyère, add mustard if using, stir to combine, then remove from heat and allow to cool slightly (2–3 minutes).

Stir in the egg yolks until smooth and combined. Season to taste. You should now have some thick and delectable cheesy goo.

Whisk the egg whites and a pinch of salt until medium-firm peaks form (don't rush this, because it is the basis of the soufflé's body!), then fold one-third of the egg whites into the cheese mixture. Fold the cheese mixture through the remaining egg whites and divide evenly among the ramekins, smoothing the tops.

Place the ramekins in a roasting pan. Pour in enough boiling water to come halfway up the sides of the ramekins, then bake until the soufflés are puffed and golden (25–30 minutes). Remove the soufflés from the oven and cool in the ramekins for 10 minutes or longer if you need the time.

Run a small knife around the insides of the ramekins and turn out onto a tray lined with baking paper. Cover and refrigerate until required. Soufflés will keep refrigerated for 2 days.

To serve, transfer the soufflés to heatproof bowls, pour over the cream evenly, scatter with remaining gruyère and bake until risen and golden (20–25 minutes). Serve hot with interesting, engaging dining companions.

13

Frankie, 1975

WHY DOES IT POUR SHIT ON THE DAYS YOU ASK FOR RAIN?

The kitchen pumps and throbs. Serge moves to the beat as he slices and dices onions like a champion. A new recipe, French Onion Soup is a tricky beast; so many attempt to overcomplicate her, muddying her delicate waters with too much low-grade stock, wine or – god forbid – cognac. No, mistress *oignon* deserves more: she deserves a tease of freshly made beef stock and an offering of decent white. What she needs more than anything, though, is time. You cannot rush her as you sweat onions. Where else would you be going, anyway? Devote yourself to her and she will repay you in full.

Tiffany spreads ganache over the Black Forest cake. Her delicate hands are luminous against the cocoa sugary decadence of the icing. Her shining black locks have been smoothed into a low ponytail that I have been longing to pull on all day. I move to her and lift her onto the bench. I take the icing spatula from her and place it in her mouth, spreading her legs as I do. I am a stickler for hygiene, otherwise her lack of interest in underwear would overwhelm me right now. Still, as I feed her I hear myself calling for Serge to watch the kitchen for a while, and I lift her onto me, her legs wrapped around my hips, and begin to carry her to the cool room.

Shit and fuck and damnation if at this very moment Helen doesn't choose to walk in with some menial hormone-fuelled domestic crisis. She's as erect, beautiful and distant as the Statue of Liberty. On her hip she carries Charlie, who gurgles his gibberish salutation.

I drop Tiffany and hand her back her chocolate-coated spatula, and my desire that accompanies it.

Helen throws us the look of the wearied soldier. Poor darling. In our first days she insisted an open relationship was what she craved too: freedom, a fluidity of sexual exchanges. All that changed, of course, as I warned it would, and the result is expulsive. Once they fall – oh god, once they fall for you the caginess appears, the neediness grows and festers into resentments and reminders of half-sentences uttered when you were off your brain and communing with the two-backed god of late nights and evasive divinity. It's our hardwiring, and regardless how honest you attempt to be you will find yourself caught in the mystifying theatricality of a woman scorned.

Bugger me senseless, *why* did I let her move in? How can she expect me to spend an entire day at home prostrating before some impotent god of domesticity and inane dinner parties with neighbours? Save me. Of course I had moments when I felt the possibility of a life of just us, especially when Charlie was first born, but then she harnessed that and rode it into a time-zone I cannot penetrate. And *why* did she turn up just now? She's a darling girl, I hate to hurt her, but that is what I do. The Midas touch in the kitchen does not extend to my home life. Why, why, *why* didn't she stay home?

'When are you coming back?' She fights back tears and I momentarily feel the outer edges of regret.

'Darling, it's Saturday, the reviewers are coming tonight, I told you.'

'You promised to spend the weekend with us.'

'When?'

'The other night.'

See, this is exactly what I mean. And now I am going to lie to her again. 'I meant Sunday.'

'You promised we would stay in bed all day. The three of us.'

'Tomorrow we will. I will get the newspapers and croissants and we will spend the day in bed spilling crumbs on each other, tickling Charlie.'

She can see the thin veneer of my false gaiety for what it is. And I love her for that.

'Why aren't we enough for you?'

No words come. What words are there for *I am a selfish shit who will not keep it in his pants*? Bar the obvious.

'Charlie and I will be at my mum's.'

One thing I hate more than feeling beholden to the Tupperware of domesticity is coming home to an empty house.

'Darling,' I say, 'please, you mustn't—'

'What?' she breaks in, throwing a glare towards Tiffany, who along with Serge has been trying to achieve invisibility on the other side of the room. 'Wait for you to break another promise? Not be lying in bed awake when you come home pissed with chocolate icing on your cock?'

I do love her, you know – as much as I feel myself capable of loving anything that wasn't invented in my kitchen.

She grabs Charlie tightly and turns towards the door. Charlie waves as they exit.

I hate myself.

Serge shoos everyone out of the kitchen and leaves me to finish icing the fucking cake.

I've done it again.

14

I DRIVE AWAY FROM THE RESTAURANT WONDERING WHAT JUST occurred. Is this a mistake of gargantuan proportions? How did this happen? What would Leith say? And then, as I sit and watch the first rays of light come up over the harbour at Mrs Macquarie's Chair and the orange burst of a new day that hits the buildings of the CBD and highlights the beauty of the white sails of the Opera House, a funny thing happens: I'm flooded with ideas for recipes in a way I haven't been for months. Reimaginings of the recipes from Frankie's book, along with new creations that will harmonise with and challenge some of his dishes. Finally I have found someone as inventive as I am with whom I can talk food . . . *really* talk food. So what if he's dead, or non-existent; he's my muse.

I race home through the first of the morning traffic to beat Mum out of bed and into the shower. The sooner I get back to work, the better.

15

Frankie

LUCILLE INFORMS ME THAT UNTIL RECENTLY, WITH THE exception of the occasional outdated French bistro, pâté has fallen almost completely out of fashion in Sydney. I find this incomprehensible: pâté, that delectable paste of meat and fat, is, first and foremost, of the people. It came to fame when Escoffier used it on his menu for a dinner he cooked in 1918 to celebrate the end of the Great War, and by all accounts – and I am happy to say I have spent time with the great man himself – it was a hit. And from that moment pâté experienced a status shift, becoming associated with celebration, luxury and privilege.

No, to me pâté is timeless. It's practical. It's simple. And it's very bloody good.

16

Lucy

FRANKIE IS WITH ME EVERY DAY AT THE RESTAURANT – WHICH isn't surprising, because he (for want of a better word) 'lives' there – and I have to admit he has been great. I am coming to relax and enjoy our conversations. I love hearing the many tales about his patrons of the past who still dine with him in the afterlife, the characters he continues to serve. But he disagrees with the new paint job, accusing me of trying to turn the restaurant into a science laboratory. I chose a pale creamy white and sanded back the Tasmanian oak floorboards that Julia and I discovered when we ripped up the faded and deeply unwell carpet. They look divine. From the edges of my awareness I hear both applause and criticism from the guests who have passed over.

'Joan asked me to tell you she'd prefer a new carpet,' Frankie says out of nowhere while inspecting his pâté recipe with great satisfaction.

'Joan asked you, or you pushed Joan into saying that?'

I've heard about Joan, the old librarian who saved him from a tough patch, wore her hair in a bouffant and still keeps an eye on him.

'I'll admit the wood is handsome, but carpet is more intimate.'

'Frankie, we can't afford intimacy, we're only open for three months. It's an experiment.'

'So you keep telling me. More madeira, would you agree?'

I only half suppress my smile; I was a tenth of a second from reaching out and grabbing the madeira, which both Frankie and I prefer to cognac when making chicken-liver pâté. Though, when it comes to consuming the pâté, a small glass of cognac and hot buttered toast or a warmed baguette are a girl's best friend.

Frankie and I connect – as ghost and living. It's so different to the way Leith and I were in the kitchen, and not merely for the obvious reasons. Frankie makes me laugh. We're the same age but he's of another vintage; he can be comical, with a few rages over his passion points – such as, the amount of salt and butter I use. To be honest, I think we both enjoy arguing simply over who is right.

We also discuss the mystery of his demise, which I have no idea how to solve. He strides around rattling off names that I add to a list; many of them belong to women.

'All of these people would seriously want to kill you?'

'I got on the wrong side of people. *Some* people.'

'Half of Sydney, according to this list. How did you manage to offend so many?'

'*How* is irrelevant, *why* is irrelevant, but *who* . . . that is the question needing an answer. Now, let's continue. I was thinking baked Alaska could be a good dessert for opening night. Shame it's too early for cherries, that's the best accompaniment.'

'Raspberries are in season,' I reply, barely having to think about it. 'There were some lovely ones at the market yesterday.'

'Perfect. You know, it was called baked Alaska until someone lit it on fire and it became a bomb. I like it being lit – more drama.' He raises his eyebrows in a way that begs for an eye-roll in reply.

I have a growing certainty that Frankie's life was never short on drama, though he's elusive as to what actually went down – him, by what I'm gathering, on many. He will talk details of my recipes, his, menu design, anything about the restaurant and its running for hours on end, but when it comes to the real dirt on him, it's a vague mumble, a one-liner and a subject shift.

He is open to my suggestions, and there is a lightness to him, which makes sense because he's not alive. He is warm and he swears a lot. And sometimes, when he gets on his high horse, he is impossible. Frankie is open . . . except with details of his family life. He says he was a failure of a husband and not much of a dad, but that's about it. He definitely likes women; going by the list, he liked them too much. Though how well he really knew any of them I'm not sure.

I try not to let myself think too hard on the reality of all this, I just focus on the work and whatever it will take to get my own restaurant open. I'm not sure whether pâté will make the opening-night menu – we are, after all, in spring – but making it with Frankie is a welcome distraction from calling people about council permits and safety inspections.

'You never soaked the livers in milk first?' I ask.

'Makes them too bland, they have nothing to apologise for.'

'Agreed, though occasionally I'll poach them in stock.'

'That can work well, but really what they need is a good sauté in butter.'

'Yes.'

'Damn, I'll have to find something else for us to argue about,' he says with a grin.

'I thought an aspic with peppercorns and blood oranges might go well?'

'Blood oranges? Are you mad, woman? *Seville* oranges!'

'I'm getting a feel for why that list of yours is so long.'

'I can't help it if I'm right.' He feigns insult.

'And all the time, too, Frankie – it's quite impressive.'

And so it goes with me and my ghost.

I have tried to contact Serge several times, but all I got was an elderly lady accusing me of being a telemarketer and a young girl who said she would go and get him . . . and never came back. Frankie insists Serge will come through for us. I try again and get a teenage boy who gives me a mobile number, though he warns me Serge rarely uses it: 'he's in and out'. I leave a voicemail and I text. So far no reply, and we have ten days until we open. Staff-wise it's just me, a ghost and a phone number.

17

Frankie

AND THE MELBA TOASTS MUST BE FRESH, FROM A QUALITY LOAF.
Some say waiting a day for pâté improves the flavour, but the way
I make it I say waiting is a waste.

She's good fun when she doesn't cry over her dreadful husband.
She has a lighter hand than I do. She is relaxing around me,
though I still see her wondering if she has invented the entire
thing. Well, we all do to an extent. All our lives are but staged
performances of our inner imaginings.

She has an elegant walk, as if she could leap into the sky at
any moment. I wish she would stop prattling about all the things
she has done wrong or isn't good at, silly girl.

I like her laugh.

18

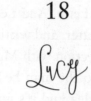

Lucy

THERE ARE SO MANY CHECKLISTS. IT'S OVERWHELMING. I'M FIVE days out and there is so much to do. How am I ever going to pull this off?

Daylight saving is yet to start. Citrus is still very good, but shouldn't the menu be more spring-themed? More strawberries? More asparagus? I wipe down the benches, trying not to get overwhelmed, but my mind races. My breath catches, refusing to go anywhere that could provide me with oxygen.

Frankie watches me, finally asking, 'What's wrong?'

'I can't breathe.'

'You're doing a lot better at it than I am.'

'It's not funny. There's no buffer, Frankie. I have four days and I'm going to die.'

'Five.'

'Four after I leave here, and no buffer.'

'What kind of buffer do you need?'

I attempt to answer while breathing in a shallow, hyperventilating, panicked way. 'Oh, I don't know. More than twenty dollars in my pocket. More than four days to make this place habitable. More than just me and you working here. There's no Serge, although right now I don't even know if maybe you made him up, which is pretty funny considering I made you up and I can't even get your sidekick right, and I'm pretty thin on back story other than you were a lousy dad and some kind of man-slut, you know a lot about food and nothing about women. Nothing! Just what I need in my life after Leith. And Leith . . . Leith is posting how Circa has never been better, and writing stupid fucking bush poetry about his deep connection with Maia that's taken him by the balls and made him into the man he always knew he could be. And this was a stupid idea and it's not going to work and I will never get another job and I hate my lousy, crummy, impoverished, clapped-out-ute-driving stupid life – I don't even own a wardrobe, for god's sake. It's a complete shambles, the lot of it.'

'Anything else?' Frankie, infuriatingly, is cucumber cool, smiling and smothering a slice of toast with pâté. He hands it to me and pours a glass of cognac. He seems unfazed by my blast-off into the stratosphere of the Lucy vent. 'Eat this, drink this and then walk out into the yard and tell me what you see.'

I stick as much toast as I can into my mouth, realising I am in fact starving, take the glass and humph outside.

'I see black.'

'That's it? Just black?' He stands at the doorway watching.

'It's night, that's usually the way it goes.'

'Lie down on the ground.'

'No.'

'Please?'

'No, it's too cold and the grass will prickle.'

'Lucille, you're wearing about seven layers of clothes – who knows if you even have a body underneath all that garb? I agreed about the artichoke hearts, you were right; now please, humour me and lie down and look up. Nothing bad will happen.'

I sit down, take a sip of the cognac and then place it beside me. Then I sigh, lie down and look up.

'What can you see?'

'Bats.'

'And?'

'Rooftops, street lamps – oh, and a bra over an old telephone line. Classy.'

'Any stars?'

'A few.'

It's an unseasonably warm night, there's a yielding in the air. The city hums steadily in the background and up past the glow of streetlights a cluster of stars curtsey to their infinite backdrop.

'Which ones?'

'I don't know any of the constellation names, Frankie. The one that looks like a saucepan.'

'Oh, you mean you can't see the Rise of Soufflé?'

'There is no constellation called the Rise of Soufflé.'

'Of course there is, it's up to your left. There's a cluster that looks exactly like the soufflés you make. And over to your right is the Banana Split. Beside it lies the Roast Leg of Lamb with Rosemary Twig.'

He speaks with such earnestness I wonder if my imaginings are melding and this is the sorry end, a few neurons firing nonsense. I look up at him and he winks.

'Keep looking, Lucille. Which other ones can you see?'

I stare up. 'Well, there *is* one that looks like a lopsided lamington.'

'That would be the Mount of Lamington, yes – well spotted.'

I start to laugh and we continue, getting sillier as we go.

'Yes, the Moulded Ring of Jelly with Mango Cubes, ah, how I miss that.'

'And there's an avocado, I think, or is it guacamole?'

'You see, Lucille, it's all relative. All this seems so big now – your opening, my death, though that *was* pretty major to me – but really, when you compare it to the smorgasbord of stars, what are we? We're made of the same carbon as they are, but they're up there, stretching out into the endless night sky while you and I, the living and not so living, are just two souls in one little single-storey terrace. The constant of proportionality, that's what we have to remember.'

I turn on my side and study him, my imaginary friend . . . and I feel the most at ease I have in weeks.

'I'm glad you're here,' I say quietly.

'I'm glad *you're* here,' he echoes.

Both of us turn our gaze to each other for a moment.

'Now, enough nonsense,' he says, breaking eye contact. 'Have another piece of toast and then take yourself home to bed. And in the morning I will tell you all the sordid details of my life and then we can revise the menu and get on with our work.'

Life feels possible again.

'Promise?'

He does.

19

Frankie

OH, HOW I MISS THE EXPANSE OF STANDING BENEATH THE FULL blanket of night. That girl has brought the world back to me, and reminded me how much I miss it.

Who took me away from it?

20

Lucy

I DRIVE TO THE MARKETS AS DAY BREAKS OFFERING ME THE morning of Fortune's reopening. Again I run the checklist through my mind. The windows have been scrubbed. The china and glassware are good to go and provide a retro sense of whimsy.

Such opulence in the seventies and eighties. Frankie was obviously worse at keeping to a budget than I am. The china is exquisite. He tells me it is the creation of a Danish artist, Bjorn Wiinblad, who worked for Rosenthal re-creating each scene of *The Magic Flute* with broad-rimmed gold-edged opulence against the finest white porcelain. Frankie claims that he was the catalyst for this creative decision, of course; he does see himself at the centre of most things. The setting offers the most baroque of frames for each dish. I can only hope my food is worthy. He had them stashed in a chest in the cool room and had hidden the key in the chimney. Apparently he knew a few months before he was killed that things were grim, and debt collectors were visiting. The china setting would be worth a fortune now, at least fifteen thousand dollars, but to him it is as vital to the restaurant's success as the quality of the food. Well, nearly. We're alike in that very little matters as much as the quality of the food.

He told me he happened across the artist when he was travelling. Frankie was twenty, which I'm guessing would have been in the late sixties. Bjorn was much older, but the pair spent what Frankie says was a highly agreeable evening in Paris following a performance at the Opéra National. Frankie had no money at the time and was in the poor seats at the opera, *The Magic Flute*. He met Bjorn at intermission and the pair hit it off. Bjorn then took Frankie to after-show drinks and dinner and ordered food that Frankie equated to a spiritual awakening. They sat and drank till dawn though Bjorn barely spoke English. Frankie told me that Bjorn's palate was one of the finest he had ever encountered.

It was during this night that Frankie had the epiphany – his destiny was to train as a chef, which he did in Paris at Le Cordon Bleu, where he received a scholarship. Up until then he had been studying medicine at Sydney University. His parents, a family of surgeons, disowned him.

The meal obviously changed Frankie's life. Bjorn, way ahead of his time, was a bit of a hippy at heart. He only ordered food that had been grown, raised or foraged within a fifty-kilometre radius of the restaurant. When staying in France he liked to meet the farmers and see the livestock, liked to pick the flowers he placed in the vase in his studio. I asked Frankie what the menu was, at which point he drifted into his own reverie: pâté, baguette, salad niçoise, beef tartare, duck confit and apple tarte tatin to finish. A classic French bistro meal and one that in the wrong hands could leave you reaching for the Mylanta for days afterwards. But Frankie insists it was the lightness of touch, the freshness of the produce and the companionship of Bjorn that elevated this meal to the music of the spheres. It's amazing what a good meal can do. Bjorn came away with the idea of transferring Mozart to porcelain, in the most beautiful of ways.

There is also the Waterford crystal: heavy, beautiful, decorative lead crystal with a medieval edge. A far cry from the paper-thin tumblers and Gen Y jam jars we have all been accustomed to using. Fortunately there are more-modest dishwasher-friendly backups, though if someone brings a Hill of Grace I'll be sure to use the Waterford. I have to do BYO until I get my licence and enough money to stock a decent cellar, though I will need to supply the customary champagne for opening night. Sadly it won't be Bollinger or Veuve or Pol Roger. I'm not sure there's enough cash to buy anything that's even carbonated. The linens, though thinned of their former damask glory, are fine. Once we have flowers in there, it will be pretty, though I wish there was some kind of signature wall.

Flemington market at dawn remains one of my favourite places. Watching the sky lift itself into a new day while I wander from stall to stall, chatting with the farmers who have been up since two getting their crops to market, is a joy.

Produce and possibilities are at their freshest. Baby chat potatoes, creamy and new, converse with fresh French beans, conspiring to be made into a salad niçoise, one of my favourites. Filling, tasty, full of contrasts, the yielding potato melting against the crunch of the beans, the spark of black olives and the tenderness of fresh tuna, the splendour of a perfectly boiled egg – all elevated by the salty playfulness of anchovies. Niçoise makes salad special.

There's a springtime bounce in my step that hasn't been around me for years. There is something quite liberating in having my own field-of-dreams chapter; opening a restaurant with a ghost is certainly that. I realise that thanks to Leith's ongoing Tweets and the uploading of my meltdown at Circa, the reason I am booked out for tonight is so most people can see a social-science experiment fail. At least I will go out with a bang; the menu, though bare bones money-wise, has a flair and sense of humour I am proud of. But . . . I am probably going to end up moving to

Manyana and working for a florist, which wouldn't be a bad life except I'm not that great at arranging flowers. Maybe in years to come I will look back and see this as my defining moment. Or the last night before I was taken away to some rural community to 'rest'. Or I will become a cautionary tale for small businesses and young chefs – the Icarus of Woolloomooloo.

I am meeting with Serge today. He finally returned my multiple calls and messages with a text at eleven fifteen last night saying he will be there today ready to help. Thank god, because I open tonight.

Julia strides up to me at our agreed stall – Josh from the Megalong, he grows the best beans. As usual she's on the dot. Attica chatters nonsense from her position in Julia's backpack. They look ready to hike the Himalayas rather than stock up for the week. Julia loves coming to the markets; she says it makes her feel like a hard-core foodie. She has been known to bargain with the farmers over three apples, but the stallholders take her with good grace. This is Julia's sport.

'You have been standing with the same handful of beans for five minutes,' she says sternly. 'You're either conjuring a recipe or obsessing over a man. Think carefully before you answer, and realise you have time for neither – you open in thirteen hours.'

'I'm thinking of adding salad niçoise with the tuna and mustard seed, just a little on the side by way of a nod.'

'Nod to what? Just boil some beans.'

Julia, classic films aside, is not one for romance by the light of day.

'A nod to spring and the restaurant's history.'

'As a derelict, undersized, glorified café that was run into the ground by its pisshead, bankrupt, moody, womanising predecessor who had good taste in china?'

I have filled Julia in on my recent Frankie education, citing a friend of Mum's as the source. Since the star-gazing night he has been more forthcoming on the shabby details of his life – well, his addictions and financial downfall; he is still hesitant to tell me much about his relationships.

'Really,' Julia continues her diatribe, 'what is with you being so fixated on the past? The past didn't work out so well – that's why it left, or was left, in a complete state of disarray. The only way you're going to get through this day is to keep your eye on the present.'

I am glad Frankie cannot hear this. He would break something.

'What about the future?' I ask.

'Honey, you know as well as I do that if you don't get through tonight in some halfway decent shape, there is no future. There is you working at a chain café in Bondi Junction and that's about it.'

'If only Leith hadn't publicised it so much! It was meant to be a soft opening.'

'Well, guess what, Luce? It isn't. It's a walk on a tightrope and your chances of success are about as high as being hit by lightning.'

'I think you're mixing too many metaphors,' I reply, attempting righteous indignation. 'And there's the constant of proportionality to consider.'

Julia shoots me a look and grabs my list. She's nervous for me.

'Okay, tomatoes, go grab, now. We're leaving here in thirty.'

'Does Attica need a nap?'

'No. I do if I'm helping.'

Oh god, Jules waitressing. She's going to terrify everyone and break the Rosenthal.

'And before you say it, I *will* be friendly, courteous and gracious.'

'That is so great of you, but I'm not sure I—'

'Trust me,' she overlaps me, jiggling Attica as she does and performing her smiling, don't-talk-rubbish flick of the hand.

'You need me. All you have is this guy Serge helping you out the back.'

'And I've hired a temp for the night, and I can shuttle when I'm not behind the pans.'

'I've watched enough episodes of *MasterChef* to know that's *never* going to happen. You'll be lip-locked with the kitchen. Would you rather a temp or champagne that you can actually swallow? Face facts, it's either me or your mum.'

The thought of my stoned mother anywhere near me while I'm trying to work pushes me over the edge.

'Okay. Great, thanks.'

'And Ken's coming too.'

'What, as a guest?'

'Nope, I've told him he's going to pour drinks. I even made him iron one of his shirts.'

'Gosh . . . Jules.'

The subject of domestic assignment is a battleground between Julia and her husband, and the ironing a wasteland no one mentions. Consequently Ken is one of the most rumpled men I have ever met. He is also terribly short-sighted and walks around with his iPhone practically glued to his face.

Julia, as usual, reads my mind. 'He's got new glasses, much better, and I've banned the phone.'

'But Ken doesn't like people, and now he's going to spend an evening surrounded by them.'

'He's doing it for you, Luce . . . that and I promised him some oral.'

'Has anyone told you that you truly are the best friend ever?'

'Not nearly often enough. Go get tomatoes.'

I obey Julia's instructions and wander over to the next stall. I am feeling and smelling tomatoes when the hand with a matching wedding band places itself over mine.

'You say tomato, I say tomato.'

He grabs the tomato I was about to take and moves to hand it to me but then places it in his bag. I exchange a look with Ned, the tomato man who has been looking after me for years; we both agree, Leith's a jerk.

'All set for tonight, LiLi?'

'All set,' I reply, matching his tone. 'Thank you *so* much for all the PR.'

'I'll bill you later. My invite seems to be lost in cyberspace.'

At that moment the shadow of Julia falls across Leith's face. 'Get out of the way, dickwad, and let her get on with it. We've got a lot of shit to get through, no thanks to you.'

'Oh Julia, so nice to see your interpersonal skills are really coming along.'

'Go fuck yourself, and stay away tonight or I'll be slapping an AVO on you personally. Now shoo, you irritating gnat.' Julia grabs Leith's bag of tomatoes and sets him on his way.

Leith hovers for a moment longer, before he walks away with a calmness that's slightly unnerving.

'Bless you,' I say to Julia. I don't have time to fret over Leith's next move, though his appearance has left an unsettling residue.

'Forget blessing me, name your firstborn after me and we'll be square.'

We head off to the fish markets to find the perfect seafood for the perfect opening night.

'Everything going to plan, then?' asks Julia.

I look over my list with its many gaps and a circle around champagne. 'Absolutely.'

I have that gripping feeling in my belly that this will be a day of calamity. But really, what else could go wrong?

21

Frankie, 1981

THE KITCHEN PUMPS AND THUMPS WITH DAVID BOWIE, THE HIGH priest of Saturday nights. I finally got my own copy of 'Under Pressure', his collaboration with Queen, and now it throbs out of the ghetto-blaster. Oh Ziggy, oh Freddie, you place me in the zone to cook. This place I'm in right now is the reason Zen masters sit on rocks for decades pouring water over their feet. All is in sync. The pans, the plates, Serge – everything I need. My sous chef has possibly the worst English known to man but my god he's as good a right hand as there ever was. I can't tell if he's Russian, Croatian, Latvian or a mix, and every time I ask he sighs and commences some drawn-out story, his hybrid English constantly abandoning him in favour of his own native tongue, with a tale involving donkeys and midnight castaways. In any case, he's Serge. He moves to the Bowie beat as he sautés scallops and follows me up garnishing spatchcocks I have steamed in straw. Serge has been with me through the highs and lows of the past five years, seen me too drunk to walk, too sad to speak and too giddy to fuck. He's a brick. He's loyal. Perennially single, caring for parents who live out past Drummoyne, and his awful sister with her tribe of offspring.

Then there are my girls. Tiffany is on tonight; she has the blush of new love. She has decided to opt for the fairer sex, and who could blame her; her affair with me would have been enough to swear her off men for life. Still, she holds no grudge, bless her, and her girlfriend, a Welsh lass with smouldering eyes and a great laugh, fits easily into our team. Stacy is on tonight too, the woman whose wardrobe choices know no boundaries: tonight it's a silk jumpsuit held together with oversized safety pins. Definitely rip-off-able, with her tight rebellious body peeking out at every turn. My god, she's a stunner and full of piss and vinegar. The perfect hostess. She can get an overly raucous drunken customer to leave while they think they're becoming best friends, and then welcome them back the following evening so they think their night was as smooth as silk. She gets the tips, too.

The last spatchcock is plated as Melanie-most-makeable, the new girl, waits at the pass. I take my time pouring some extra jus around the succulent bird, milking the moment. Serge laughs as he watches. Melanie quivers in her sweetness. What an arse I am; still, it's too tempting not to. I send her on her way as Tiffany returns with the nonentity Paul Levine. A food critic who broadcasts his expertise via turtleneck jumpers and horn-rimmed glasses. A flaccid style of man whose self-importance vastly exceeds his talent.

'What the fuck are *you* doing here?'

'I wanted to explain.'

'Explain? *Explain* why someone who has sung the praises of my restaurant since I opened and has tried to take up residence up my arse at every moment possible would write a pretentious, fabricated, unworthy review that doesn't deserve to even mention my food?'

I'm met with an obsequious smile; he dithers and nods. 'I agree.'

What is this fool doing in my kitchen?

'Your food is first rate.'

'You have a strange way of expressing your appreciation of it, Paul. Are you willing to write a retraction in tomorrow's paper?'

'I can't. It's not your food, it's . . . you. Some of your creditors are getting antsy.'

'So, how does ruining— Oh, I see: ruin my reputation, drive me to closure. But that won't get them their money back. What's your involvement with them, anyway?'

The weasel wit looks away.

'Or is it another restaurant, another chef who perhaps wants me shut down and is prepared to pay my debts to help make that happen . . . but who could that be?' I have no time for this; Serge and Tiffany hover, waiting for my fury to unfurl.

In truth, the line-up of chefs who would love to see Fortune close is growing. Via my connections I'm able to get the first and best of everything, and I can cook them all under the table. And yes, I have been an idiot with money, a few flutters on the ponies and a taste for a lifestyle that belongs more in Monaco than Woolloomooloo.

'Here, I could do with your advice,' I say, my blood bubbling along with the coq au vin for Tuesday. My voice remains calm, sage-like.

Paul looks at me hopefully with his beady eyes. 'You know I'm sorry, Frankie. I'm new in this role and it's not like I had any choice in it – the review, I mean.'

I wave my hand with an air of nonchalant and magnanimous dismissal. 'What do you think of the sauce?' I pass him a spoon. 'Too little salt?'

Paul shuffles towards my coq au vin and slurps greedily. Tastes. I have to admit his palate is good, not great but decent, which demands my begrudging culinary respect, but watching him taste is barely an act of beauty.

'Perhaps some more pancetta?'

'Really?'

I grab the spoon and taste. The bastard is right.

I pass him back the spoon and, emboldened, the greedy guts goes in for another mouthful.

'I thought you had potential,' I say as he swills my flavours in his greedy gob. 'I thought you understood what we are doing here. It isn't just about food – the textures, the bite, the taste – it's the alchemy. Every meal is imbued with your mood, your history, the conversation you're having, the lighting, the table next to you, the scent of your waiter. I want that to mean something.'

Paul nods as he gorges. 'Yes, yes, it does.'

'Jesus, you're a lily-livered git.'

Paul straightens, looking wary. I watch him. I decide not to do anything. But then again . . .

'Oh, fuck it.' I push his face into the coq au vin: long enough to hurt, short enough not to scar.

'You were right, it needed more pancetta. Serge!'

As always, Serge is by my side in an instant.

'We need to start another coq au vin!'

Serge passes Paul a tea towel, nodding, 'Yes, chef!' as I head back to my plates.

A man can only stand so much.

22

Lucy

THE FISH MARKETS PROVIDE ME WITH SOME EXCELLENT TUNA and scallops for tonight. As I pull up the ute in front of Fortune I see a crumpled form in the doorway, who I assume is Old Bill. I've picked up an extra coffee for him by way of apology for making him move from his preferred sleeping venue when he's not up at the shelter. I honk and call, 'Bill!'

To my surprise, Old Bill appears around the side of the house. He kicks the wall and approaches me. We don't so much speak as nod.

I hand him his cappuccino.

'Sugar?'

'It's in there.'

His eyes are the red beads of lab mice; obviously a big night on the turps. I still have no idea about his past.

'Who's that?' I point to the door.

Bill laughs and looks skyward. 'That's Serge.'

'Huh?'

'Serge. He's here to help you, he said.'

I look at the motionless form on my front doorstep, and the ocean roars in my ears once more. Bill shrugs and moves away, clearly wanting no part in my meltdown.

As I approach I note that Serge holds a lit cigarette with a gigantic ash like a dragon's flare as he snores blissfully. He looks about eighty, though if he's the same age as Frankie he should in my time only be in his early sixties.

Deep, cavernous lines score his face. His hair is uncut and unclean. A stench of garlic and bourbon is emitted with each exhalation. He farts himself awake.

'I was nu sleepink, I was waitink.'

Serge struggles his way to standing; he stumbles but somehow manages to keep the cigarette ash in place until he stands, then releases it in a single, practised tap.

He nods at me and coughs the cough of a terminally ill man in a palliative-care ward.

'Serge, is it? Here, let me help.' I move to him; he places his hand on my shoulder and continues to hack.

'I help you unload car.'

'No, it's fine. Is there a hospital you should be in?'

'I'm good, just waking up. Been a while since I work.'

'Oh. How long?'

'Thirty-three years,' he says precisely. 'I work for nobody after Frankie. I nurse parents, then I have holiday, then I look after niece, then her kids, then I forget what I do.'

Oh my god, this is a freaking disaster.

'I'm sorry. I didn't realise you'd retired.'

'I come out of retirement to help you. You friend of Frank.'

'I didn't know him when he was here – I was two when he died – but my mum knew him a bit.'

Serge whistles, then has another hack. 'All the girls knew Frankie.'

Please don't tell me this, I don't have time. 'Really?' I say politely but, I hope, distantly.

Serge nods proudly. 'He what you call excellent mover. Womaniser but even better cook.'

I nod. 'Serge, I'm not sure you're up to an opening night.'

'No. I good. I'm here. Let's go it.'

He follows me back to the ute where I begin to unload. He takes the bulk of the goods in his arms. Moves two steps and stops.

'Serge?'

'Is okay. I still got it.'

Old Bill reappears and miraculously also grabs a bag. For a moment I'm not sure if he's going to do a runner with it or carry it inside. He chooses the latter, though after I unlock the side gate and back door leading into the kitchen he leaves it at the entrance.

'Bill, you can come in.'

Bill shakes his head firmly. 'Not yet.' He performs a bow and is on his way.

Serge is already inside unloading produce into the fridge. The man certainly knows his way around the space.

He wanders through to the dining room. 'I am home, I am home.'

I follow him. Serge cries openly as he wanders around.

Frankie appears. 'Serge?'

Serge can't see him, and continues to wander about. 'Where is wallpaper?'

'It was ruined with mould. I know it looks plain, but the paint's nice.'

'Wallpaper better.'

'I agree, Serge. Lord love a duck, what's happened to you?' Frankie says.

'Frankie and I lived our most good times here.'

'That's true,' Frankie laments.

'I can still smell him.'

'Because I'm right here.' Frankie circles Serge and Serge leans into him as he does. So close it bruises my heart to watch. 'Serge, you were so young and handsome. The girls loved you.'

'Not as much as they loved you,' escapes from my mouth.

'Pardon? No, everyone loved Frankie more. Especially women.'

'Of course, and he loved them too, right?' I cannot help myself.

Frankie throws me a look of irritation mixed with the edgings of pride.

'Oh, so many,' agrees Serge.

'And I bet he broke a few hearts.' I am enjoying this now. Frankie is not.

'Lucille,' he warns.

'Yes, many, many, he always brought in Serge to help clean up the mess. I would dry their eyes, put them in taxi.'

Frankie attempts to backtrack, badly. 'There weren't *that* many.'

He is of course corrected by Serge who, lost in his own memories, recounts their glory years.

'Hundreds! Many hundreds.'

'Serge!' Frankie snaps.

'Frankie!' I snap in return.

Serge looks at me, baffled. 'Yes, Frankie, that's who we talk. I miss him with my whole heart.'

'Oh, Serge, why can't you see me?' Frankie's voice softens as he watches his old friend closely, absorbing the changes in him.

'He was one of kind. We made something you believe in and then they all come and took it away, and him too.'

'What happened?' Perhaps Serge has a clue.

Frankie continues to study his smelly former sidekick.

'He was too generous, too free, he owed much.'

This I can relate to. Frankie nods reluctantly. 'It's true, I was a train-wreck with no track.'

'He was about to declare bankruptcy, close doors.'

Frankie stamps his foot and blusters at this. 'No! I never wanted that to happen. I was owed money, and I owed – they just had to wait.'

'But what he create in that kitchen . . . no one else could touch him.'

'Oh, how I wish that was true,' Frankie laments. 'They touched me all right – grabbed me from behind, the cowards. I never saw their faces.'

Serge cries some more. 'He was one of kind.'

'Oh, Serge, stop weeping, you look like my aunt Ethel,' Frankie says.

'Now I have bad back and I no drive.' Serge pulls out a chair and takes a seat. He looks down. 'I like floorboard. Bit noisy, though.'

He's right.

'We're going to get some big rugs when we can.'

'You is brave gal.'

Frankie claps his hands together. 'That's more like it.'

Serge follows his thought through. 'Everyone in town saying this will be lemon.'

'Everyone in town?' I repeat. 'Serge, who did you hear that from?'

'My niece, she send me Tweets.'

Oh great, even my down-and-out sous chef can see I'm sailing into failure.

'Are you sure you're up for this?' I ask him.

Serge stands back up, attempts to puff out his chest, coughs. 'Serge will help save your day. Besides, what else I do with my days? This give me meaning, I believe you can.'

I smile. 'Thanks, Serge.'

He moves in for a hug. Frankie looks displeased.

I give him a quick embrace, as much as my nasal passages can bear, and his hands place themselves on my bum. I slap them and pull away. Serge shrugs, unfazed.

Frankie shakes his head, laughing. 'He always does that.'

'It was worth a try,' says Serge.

'Kitchen, now. There's a pile of carrots, get chopping,' I say firmly.

Serge cheerily accepts my sternness. 'Yes, chef!'

I wait until he's out of earshot. 'Man-slut!' I chide.

'Reformed,' Frankie coos.

'Only because you're dead!'

'You don't have time to hate me, Lucille.'

I look at the time. He's right. Again.

23

Frankie

FUNNY, ISN'T IT, HOW YOU SEE SOMEONE YOU HAVEN'T CLAPPED eyes on in years, decades even, and at first you're struck by this faded, balding, stooped, lined and flattened impostor who stands in your friend's place. Like those terrible magazines in which people are encouraged to send in a photo of themselves alongside one of the star they think, or were once told, they resemble. It's not right.

Yet with each breath, each gesture, each moment that passes, your sense of recognition expands and adjusts. Maybe it *is* him.

And then they perform some familiar, moronic gesture, like Serge attempting to grab Lucille's derriere, and instantly you see the original again. Halleluiah for that.

24

Lucy

I WONDER WHO IT WAS WHO FIRST THOUGHT OF PAIRING PORK belly, so succulent, so salty, so crispy on the edges, so right, with the dreamy light freshness of seared scallops. Drizzled with basil oil, bedded on a wellspring of peas and accompanied by baby carrots with a honey glaze. Ladies and gentlemen, we have a main that is a fun reinterpretation of surf and turf.

The morning progresses as smoothly as a morning spent with a skirt-chasing ghost and a hungover sous chef who hasn't worked for thirty years can. Possibly a bit better.

Frankie and Serge echo each other in their speech and ideas. But where Frankie is impatient, compulsive and compelling, Serge is considered and deferential, and even though he's out of practice he is a hell of a good sous chef.

We've talked through the menu, which has his approval, though terms such as 'infusion', 'deconstruction' and 'soil' are lost on him and sworn at by Frankie. That's not a bad thing. It is far too easy to overcomplicate recipes in the hope of sounding fancy, something I wish to get away from; Circa was full of it. As Frankie says, writing 'juicy' on a menu is as bad as saying 'yum!'. It should be obvious that the pork is juicy by its texture, its flavour, its ooze. In the past few years I guess we have all in our restaurants become guilty of menu masturbation.

A century ago you would simply say entrée, main and pudding; the rest was left to the discretion of the chef. I think with the popularity of TV food shows we have all become a lot more creative with our dishes and I am all for discussing the food we consume – we should be informed and aware. But it has got a bit out of hand, to the point where the more words on the menu, the more nervous I become, both as a diner and chef.

Serge is removing the sesame crackers from the oven when there's a knock at the back door. Frankie has ventured off some-where – no doubt serving his customers in some alternate universe.

Hugo appears, his arms full of craft supplies and a case of Veuve Clicquot.

Frankie reappears and eyes the champagne. Then he and Serge declare in unison, 'Ah, velvet clitoris, my favourite.'

Hugo and I both turn and stare at Serge, who comes as close to a blush as he ever will.

'When I started here my English was not good. Frankie short-staffed one night, so I help on floor. Some big fancy man orders bottle of champagne but he pronounce it wrong. I try help him but he thinks I tell him "Velvet Clitoris". I tell Frankie, who laughs so hard he give another bottle for free. From then, everyone at Fortune who have some lot of dough order loud and proud the velvet clitoris.'

'It was a bloody lark, velvet clitoris,' chimes in Frankie. 'Mind you, it was the widow Clicquot who made the fizz what it is, moved it on from its sickly sweet origins and led a failing cham-pagne house to superstardom, bless her; I think she'd appreciate the name.'

'Right,' I say, because what else can I say?

'Lucy, are you going to help me or are you going to keep talking to your basil?'

I race to Hugo's side and grab some of the rolls of paper on top of his case. 'What are you doing here? I thought you said it wasn't worth the torment of Leith?'

Hugo is an exquisite being. He works a crowd with a panache usually reserved for Hollywood starlets. He has the perfect balance of deferential and just enough sass. He is a gifted waiter, organiser and lifestyle connoisseur who knows his food. Hugo is always chasing young boys who break his heart. He is bossed and adored by his Jewish parents, has been asked by billionaires to work on their private jets, and every other decent restaurant has tried to poach him, for good reason. But he is loyal and he hates change. He was one of the major factors that kept me at Circa when things felt grim, his wisdom and wit were what helped get me through many a night in the kitchen when my husband had deserted early and left me with the mess.

'Julia called my dad to sort out your insurance. Dad still says Julia is the most cutthroat lawyer he's ever worked with. Julia told Dad about you and Leith. Dad told Mum, and Mum summoned me to the house. When I showed her the Instagram pics of you yelling at Leith at Circa and told her how many arguments it set off among our customers for the rest of the night, Mum laughed. Then she rang her girlfriends, booked a table for eight here tonight and told me she'd pay for any breach of contract Leith tried to lay on me for leaving Circa. Then I had a conversation with Uncle Harvey, who drafted up a letter as a backup to keep Leith in his place; it listed a few things Leith has done which aren't by the book. I took it to Circa along with my letter of resignation, and Leith went pale. So, here I am, if you still want me. Oh, and the bubbles are from Mumsie.'

Before I can get a word in, Hugo turns his smile on Serge. 'Hello, I'm Hugo.'

Frankie interjects approvingly. 'I like him. Some of these fairies have more backbone than straight men.'

'Frankie!' I admonish.

Hugo and Serge look at me blankly. Serge, bless him, saves me. 'No, I Serge. Frankie was owner.'

'Yes,' I say hurriedly. 'Of course. Serge, this is Hugo, my lifesaver and maître d', and sommelier when we can afford our licence. Hugo, Serge is my sous chef.'

'Number one,' Serge enthuses.

'Charmed.' Hugo maintains his wide-eyed, democratic-lefty-non-judging smile.

I owe a lot to Hugo's mum. She's the kind of woman you daydream about having as your mother: smart, driven, stylish as all get-out; a psychotherapist, she's also a society queen on every single board of every single cause.

Stella can be seen at dawn power-walking her dogs and her husband, the fabulously debonair and clever John Supera, on the promenade by Bondi Beach. After sunrise she's home on her exercise bike talking on speakerphone conferring with an assortment of high flyers, lobbying them for her causes. At lunch she's usually chairing or hosting a function, late afternoon she's back in her office seeing patients, dinner is at a restaurant to see one of her four children, or at another event. It's not unusual to receive emails from Stella at 3am with the title: 'Just a thought'. Stella is a social reformer, a brilliant mother, a devoted wife and the woman you definitely want at your opening night. She could run the country, possibly even the Western world, in a blink. During the Sydney Olympics she actually carried the flag for some bizarre tiny country that no one knew the name of because she didn't want them to miss out; the country had one Olympic representative, for something like ping pong, but Stella would not hear of them missing their moment. Having Stella come to your opening night is a bit like having Jackie Kennedy wear your fashion house's dress to a gala opening.

'What's that smell?' Hugo asks. Frankie is circling him, making a close inspection.

'Is it the pork belly?' I offer.

'Not a food smell.' Hugo sniffs again, not pleased.

'Are you wearing Kouros, Serge?' I ask.

Serge proudly puffs out his chest. 'A little behind each ear in morning. The ladies love it.'

'I'll bet they're lining up,' Hugo jokes.

'Not for a while,' Serge muses.

Hugo laughs at this, as does Serge. Frankie slaps Hugo on the back. Hugo looks behind him but says nothing.

'What's with the art supplies?' I ask Hugo.

Hugo shrugs, feigning nonchalance. 'Just some Florence Broadhurst left over from Mum's powder room. Julia said it was looking a bit bland out front. I thought we could do a feature wall.'

I clap my hands with joy. Stella's taste is both flamboyant and impeccable.

Frankie looks perplexed. 'Yes, of course she's right about it being plain, but a feature wall with wallpaper? Why not just cover the lot?'

Hugo moves through to the dining room, and whistles. 'Not bad, Lucy Lu. This will lift it.' He unrolls a perfect, gorgeous golden brocade that will bring out the golden rims of the Magic Flute china. When I show Hugo the Rosenthal, he breaks into applause.

'I knew Florence. Wonderful woman, she dines here on occasion. I think she would approve.' Frankie is warming to the wallpaper idea.

Serge is less convinced. 'But where is paintings?'

Frankie sulks. 'They were taken by that dreadful woman I dated.'

Serge plucks Frankie's line of thought from the ether. 'Oh, yes, I remember. Girlfriend of Frankie walk into restaurant, take it off wall and walk out with one night after they have fight. He bad boyfriend, but it such a pity, it was Whiteley.'

'You owned a Whiteley?!' I pretty much shout.

'Not me,' replies Serge. 'Frankie.'

Frankie nods stoically.

'Where is the girlfriend?' Hugo is intrigued.

'Very successful art dealer,' Serge reports proudly.

'I bet,' Hugo says.

'She live in London now. Frankie, he had a few. What about other paintings?'

'What other paintings?' I ask.

Frankie slaps his hand to his forehead, his performance for multitudes, though I'm his only audience. 'Oh lord, of course. But you don't want those.'

'Want what?' I ask.

'Other paintings,' Serge continues. 'Frankie always liked the artists, he used to let many of them pay with their work.'

'And I wonder why I was going out of business,' Frankie scoffs. 'Bloody artists, they ate everything, drank everything, stayed all night. Best fun, though.'

'Where are those works now, did someone take them?' I ask.

'I hid them on one of the pantry shelves. I was going to use them as lining.' Frankie snorts.

Hugo claps his hands. 'It's just like La Colombe d'Or.'

La Colombe d'Or, or the Golden Dove, is one of the world's most romantic restaurants, located in the French Riviera. It's become legendary for the artworks lining its walls.

'But without the artists being Chagall or Picasso. That was my inspiration too,' adds Frankie.

I go back into the kitchen and drop to my hands and knees to search the bottom of the pantry.

'Why are we in here?' Serge asks, watching me crawl about.

'Just a hunch.'

'Luce, darling, have you got time for this?' Hugo asks. 'Why would he leave them there?'

'To line the pantry shelves,' I answer matter-of-factly.

'I think it's bottom right, or no, maybe left,' says Frankie. 'Or maybe I took them home or binned them.'

The others join me, and the three of us are on our hands and knees when Julia enters. We look up to her as one.

'I'm assuming you're praying that you'll get through tonight?'

'Why are you here now?' I ask.

'Ken came home from work early. The thought of a full house pushed him over and he broke out in shingles. I've quarantined him until further notice, and the nanny is with Attica, so I'm all yours. Please tell me you don't expect me to join you down there.'

'Serge thinks there might be some paintings, sketches.'

'And you're hoping one of them will be a Rembrandt?'

'An Olsen would do.' Hugo sounds hopeful.

'No, he never gave me one,' Frankie muses.

'Damn.' I love Olsen.

And then I see a small rise beneath the linoleum. 'Under the lino?' I ask my ghost.

'Possibly. I may not have been sober when I stored them.'

Julia passes me a knife, which I use to lift the lino tile, which needs replacing anyway. There lies a perfectly sealed plastic bag with the label: 'Bad art by poor patrons'.

'He labelled it: I like that.' Julia nods approvingly.

It's the first positive thing Julia has had to say about Frankie, and he basks in the compliment. I carefully unwrap the package, which contains close to thirty sketches, most of them unremarkable.

'I told you,' Frankie murmurs happily.

'Oh, boo,' chimes Hugo.

'Most artists not so talented. Frankie hung the good ones,' Serge reflects.

'It was worth a try.' Then I see another bump. 'What's that?' I ask Frankie.

'No idea,' is the chorused answer.

Another sealed thin pile, this one unlabelled. I open it. Beautiful free-flowing sketches and a few paintings appear, including a portrait of Frankie created by a well-known artist.

'That's a Matthias Drewe!' Hugo beams.

Matthias Drewe, now in his fifties, is known in the Australian art scene for his terrible temper and his serene, beatific work. He is a regular finalist in the Archibald prize for portraiture.

'Matthias Drewe. He was kitchen hand, very bad at sink, but good with pencil,' Serge informs us.

'Oh, him. I forgot about him, little troublemaker.' Frankie is underwhelmed.

'He was a kitchen hand here?' I say incredulously.

'He was streetkid, and thief – he was always pinching Frankie's bread delivery. Frankie found him and wanted to smack him, but he was only thirteen, so instead Frankie give him job.'

'Gave him a job? That's child labour!' Frankie's approval rating descends for Julia once more.

Frankie laughs. 'That kid was never a child. One of the most conniving, clever and talented little shits ever.' He says this with a certain level of respect.

Hugo is enthralled. 'What happened?' he asks Serge.

'Matthias always more interested in trouble than work. He always here, he would come in early and sit and sketch while me and Frankie did the menu and recipes. Then he came up with idea: he would tell other restaurants our idea for a price.'

'He was a rat!' Hugo is impressed.

'He wanted money for new bike. Frankie found out and tried to fire him, but he cried so hard, Frankie soft and let him stay. He was always pinching stuff but he stayed till he got into art school in London. When he left he give Frankie these.'

We look over them again.

'This is Frankie?' Hugo points to his portrait.

Serge looks at the picture adoringly. 'Yes, is him.'

'Hello, he's a total spunk!' enthuses Hugo, and I try not to nod my head in agreement.

Frankie laps it up, a cat with cream. 'I like that man.' He nods at Hugo.

Julia inspects the portrait. 'Yes, good bone structure, but he looks arrogant to me.'

'Yes,' I agree.

'Steady on!' the subject says.

Serge studies the painting. 'Yes, very arrogant. And very kind.'

I wrap the pictures back up.

'You could sell them? Cash to inject into the restaurant?' offers Hugo.

'They aren't mine to sell. I'm the tenant, not the owner.'

'Frankie would not mind.' Serge is confident.

'No, I don't mind.' Frankie studies me. 'Use them.'

'I'm going to frame them and keep them here. This is Frankie's place too,' I announce.

'Oh my god, you aren't going to last a week, you and your romantic principles.' Julia unsuccessfully suppresses a headshake.

Frankie looks pleased. 'You're sure?'

'It will bring us good fortune, and he would have hung them if he'd stayed. It's like his blessing.' I am thinking on my feet. I love the work of Matthias Drewe and these are exactly what the restaurant needs. I am also becoming too fond of looking at Frankie.

Serge begins to cry again.

Julia eyes me warily. 'Just don't hang his painting over the fireplace.'

'Agreed.'

Strange, isn't it, how sometimes you reach the point of surrendering to whatever is going to happen – and how you often find yourself at your happiest in those moments?

When I return from picking up more flowers, I find Julia and Hugo laughing as they set the tables in the dining room, the Broadhurst wallpaper now hanging thanks to some strategically placed Blu-tack – and then I realise what they are laughing at: Serge is singing. I peek through to the kitchen and see that he has taken the old busted-up ghetto-blaster from one of the bottom shelves and plugged it in, and is singing merrily along to Barbra Streisand and Barry Gibb's 'Guilty'. What Julia and Hugo cannot realise, of course, is that Frankie stands beside him, as Serge preps the beans for the niçoise, harmonising perfectly. It is obviously something they have done together in the kitchen many times. And just in that moment, before even Frankie realises I am there, I feel grateful. Grateful to have assembled these oddballs, who are all in their own way going out on a limb to support making Fortune live again . . . and me too, I guess. Then, of course, I begin to cry. Serge stops singing.

'This song make you sad?'

'No,' I reply. 'I haven't heard it since I was about eight, but it makes me glad.'

Serge nods in agreement. 'She is good woman, our Babs. We listened to her here a lot.'

I smile at Frankie while I ask, 'Frankie liked music in the kitchen?'

They both nod, and then overlap in reply.

'We listen to all kinds: Bowie, Van Morrison, the Stones,' starts Serge.

Frankie continues, 'Led Zeppelin, Dylan, Bach.'

'Olivia Newton-John.'

'What? We never listened to Olivia Newton-John!'

'Nana Mouskouri.'

'Serge! He's lying. We banned his tapes from the kitchen in the end!'

'The lady who yodels . . . and ABBA.'

'Never ABBA!'

Hugo and Julia re-enter the kitchen, both of them singing away.

'This music is retro fab.' Hugo performs an elegant twirl.

Frankie is now in a huff. 'Not retro *anything*. It's just good music! What is it with this obscene desire to re-label everything? That music is still current.'

'To *you*,' I say.

'Don't tell me you don't like it, you're about ready to break out into a solo.' Julia attempts a dance move of her own . . . all of her own.

The problem with being around people you know so intimately is that they also know your daggy tendencies, particularly those of singing eighties power ballads when intoxicated, and dancing to Bananarama.

'I say we use it as our playlist tonight, add to the fun!' Hugo is now on a mission.

'Good lord,' Frankie says. 'It's a restaurant, not a circus. But there must be music, yes.'

'I've already made a playlist,' I counter. 'It already includes a lot of seventies and eighties tracks but they're more indi–folk: Joni Mitchell, Nick Drake, that sort of thing. And yes, I made it with Fortune in mind.'

Serge looks worried. 'Does it have Bee Gees? It must have Bee Gees.'

I look to Frankie, who nods solemnly. 'Take a risk. Take the diners for a ride that reflects where their palates are going. Take them from Philip Glass to Nina Simone, leave them with the Bee Gees.'

'I have the Bee Gees,' I assure Serge, making a mental note to add some more tunes.

Julia turns to me now and switches on her matron tone, the one she uses when she thinks my hair needs new highlights or I'm wearing a worn-out jumper in public. 'Lucy, you should go home now. Have a little lie-down, take a shower, wash your hair.'

'I was going to stay and work,' I argue. 'I brought a different shirt to change into.'

Julia and Hugo synchronise their headshake. It's not going to cut it. I look to Serge, who shrugs and says, 'May be good to wear dress after work. And lipstick.'

Oh my god, I am being given fashion advice by a man whose nasal hair pretty much touches his top lip.

Frankie groans. 'Yes, a woman should look like a woman.'

'Are you saying I don't look like a *woman*?' I demand.

'No one's saying that, honey bun. You're our blonde Nigella,' says Hugo.

'But scruffier,' adds Julia.

'A little primping wouldn't go astray.' Hugo is being as diplomatic as he can.

And it's true. You hardly think of great fashion choices, waxing, or Chanel No. 5 when you're strung out, broke, haunted, and opening a restaurant. But I guess it *is* my restaurant, and since most of the customers are turning up to view the mad woman of misfortune, it might be a good idea to shower and, yes, wash my hair.

'Okay, fine,' I announce with very little grace. 'But know this, it's what I do, how my food tastes that matters, not how *I look*. I will not be bullied by anyone's patriarchal objectification of me.'

The four of them nod slowly, laughter not far from their lips.

Indignant, I turn to walk out, and as I open the front door I hear Frankie call after me, 'And bring some heels for after you finish. I know you've got a good set of ankles hiding under those boots.'

How does he know that?

He noticed my ankles?

25

Frankie

WHEN DID PEOPLE STOP LISTENING TO THE BEE GEES?

When did they begin to use walkie-talkies to check the weather, take photos and type novels?

Why didn't I frame those sketches?

Will they come tonight, the culprits?

26

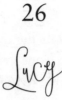

I DRIVE HOME THROUGH A MAUVE STORM OF JACARANDA AND wisteria. This is my favourite time of year in Sydney: everything is opening up again and the lavender canopy creates the feeling of a utopian wonderland.

I walk in to see Mum on her throne viewing another medical show.

'Oh, you're back,' she says, as she always does. The tone is never surprised, distressed or euphoric, more like the greeting you might give your postman after his return from holiday. 'You've got a visitor.'

I look around; there's no one there.

'Leith.'

'*What?*'

Mum signals to my bedroom.

'Why'd you let him in *there*?' I hiss.

'Well, I didn't want him in here annoying me while I'm watching my shows.'

Panic rises. 'How long has he been here?'

Mum shrugs. 'He arrived sometime during *The View*.' My mother's schedule is punctuated by her programs.

'Thanks, Mum.' I pull an adolescent face and then head to the room of Leith. Ugh. Why is it that whenever you start to feel anything like optimism your ex shows up on your bed?

The room is not a sunny one, but even in the gloom I can make out Leith on the bed, shoes off, staring blankly through the window.

'Leith, I thought you—'

'Shh . . . come.' He beckons me over, his voice a whisper. As Julia says, the guy has more front than David Jones.

'What?' I ask, not bothering to lower my voice. The last thing I need is to be sitting on a bed next to Leith.

'Please, just come.'

I know this man, he won't leave until I seem to cooperate. I plonk down beside him. 'What?'

'See. See there, next to the fern, there's a spider weaving his web.'

I'm not sure what parallel universe I've transited myself to. 'Leith?'

'Isn't it amazing? It's a miracle, really – just watch. Watch it with me.'

'Are you okay?'

Obviously not. Leith barely spares the time to watch his preferred footy team score a winning try in a grand final, let alone watch a small, unremarkable spider weave its web.

'It's like, here is this moment, and I am viewing this amazing creation in this moment, like, this thing is never going to happen again like this and I'm here seeing it, which makes me part of the web, and now you're here and we are the only living humans who will ever know it.'

'Wow. Yep. Leith, have you been eating my mum's cookies?'

'I needed to relax.'

'Sure . . . How many did you have?'

'She only let me have half, but I was still hungry and nothing was happening, so I crept to the fridge and took two more.'

Brilliant. 'Do you have any idea how stoned you are right now?'

'Yes. No. Pretty stoned.'

'Very stoned. Do you need to vomit?'

'Every word has a big gap till the first letter of the next word starts, you know?'

'Not really. No.'

Leith begins to unravel on the bed. 'I might need to lie down for now.'

And he's horizontal, his limbs splayed. He pats his shoulder, indicating just the spot where I should place my head.

'Leith, no.'

'Shh, just shh, it's all good. Lie down. Just for a minute.' He pulls my head down to his shoulder. This was not the nap I had in mind. How am I going to get him out? So much for my mini personal one-hour overhaul.

I lie still for a minute, hoping he will commence snoring so I can get on with it. This, of course, is not what happens.

'This is nice,' he murmurs.

'Hmm . . .'

'Hmm, yum. It would be better if we were naked.'

'What are you doing here?'

'Shh, let's just listen to the sound of the fan.'

'The fan isn't on, Leith. What are you doing here? Where's Maia?'

'I wanted to wish you well.'

A knot in my stomach tightens. Stoned or sober, Leith is incapable of wishing someone well if it isn't of benefit to him. I play along; alternative options are scarce at this point.

'That was very kind of you, especially after the past week.'

'Every marriage has its ups and downs, babe. I want you to be happy.'

Do not fall for this. Do not fall for this, Lucy.

'Really?'

'Hmm . . .'

He snuggles into me and kisses my forehead, then he kisses my cheeks, and I wish I could say I am repelled. I blame pheromones and loneliness, but it feels good, too good, and my body involuntarily begins to move into his. We kiss on the lips lightly, and then again, and with each kiss I feel myself being sucked into the vortex of him.

'Leith, I can't. This isn't . . . I have to get ready for tonight.'

'No, you don't,' he says, a dreamy puss with unlimited cream.

'I do. In case you haven't looked at me lately, I resemble Catweazle.'

'We can go home and have a long bath, open some wine, I'll make spaghetti carbonara, loads of it, we'll eat, just sit, eat and listen – sound good?'

For a nanosecond it sounds perfect. And then I think of them all singing, and of Serge and the china and the soufflés. And then I think of Frankie.

'Sounds fictional. I have the restaurant opening.'

'No, that's all done.'

I laugh at how stoned he is. 'No, it's tonight.'

'You don't need to worry about it now. I posted the message. I was taking care of you.'

I sit bolt upright. 'Leith, what have you done?'

'Shh, it's all okay, no one's angry with you. It was dangerous, and fine print isn't your strong suit,' he says conspiratorially, two runaways in on a fun caper together.

I try to stand, but he pulls me back onto him.

'What have you done?' I ask him slowly.

'You didn't get a council permit. That place is a fire waiting to happen. I told them, for your own good. Leithie knows how to look after his girl.'

I'm slapped with the realisation. I have completely forgotten the council permit. Part of me has kept putting it off because I am scared of dealing with the expense of any changes they'd want me to make. Sydney is notorious for its strict regulations.

I am officially fucked.

Leith twiddles a piece of my hair between his fingers. I pull it away. 'You really are a dick.'

'Don't say that, LiLi,' he coos, touching his crotch, which is hard. 'How about I give you a bit of it now, make it all better? Come on.'

'Are you fucking kidding me?'

Leith begins to writhe. He reaches for my breast, turned on by his sabotage. 'Come and fuck me, you need it.'

In his stoned heaviness he rolls me beneath him. Feeling the hard-on I once spent my days yearning for is too much. I knee him. He yelps and slaps me. I slap him back.

'It's over, Lucy,' he spits. 'Your restaurant is over. There's a council guy on his way to make sure you don't open. It was a harebrained idea to try to punish me, now stop being pathetic and come home.'

I try to scramble out from beneath him, but he holds me tightly.

'Let me go now, you stoned cock-jockey.' I'm about to scream when—

'You stole my cookies.' Mum, also very mad, stands at the doorway.

Leith is terrified of my mother. He winces and moves off me. I jump up.

'Sorry, Sara.'

'I told you *half*. You're a big fat guts, Leith, and a sneak, and I've never liked you.'

Leith looks slightly ashamed. 'I know. You told me.'

'How you are in any way coherent after ingesting four cookies is beyond me.'

I turn on him. 'You said you ate three!'

Leith puts his hand in the air in a guilty-as-charged hang-dog manoeuvre that used to get him out of all manner of shit.

'You're also a liar,' I spit.

Mum inspects me. 'Lucille, get in the shower and wash your hair, it's a ball of grease. Leith, lie there till I drive you home.'

'I can't,' I say to Mum. Panic floods my voice. 'The council inspector is coming to close us down.'

'Well, he'll have a harder time rejecting you with clean hair. It's my condition for helping you. Go. I'll guard this one.'

'Really?' I kiss Mum and head to the bathroom hearing her quote Germaine Greer mixed with Dr Phil to Leith.

Half an hour later, Mum drives her Kombi van with me in the front passenger seat and Leith, who is now comatose, in the back.

'I just need to check him every half-hour, give or take, to make sure he's still breathing,' she says.

'He'll be okay, though?'

Mum responds with an unenthusiastic nod. She wears an ensemble I'm still attempting to digest; it involves a classic Diane Von Furstenberg wraparound dress in red with tiny, dainty white-and-green flowers, a series of diamante hair clips she ordered online, an old orange mohair cardigan-cum-bedcape my grandma made in the sixties – and Birkenstocks. Her hair is in huge white loopy waves, and a pair of emerald earrings dangle from her ears. My mother is nothing if not counter-cultural.

'Thanks, Mum, for helping.'

'Can't let that little prick keep you from your future. You need to toughen up a bit, kiddo.'

'Are you going to stay for dinner, if we open?'

'May as well; Mr Fuck-Knuckle's going to make it impossible for me to watch anything in peace.' She squeezes my knee. 'Besides, never know who I might meet.'

'Oh, Mum, you're not going to—'

'Just teasing. I couldn't be bothered, but it would be nice to have someone to chat with now and then. And I want to see what you've done to Frankie's.'

I eye her narrowly. 'You're *sure* nothing happened between you and Frankie?'

Mum laughs, then shakes her head. 'As sure as I can be of anything that happened that long ago.'

Which is about as much surety as Mum has ever given me over any of her past actions or non-actions.

We pull up outside to see a stand-off taking place between a notice-wielding council guy and Julia, Hugo and Serge. They all look to me as I climb out of the van and Mum goes to park.

Julia looks relieved. 'Luce, tell this idiot you got the permit, will you?'

27

Frankie

THE RESTAURANT SITS IN A HONEYSUCKLE GLOW OF REOPENING anticipation.

Where is Lucille? Why do women doubt themselves so frequently? The majority of the time they do things twice as well as men while attending to three other matters.

Lucille. Watching her cook, scour recipes, attend to the pantry and cool room as though it were some spewling infant. She truly loves it and is the epitome of dedication.

When I was alive I spent my time here chasing skirt and the ultimate bite. Desiring both consistently. When I was rattling off names of potential culprits of my murder, the number of women who may, for fair reason, have wanted me dead was unnerving. What made it worse was the number of names I couldn't recall, because I'd barely taken notice of them in the first place. My appetite went beyond voracious and into addiction, and then my indulgences with the bottle caught up with me. Why was I so hungry for life but never able to savour a meal? I always wanted more, and that went doubly for women. My appetite was insatiable. I had no real desire to know who they were beyond their warm curves and their cries of joy when climaxing. I loved to charm and sway them, to win them back when I'd pushed them too far. It was such a game, but Lucille is right, I didn't really know any of them. I never considered myself a misogynist, I love women, but I never took the time to really get to know any of them beyond my own needs and bedroom behaviours. It seemed pointless: they were always so much brighter, so much more in control than I was; their lives were about children and feelings, and who knows what else because I didn't stick around long enough to find out.

I feel the worst about Helen. I broke her heart and left her to raise Charlie. I would pick him up for the occasional paternal excursion, feed him and take him to visit my current romantic pursuit; there is no carrot sweeter than an adoring child to soften a woman you are attempting to woo. And Charlie was a smart kid; he knew his role and played it to a tee. But I was never there for school reports, or tuck-ins or chicken pox. Poor mite. I went to a school careers day once, where Charlie announced I cooked pancakes and kissed women for a living. I was trying to pick up his teacher at the time, so it didn't go down a treat. He knew what he was doing.

It has taken becoming a leftover from death for me to see that women, aside from being the alluring muses of carnal cravings, really are worthy of being known. Lucille attempts to look as asexual as possible – I think it's the breakup – but seeing her so critically vulnerable on a daily basis means, well, I am beginning to actually care for her.

Not that she isn't straight-out pretty. Her aqua eyes dance, her fair face has grace and her lips are as sexy as they come. She's lithesome, a racehorse and a fairy queen with just enough steel to keep you on your toes. Surely she can find a decent man who knows the right way round a woman, instead of, from what I understand, a collection of jealous, insecure losers? Why can't women trust themselves and see that they are entitled to this planet much more than men?

If she would quit the excuses and the tears, and just let herself be as magnificent as I have seen her be when she thinks no one's watching, the woman would be a culinary rock star in her own right and this restaurant could shine once more.

Why are they all still outside?

28

Lucy

JULIA'S FACE CRUMBLES AS I ADMIT THE TRUTH. 'YOU *FORGOT*?'

Serge eyes me with regret. 'You are like Frankie, not for the details.'

Ewan, the council ranger, hands me the notice he was going to stick on the door. 'I have some masking tape if you need it?' He seems as sad as we are.

Serge, in all his mid-European determination, digs in. 'I have one hundred buck in wallet, or close to. I give you, you walk away and forget.'

Ewan declines Serge's generous offer. I'm not really sure he has any cash anyway.

I'm thinking on my toes. This cannot be it. I cannot stop now. Frankie's inside, I know he's watching. I cannot let him down.

Hugo, who is panicking, gushes, 'My uncle is one of the biggest lawyers in town. If you don't let us open, we'll sue.'

'You can't sue the city of Sydney for making us obey the council laws,' Julia laments. 'Trust me, enough of my clients have tried.'

'Is there any way we can make the necessary repairs in the next hour, before we open?' I plead.

Ewan looks over his pad. 'Fire alarms need to be replaced, ventilator cleaned, the step to the outside lav needs a rail.'

Hope beats in my chest. 'We can do all that!'

'Wait, I'm not finished. The front door needs to be widened to accommodate wheelchair access. And even if you get that done, there's the matter of the licensing fees.'

'We can pay!' volunteers Serge, determined to triumph.

'Office hours are Monday to Friday, nine am till five pm.'

I take a quick look at my phone. 'But it's only five past five!'

'Sorry, lady, rules are rules.'

Julia looks at him steadily. 'I'm not sure you're using the correct handbook for pop-up restaurants.'

Ewan studies his papers. 'Yes, I am.'

Shit, shit, shit.

'Sorry,' he says to me, looking a little longingly through the front window. 'My wife and I live in Zetland, we would have loved to try this place. She writes food reviews, as a hobby. Has her own blog and everything.'

I can't believe I've come this far and a bloody council approval has stopped me. I've had nearly three weeks. I did call, I remember now, and, as is the way of the modern world, I got through to an automated message, was offered countless options and then placed in a queue for forty-five minutes only to be disconnected, and then . . . then I forgot. Shit, fuckedy-fuck arse bum-wipe . . . I forgot.

'You may as well stay for staff dinner.' Hugo winks at me as he says this. He mouths the word 'plan' and runs out of earshot, dialling a number on his phone.

'You don't have to do that.' Ewan looks at us apologetically.

Serge swears in gibberish and then moves away, chanting, 'I check pork.'

Julia makes a beeline for Hugo, and I'm left with Ewan. I spot Mum making her way down the street, just as Bill rounds the corner to check out the action. He stops and studies Mum, who performs her Duchess of the Western World march. He disappears again before she notices him.

'What's going on?' she demands. 'I have to check on dickface and move the car in an hour.'

'Mum, this is Ewan. He's stopping us from opening the restaurant tonight because I forgot to get my council permit.'

Mum, having dealt with trying to find a parking space in the inner city on a Thursday evening and being a rebel with no cause or respect for laws, is unimpressed. 'What are you, some kind of fascist?'

'Mum!'

'You'd better not be one of those idiots walking around taking photos of number plates all day. This kid has worked her guts out for this, she's got a dead-end husband and has all her apples in one basket – and you're going to stop her because she forgot to sign a form?'

'There's more than that to a council approval, ma'am.' Ewan recites politely from some invisible guidebook.

Mum turns to me. 'How hard are you prepared to fight for this?'

Oh god, she always gets me.

'We could tie him up and put him in the back of the Kombi van with Leith,' she suggests.

I wouldn't wish that on anyone, so the fact that right now this seems a plausible idea should suggest I am not thinking straight.

'Let's tie him up!' Mum seems quite pleased with this idea of hers. Of course it won't be her going to jail when we're arrested.

Julia reappears with Hugo. 'That won't be necessary,' she announces. 'We're going to sit down and have a nice staff dinner outside so we don't break any rules.'

Serge, now whistling again, assembles a table. I look in the window. Frankie stands looking outraged, pointing to his watch.

'I know, I know,' I mouth.

'What do you know?' Mum stares at me curiously. 'You have a better idea?'

'Sit.' Hugo pushes Ewan down into a chair as Julia pours him a glass of wine. They're definitely up to something.

'I'd like some of that.' Mum hates to miss out on anything, especially if it's free.

Serge reappears with a huge bowl of linguine with scallops, peas and chilli. The perfect staff dinner.

'That smells good.' Mum is already reaching out.

Ewan's stomach grumbles. 'Sorry, early lunch. Katherine's been making me do the five–two diet.'

'But you can eat now.' Hugo piles Ewan's plate high with pasta.

'*Serge?*' Mum stares at Serge for a moment before performing a charming, flirtatious, girly giggle.

Serge clearly has no idea who she is but that isn't about to stop him. He kisses Mum's hand. 'Charmed.'

'Serge, this is my mother, Sara Muir-Lennox-Sari,' I mumble.

'I used to come here, you always gave us extra cocktails.'

Serge shakes off the years of pain and loss with a joyous nod and a mostly full-teethed grin. 'You sat back left corner, you were never alone, all the male customers wanted your number, you looked like a movie star and nothing has changed.'

Mum's matronly stoop vanishes as she moves her shoulders in a faux coy shrug that would do Marilyn Monroe proud. 'Oh, Serge.'

Julia and I exchange an eye roll. She, like me, has been mystified by my mother the man magnet over the years.

Quite soon we are all sitting and eating pasta. The others are as happy as clams. I watch Julia and Hugo in action, unrushed, topping up wine, asking about Ewan's wife and her food blog.

'You know,' says Hugo, the natural charmer, 'if we were opening we'd make you grab Katherine and bring her back here tonight so she could review us.'

Ewan looks tempted as he munches steadily. My eyes are drawn through the window to Frankie, who is still in the throes of conniptions.

'Except it's not really an opening night,' Julia corrects him, pacing her words slowly for full effect.

Ewan takes the bait. 'Yes, it's down as an opening night.'

'Only on her awful ex's terrible social-media sites and in gossip columns,' says Hugo.

Ewan looks wary, but Hugo continues, as light as whipped cream, 'In reality it was just an invitation to friends.'

'A soft, informal opening,' Julia follows on smoothly, 'for Lucy's nearest and dearest, to wish her well and taste what is ahead when she officially opens, *with* a council permit.'

Ewan's desire not to be had struggles with his wish not to be the guy half the restaurants in Sydney will look upon harshly. 'So, there's no charge for tonight?'

I inhale slowly. I have fifteen dollars left to my name. I have to make some money tonight or there can be no tomorrow night.

'Oh, god no,' breezes Julia.

'Serge has lots of money,' Serge adds, winking at my mother, who, oblivious, is busily shovelling linguine into her gob.

'Of course, if some of the guests wish to make a donation, then that's a private matter.' Julia is at her best in situations like this; there is a fair whack of *LA Law* in her manner.

Ewan considers. Then, finally: 'Do you think you could find space for Katherine and me?'

'We couldn't *not* open without you, best seat in the house,' escapes from my relieved lips.

Just then a still very stoned Leith makes his way towards us. He walks straight up and places his hand in the bowl of pasta.

'May I offer you a bowl, Leith, and perhaps some utensils as is customary in the civilised world?' Hugo suggests with a crisp primness.

'How stoned is he?' Julia is elated.

Mum inspects him. 'Very. He shouldn't be upright. Lie him down somewhere hard.'

Leith attempts to form words, something beyond his current grasp. He points at Ewan and grunts, 'Council.'

Ewan nods, stands and tries to shake hands. Leith falls on top of him.

'You stop her,' Leigh manages.

I help to disentangle Ewan from Leith. 'This is Leith, my ex-partner, the guy who got in touch with you about our permit.'

Ewan takes an awkward step back from a swaying Leith. 'Yeah, Leith. He's been calling and emailing every day.'

Hugo steps forward. 'How sweet of you, Leith, to be so concerned about Lucy's OH&S situation, especially considering that dreadful plumbing issue we've been having over at Circa.'

Oh, how I love Hugo.

'Shut . . .' Leith lapses into gibberish once more.

'Yes, exactly what I think, Leith, it's getting worse every day, and then there's the electrical crackle in the kitchen and the fuse box being so exposed, really things Ewan should look into for you – if you have the time, Ewan?'

'Happy to oblige. I can be there tomorrow lunchtime.'

Hugo claps his hands. 'Oh, happy day. I will let his sous chef, Maia, know. She's got a lot of hot water to deal with already.'

I shake Ewan's hand in thanks as Hugo and Serge dispose of Leith. Mum looks longingly into her glass.

'See you at seven thirty. Thanks so much, Ewan,' I manage as Ewan tears off his report and passes it to Mum, who rips it up.

'Mum!'

'I knew she was going to do that. I'll do a proper report at the end of the week. Make sure you move your car, Mrs Muir-Lennox-Sunny. See you soon.' He walks away with a skip in his step.

'Mum, did you and Serge ever—'

Before she can answer, Frankie catches my eye, making a hanged-man gesture. I rush inside.

'Woman, get behind those pans now or this whole night will go south. Your hair looks better, by the way. Now, go!'

I attempt not to feel flattered as I race out the back. This is it. Within an hour guests will appear – hungry, curious, cynical guests with their teeth sharp and ready to dig into any fault.

'What's the matter?' Frankie inspects me as I pull back my hair.

'Is this a good idea?'

'A brilliant one. Now get cracking!'

'But what about solving your murder?' I've always been good at the sidetrack.

'For god's sake, woman, stop looking for excuses! It's your opening night! Get through that first and we can continue our sleuthing later.'

'I don't know, Frankie. Maybe the council guy was a sign from the universe?'

'He was a sign from your ridiculous husband, and a reminder that you hate red tape. Now, I want you to listen to me, Lucille, and I want you to listen very closely. Okay?'

I nod obediently. He looks intently at me, placing his face close to mine. 'I could give you a spiel about not worrying, and trusting, but the words you need right now are these: your whole life, not to mention my last one, depends on you doing an outstanding job with this meal. This is your restaurant and you need to stand behind every bite that leaves that kitchen. There is no room for faff, or flakedom or doubt. You have to muscle up and cook as you know you were meant to cook. I will be right here with you every step but you are the only one who can do it. This is your gig. I will manage Leith, you focus on your Fortune. Do *not* cry. Not until after it's done. Now, get in there and go!'

He is one step off humming the *Chariots of Fire* theme. Tears are in his eyes. I want so much to hug him. Existent or not, he knows what I need.

Instead I nod and head to the helm.

Whirling with the action of flesh, blood and heat from the stoves that she hasn't felt in too many years, the restaurant comes to life again.

She has held the dead in a spiritual culinary haven, but she now has the pulse of life throbbing through her once more.

This is exactly where I am meant to be.

And she, Fortune – she was made for this, her song of renewal pushes me on.

29

Frankie

HOW DID SHE EVER MARRY THIS GIT? WITHIN MOMENTS HE HAS begun to harass Serge, who duly places him in the cool room. I'm sure Serge looks over his shoulder and sees me as he shoves the fool through the cool-room door.

Dealing with an imbecile is rarely this much fun. It's the stuff of Saturday morning comic strips. I place my leg over his and manage to trip him. As he gets up I lift a bag of flour and throw it at him, duly hitting him in the guts, winding him and leaving a nice white trail. By this time he's rubbing his eyes and calling out to Lucille, who can't hear him. Next I do the usual, dancing a few tomatoes in front of him in an impromptu pantomime. I place an apple on his head, throw a handful of walnuts at him, and finally, the *pièce de résistance*, I pour a litre of milk squarely over his head. In his ear I whisper to him to leave Lucille alone, then push him to the corner and tell him to go to sleep. Perhaps his stoned state allows him to hear me: he nods, terrified. Within moments he is snoring. I perform a quick cleanup then take myself away from the scene of the crime into the main dining room.

Entering it, I flash between worlds, switching from now to see a very young Tiffany ushering in my own opening-night parade back in the day – oh, the guests who came, so many of them dining with me in the afterglow now, but I still see them as they

133

were. Mickey strutting his stuff to a team of high flyers. Many a well-heeled dame with a split in her dress and heels with wrap-around straps, red toenails, glossy lips, curls; some wore leather with zips. Men with ever-widening blazer lapels – so chic in 1975 – and big glasses as worn by Yves Saint Laurent. My dear old librarian, Joan, with her fur and her husband and her bridge club, entering with delight. A few straggly, hungry artists and thespians with deep voices, constantly dragging on cigarettes. They were all so beautiful in the full flight of life. And now here they are all over again, though in another lifetime.

Lucille tells me that this group of women in black, with nails to match, who endlessly discuss other restaurants and other meals are the serious foodies, many of whom run the food magazines in this country. What they lack in colour they make up for in knowledge. They know their wines, their dishes, their food history. One can even state the exact stall at the markets she thinks the beans come from. Quite the party trick. A few gay male couples, looking so much more at ease than they did in my day, confidently holding hands as they enter, relaxed in their status, a few with wedding rings; blow me down if one isn't old Rupert, the cardio surgeon. He used to come here, always so worried about being seen with his current beau. Now he couldn't care less and he camps it up with aplomb, bless him.

Young lovers, just like in Fortune's last time round, sit gazing at each other, seemingly decoding the mysteries of the universe, toasting each other whenever possible, linking ankles beneath the tables.

And their elder counterparts, one couple is here who dined with me years ago when they were so young and in love; I fear they have become part of the dining dead, both spending all their time on their minuscule phone computer devices. She sends notes to girlfriends about how 'super-excited' she is to be here, while he looks at sporting results. They used to be unable to keep their hands off each other. Used to race to be at dinner alone together and talk and talk and talk until Tiffany told them it was time to go, helping them into their coats as they still chattered and laughed and made their way down the street. What happened? What is between them is not a companionable silence, it is avoidance. Either one has strayed or one wants to leave . . . or both perhaps, yet here they are performing the charade of their former selves. Pity.

The brassy, bossy, full-figured woman drags the council man in. As she types notes about what she is eating I see that she is in possession of little subtlety in her palate but an abundance of forthright opinions. People fell for that guff in my day too; some things never change. I tickle her nipple tenderly and she spills her wine over herself, distracting her for a moment as her face fills with a lovely glow. *Be good to my girl*, I tell her, *she's earned your respect*. Her husband is an anxious fellow; working for the Sydney council will do that to you.

And then I spy them: the table of my demons. Could this have gone more to plan? It takes a moment, but the weak chin of Paul Levine, poorly offset by a turtleneck, is what I recognise. He has lost all his hair and half of his tastebuds. He is as obsequious as ever, smarming up to some coal tycoon who was trying to get into politics when I knew him back in the day; he was one of Paul's backers and one of my creditors. Then there's Len, who considered himself a bookie on his weekends and ended up making nearly as much on other people's gambling debts as his mate made in resources. I owed him too. But is he capable of murder? He had enough money to buffer himself from the actual deed, but really what would he have got out of it? And John: we played footy together in high school, made toasts at each other's twenty-first. He turned professional, then became a legend of a coach and a stranger to himself. The property dealer Bernard is on his left. It's hard to believe we were in the first year of medicine together before he took to real estate and I to coq au vin. We got along well enough then; now he owns a fair chunk of the prime real estate in the eastern suburbs of Sydney. Good move, Bernard – you may not be saving lives but have you taken any, in the name of property development? Still, there are rules with this building, in a heritage-listed area, but having a crooked friend on council – like Mickey's mate Pete – might have tempted you. Back then they were thwarted. And they were none too pleased.

These men who got to live, they don't wear the lines of hard living like Serge or, bless him, Bill. They have something else: fattened necks like geese bred for foie gras, their self-preservation and their golden nest eggs. They have jowls, good lord, they do, everyone at the table has jowls, thinning hair, and a slackening of skin around their once-defined cheekbones. They say women feel invisible after a certain age – do these men feel the same? Do they see how ridiculous they appear with their lewd remarks about the young lass's cleavage at the next table? How absurd their guffawing; private-school boys now verging on senility with their snide remarks at Hugo when god knows how often they've taken it up the arse in a dark alley. But the pack mentality of a fraternity makes them drink hard, laugh loud, talk crap, sing crass ditties. Oh god, I was one of them.

Two tables up I recognise the blown-out features of Matthias Drewe. He sits with three others. The beautiful, gazelle-like woman with wavy red tresses and alabaster skin sports a wedding ring; she would have been one of his models for sure, possibly a former muse. And another couple, male, older, companionable, discussing furniture design and holiday destinations. Are they art lovers, investors? Time has not been kind to Matthias either. Now in his early fifties, he has thinning hair, a bulbous nose and an alcoholic's tendency to keep his eye on the wine bottle and the bottle in close proximity to his glass. He guzzles more than tastes and spends much time looking at his works that we have pinned up. The portrait of me. He looks blank when he sees it. Yes, it needs a frame. Yes, I kept it even after what you did. Yes, I believed in you and your talent. It believed in itself, but you, you poor waif, remain unclaimed by love, and that has paralysed your paintbrush and soured your temper. I can see his party maintain a hypervigilance, preparing themselves for his mercurial temper to turn on them. For him to begin an argument for the sake of being contrary; he stands by no true convictions. Hollow man. I turn from him and my eyes light on what I never again expected or allowed myself enough hope to see.

30

Lucy

MAYBE IT'S LIKE FRANKIE SAYS: SOMETIMES WHEN THERE'S NO alternative, life works. Is it because you finally believe it has to, out of sheer desperation, and that allows for some vibrational shift in the way things play out? Or does some kind of divine providence call out, 'Jeez Louise, give the kid a break!' and pushes off the nasties for a few hours? Or was this all predestined by the scientific mechanics of life? Or just pure luck?

Whatever the case, my blowtorch eases over the gruyère-drizzled baguettes sitting proudly atop the French Onion Soup, and out they go. The restaurant is packed. Ewan and Katherine have the best seat in the tiny house, followed by Stella Supera. Julia is holding her own; we are only letting her carry two plates at a time. Hugo is a force of excellence. He has been so delicate when turning away the people we couldn't fit in tonight, we are now three-quarters full for tomorrow. When Ewan appeared in the kitchen to question this, I assured him that all council requirements will be ticked and lodgement will be made at exactly 3pm tomorrow. He is popping by just to make sure. Apparently Katherine is taking copious notes (please let them be positive) and has been approached by one or two editors about submitting her impressions. Fortunately, Leith is nowhere to be seen.

Stella, looking superb, has made a huge fuss over Mum and Sandy, whom she summoned over to her well-attended table, so they are all seated together. Mum must have sprinkled her bizarre spiritual fairy dust over Stella – either that or Stella considers Mum a worthy underdog. Whatever the case, Stella has declared Mum's outfit a brilliant nod to Vivienne Westwood. Of course, now that Stella has said this, gossip mags and fashion editorials will take note, and in a month or two Sydney will be awash with orange mohair, Birks, box-pleated silk and kewpie-doll hair. My mother the trendsetter once again. Serge has also twice attempted to present her with her 'special treats', and burned a round of baguettes because he was trying to crane his neck far enough to catch sight of her in the dining room.

Hugo sweeps into the kitchen, triumphant, to announce that when some society queen turned up her nose at the earthy plainness of French Onion Soup, he corrected her, saying it was actually 'soupe à l'oignon', which seemed to elevate it to something worthy of her palate. Shortly after, Julia comes in laughing at an overheard conversation that had two guests discussing a Twitter feed that claimed the place looked 'low-rent as a way of reinvigorating diners' tastebuds'.

The room swirls with gossip and anticipation. Another couple confides loudly in each other that I have gone to great expense to fly Serge back from Zagreb to cement the authenticity of Frankie's Fortune. I'm surprised the entire restaurant doesn't hear Frankie's laughter at this one.

Soufflés have been sauced and placed back in the oven. Garnishes are ready to go, plates are lined up, cayenne pepper is at the ready.

'Lucille!' I feel Frankie's warmth against my neck. I turn, startled. 'Have you checked all courses are ready to go?' He has been absent for the last while, who knows where, and now he looks flustered.

'Of course I have!'

He squints. 'Where is your dessert prep?'

'Serge has made the choux pastry. The vanilla-bean ice-cream is done.'

Serge looks up at me, bewildered. 'You mean me?'

'Yes, Serge, where did you put the choux pastry? We need to pipe them and get them in the oven or they won't be cool enough for the profiteroles.'

Serge looks grief-stricken and begins to hit his head. 'Choux pastry, no, no, was forgotten with council man. You want I make it now?'

Oh shit.

'It won't have time to sit, it will be oily and – arrrgh, get the soufflés out and start garnishing.'

'Yes, chef.'

I walk to the cool room, accompanied by Frankie, in a bid to find some kind of replacement dessert. I open the door to find Leith asleep in a chilly corner, his lips turning blue, his hair wet with milk that is beginning to freeze.

I look at Frankie, who shrugs innocently. 'What happened?' I ask.

Leith opens his eyes. 'This place is creepy,' he mumbles. 'And cold.'

'Serge!'

Serge appears, looking terrified.

'Did you do this?'

'No. I no see him for last hour. I thought he go home.'

I stare at Frankie.

Serge stares at me.

Hugo and Julia appear, and I turn to them gratefully. 'Can you please make sure he gets in a cab?'

Julia sizes up the stoned, semi-frozen life form and nods briefly. 'Hugo, you go out and open people's wine, the champers is done. I can deal with Leith.'

Hugo looks relieved and hightails it out to the front.

'You sure he's not too heavy?' I ask, half watching Leith while making a mental stocktake of the cool room for dessert potential.

Julia eyes him confidently. 'I reckon I could get him in a fireman's hold.'

The thought of being lifted and evacuated by Julia is enough to get Leith to his wobbly feet and out the door.

Frankie's gaze follows mine around the contents of the cool room. 'Chocolate mousse?'

'Not enough setting time,' I reply, eyeing him. 'What did you do to him?'

'Him. What? Don't be silly. Mango bavarois?'

'Hmm . . . I've got it. I have pistachios, I think.'

'You do. Middle Eastern trifle?'

I grab the eggs; still plenty left, thank fortune. 'That sounds good, but no. Meringue with raspberry cream, vanilla-bean ice-cream and a pistachio praline, or crumble, depending what I have time for.'

Serge arrives just in time to hear my pronouncement, which he presumes is intended for him. 'Meringue is good. Frankie could never pull one off.'

I smile at Frankie as I reply to Serge. 'Seriously? But he's the world's greatest chef.'

Frankie, of course, is incensed. 'We all have one dish that haunts us.'

'I have more than a dish,' I laugh.

Serge looks at me as though I am unravelling. 'Is okay, chef, we have more than one dish, many, enough for dessert.'

'Good. Pistachio crumble or praline?'

'Are you insane?' queries Frankie. 'It has to be crumble, otherwise you will over-sugar it.'

'Crumble,' nods Serge. 'Looks pretty and not so sweet.'

'Thank you, Serge.' I smile at Frankie and then return to the kitchen to remove the soufflés from the oven.

My voice is chorused with Frankie's as we inspect the soufflés about to head out to their destinies.

'More garnish, Serge,' I instruct.

'More garnish!' Frankie shouts. 'You want them thinking we're stingy?!'

'Temper,' I whisper.

Frankie laughs. 'All part of the drama. Serge used to love it.'

I figure I'll give it a go. 'Out! Now!'

Serge braces himself, looking impressed. 'Yes, chef!'

Frankie considers me. 'Not bad. Decent conviction, but your execution could be louder.'

'Or I could just get on with my job?'

'Yes, chef!' Serge barks again, saluting my orders with an increase in garnish.

Amid the kitchen chaos Julia returns minus Leith, and Hugo announces that he has seen the *hottest* man, unfortunately straight and on a very boring date on table eleven.

Twice-baked gruyère soufflés are served and are seemingly enjoyed; a few glasses of wine with compliments from different guests make their way into the kitchen. I'm too busy to drink, but Serge has no qualms in helping me out.

'What are you doing?' demands Frankie when he sees the way I plate the salad niçoise.

'It's deconstructed.'

'Decon – what are you on about?'

'I don't have time to give a class on modern cheffing vernacular.'

'Thank Christ for that. What *are* you doing, woman?'

'It's the same dish in a different way. I've pulled it apart and then placed the anchovies in a sauce over the top.'

'Why not mix it all together?'

'Because it's a different way of experiencing it aesthetically, as well as each of the tastes and textures.'

Frankie looks unconvinced.

'And it looks pretty.'

Frankie begrudgingly agrees. The produce is so fresh. The tomatoes are welcoming. The beans show off their green lustre. The crudo of tuna is achingly tender and promises to melt in the mouth. Golden yolks gleam inside their steamed white encasement. Black olives glisten like jewels framed by the anchovy sauce, scattered around at careful intervals.

'This is art,' Serge nods proudly.

'Shut up, Serge,' Frankie grumbles.

'Thank you, Serge,' I sing as each plate is ferried out to its destiny.

Apparently it is the most photographed dish of the evening, something that mystifies Frankie but pleases me.

Pork belly is crisped, scallops are sautéed, and they are assembled on top of an apple and sage reduction and surrounded by garden-fresh peas that Mum shelled while flirting with Serge, her one culinary contribution to the evening. I can hear her laughter from the front. Why did she stop going out? The woman loves to socialise.

A feeling of jubilation within me increases with each plate that we send out. There is something harmonious about a shared menu. It is also one of the few luxuries a pop-up could afford me. A set menu makes a lot more sense financially and is a growing trend.

To share a meal that arouses and inspires and expands your world of taste. I can release the menu the week before, or the surprise could be part of the experience: come and sit and be fed the menu I have planned for you. But what about dietary requirements, adjustments and the war against gluten that continues to rage in this city? The majority of people who live in this area possess a food allergy, be it real or imagined. Frankie would tell me to ignore this, but it's good business sense to prepare.

Whisking egg whites into strong peaks usually gives me time to think of new dishes – but tonight I need to stay in the present, to get the meringues into the oven right now. Serge assists with the crumble, making amends for his choux faux pas. Really, though, the buck stops with me. I need to stay on top of the entire meal. Serge is obviously more of a craftsman than a time slave.

I wonder: who are these people here tonight? Are they taking a punt, or satisfying their curiosity? I know that Mum, Sandy, Stella and two of my foodie girlfriends, Lana and Polly, have come to show support. They will tell me I'm a success even if I'm living in my car. I love them for that. But what about the rest?

Time melts as raspberries are puréed and whipped into cream. The meringues have cooled. Frankie looks astounded when I bring them out of the oven. No matter what else is going on, I know how to make a decent meringue.

'Frankie would die if he saw these,' applauds Serge.

'Too late,' Frankie jokes darkly. 'How did you do it?'

'I don't add cornflour. And I love whisking.'

'No cornflour!' Frankie's nostrils flare slightly and he raises his chin in opposition to what he's just heard. 'But it will be thin to the palate!'

'It's not thin to the palate, it's light and airy. You will have to try.'

'I will! Frankie's meringues were too hard, not very high. Maybe yes, too much cornstarch,' Serge observes.

'Traitor.' Frankie attempts to sound offended but there's a grin in his insult.

Serge sets aside two meringues; I know one is for Mum. She has already put in a request for seconds for dessert – the woman can tuck away sweets like no one's business, even when she's not stoned.

As the night wears on I grow more adept at responding to Frankie's questions and remarks with statements that also make sense to Serge. The three of us are a team, albeit an unconventional one.

I assemble the dessert: it looks timeless and tastes divine. Frankie eyes it and then suggests another layer of un-raspberried whipped cream to provide a contrast. It adds an even more decadent elegance to the ensemble.

'That is the Audrey Hepburn of desserts. Superbly done.' He crowns me with his compliment and a look that seems to make all the movement in the kitchen cease.

After Julia and Hugo have taken out the last of the desserts, Hugo rushes back, dewy with excitement. 'Mother says you must come out and take a bow.'

'Oh, I don't need to, I'm a mess.'

'Blow that, woman, get out there and grab your moment!' Frankie rumbles.

'I have a dress . . . somewhere.'

'Don't be silly, you're a chef – *the* chef – and this has been a superb opening night! I meant you should wear a dress out later, when you go to the disco to drink champagne and celebrate, not now. *Now*, go out there and show them who you are!'

I untie my hair, then Hugo wipes some meringue from my face and escorts me out, closely followed by Frankie.

Hugo leads a round of applause. Stella, always one for a standing ovation, takes to her feet, which of course leads the rest of the diners to follow suit.

I look to Frankie, who urges me forward. I mouth a thank-you to him, but he shakes his head. 'This is all yours, go greet your fans.'

Stella swamps me in an ultimate Jewish-mother embrace and showers me with kisses and accolades. 'Baby, it's a tour de force! You're going to have to find a more permanent location, you'll be booked until next July.'

Mum, through mouthfuls of her second round of meringue, nods at me and says, 'Yeah, it's good, love, needs carpet,' and returns her focus to the raspberries. Sandy would like to discuss a more humane, vegetarian menu going forward. Katherine promises to email me her notes with suggestions for improvements; Ewan will bring a printed copy tomorrow. A drunken middle-aged man slurs at me to get my painting of Frankie a decent frame, or, better still, burn it. His beautiful wife, looking used to apologising on his behalf, says they love the restaurant. At the same time, Frankie waves me towards a table of older men, warning me: 'Take note, they may have had something to do with my death.'

I attempt to take this in as the men, all pissed and trying to chat up Lana and Polly, slur their praise. A bald older man takes me by the arm and commences what he clearly believes is his charm offensive. 'Paul Levine,' he introduces himself. 'I see you've used some of Frankie's recipes. He was the champion of our palates.'

'So I understand,' I reply. Frankie performs a throat-slitting gesture, rolls his eyes theatrically and shakes his head.

'How did you find them, if you don't mind me asking?' Paul Levine goes on. 'He was obviously before your time.'

Again Frankie shakes his head vigorously. 'Don't tell him, Lucille.'

As usual when called upon to lie, I begin to blush and fumble. 'Just plucked from the ether, really . . . and Serge helped me, of course.'

Frankie considers my response and performs a *so-so* gesture.

'Of course,' Paul echoes with a Cheshire cat smile, clearly not believing a word. 'Though I would have imagined he'd have written them down somewhere. He was very precise, when it came to his food.'

I flounder. 'Perhaps they're with the building owner?'

'And who is the owner?' Paul feigns mild curiosity but there's a quiver of desperation in his smile.

'I have no idea, I went through a real estate agent.'

That at least is the truth. I have spent the past weeks thinking of Fortune as Frankie's and mine, when in fact I have no idea who holds the deeds to the building and has given the real estate agent permission to lease it to me.

'I see. Well, best of luck. You will see me here often.' He releases my hand and I'm left with an unsettled feeling that seeing him often won't be a completely joyous occurrence. He takes a step away, then turns and adds, 'Who's your backer? Are they here?'

'He was, but he prefers not to be seen.' I think I do well with this line; it's no lie.

Paul nods and then walks away, eyeing every other man in the room. The guy makes my skin crawl.

Lana and Polly, both tipsy and exuberant, provide obligatory girlfriend squeals. I look over at Julia, who has taken her shoes off and is massaging her feet and downing a glass of red. She performs her cross-eyed, keep-me-away-from-the-squealers-and-don't-get-too-drunk look.

Lana is the publicity doyenne of Sydney's oldest publishing house. She spends her days dealing with difficult oddball writers and celebrities, encouraging them to get on planes, go on tour, join Facebook, speak nicely to the press and shake hands with media barons. She is used to dealing with awkward people. Polly is an anaesthetist with an obsession with palliative care and experimenting with alternative states of consciousness, be it through meditation, chardonnay or bizarre combinations of pharmaceuticals. Over the years she has often come to Mum's to hang out, eat brownies and discuss death. It's a wonder she doesn't see Frankie, although she does comment that the restaurant has a 'hot' vibe. Polly might look like Morticia Addams with her waist-length, jet-black, dead-straight hair and her sexy black skin-tight dress that the table of old men cannot keep their eyes off, but she is one of the most on-the-pulse trend-diviners known to man. She can sniff the difference between fashion and fad before it has been served. Her pronouncement of Fortune as hot is a very big thing.

Lana passes me a glass of wine. 'I'm getting you a one-pager in the weekend mag, rags-to-riches story.'

'I don't think so,' I argue. 'It's still rags right now, this is our first night.'

'Darling, that's the nature of publicity.' Lana points towards a couple sitting in the corner. 'He keeps asking for you. Go.'

I make my way over to a bored-looking supermodel in her twenties and, to borrow a term from Polly, a positively hot-looking guy with piercing green eyes and a head of brown curls. The supermodel yawns. The hot guy hops out of his seat.

'Hi. Charles Taylor, Charlie . . . nice to meet you. Well done tonight, it was a knockout.'

'It was like a dinner party at my aunt's,' adds the supermodel, looking blank.

'Thanks, and thanks. Are you Charles Taylor the food critic?' Charlie nods.

'Oh. Oh, I like your reviews . . . they're fair, at least.'

'High praise from a chef. I can see how your own style has been developing. I've been watching you at Circa.'

'Me? Don't you mean Leith?'

'The meringue – you did something similar but with blood orange in winter 2012.'

I had forgotten about that; it appeared in one of Leith's man-of-the-minute magazine articles. How did Charlie know it was me?

'This was better. A beautiful evolution.' Charlie smiles warmly. His date does not. I offer my hand to her.

'Hi, I'm Lucy Muir.'

Charlie jumps to it. 'Sorry, how rude of me, my mind is in several places being here. This is Sonja Hill, Lucy Muir.' Sonja provides a limp attempt at a handshake and throws Charlie a get-me-out-of-here-before-I-die look.

'We'd better make a move,' he says. 'Sonja has school in the morning.'

I laugh at that. Charlie smiles with a glint in his eye. Sonja does neither. 'I have uni, I'm studying anthropology.'

'Great.' I nod, smile and start to back away, but Charlie keeps me hovering.

'The, um, French onion soup?'

'You didn't like it?'

'I did. Is that your own recipe?'

'Actually, it's one from the previous owner.' Unfortunately I say this within earshot of Paul, and of course he turns to me and smiles. Shit.

'Thought so,' says Charlie. 'Well, I look forward to coming back.'

'Wonderful, I look forward to seeing you again . . . both of you . . . together again.' Oh god, get me out before the scary supermodel anthropologist slaps me. I look for Frankie, but he has gone. I can feel colour in my cheeks and Julia is throwing me an inquiring look in which she performs an eyebrow lift three times in fast succession. The restaurant is emptying out, so I walk over and sit beside her, figuring I have greeted just about everyone.

'He was cute,' says Julia.

'With a penchant for dating teenagers,' I reply. 'Besides, he's a food critic.'

'Well, that's a challenge.'

'I've been officially single for less than a month, Jules.'

'I know. I'm not saying . . . I'm just saying that you're meeting new people on your own terms. And you *were* blushing while you were talking to him. Though you've been blushing a lot this week – you're not perimenopausal, are you?'

'Julia, I'm thirty-five!'

'It can happen. My aunty Moo, she started when she was thirty-two, though she'd had four babies by then. I think she was relieved.'

We clink glasses as Serge takes control of the iPod and cranks up the Bee Gees. In a dance move that would do Leo Sayer proud, he makes his way across the room to Mum, who quickly throws off her cardigan and joins him. It's the fastest I have seen my mother move in years. She's light on her feet, and before long they're busting out all their best moves; it's like watching a wildlife documentary on middle-aged courtship rituals.

I look around for the one person I want to see now. I cannot wait to hear his views on the customers and – after one more glass of wine – face his impressions on the food. But there's no sign of him.

Hugo pulls Julia into the centre of the floor as the steady thud of 'Jive Talking' sounds, and Stella takes on Sandy, her latest project. Lana and Polly, never shy of a dance floor, are up soon after. I watch them, the kaleidoscope of supporters, all of whom have made this night possible, and I think how truly blessed I am.

Mostly that I got through tonight, but also that I actually have started something to which my name is attached, for better or worse. Really, Frankie is the one who made me do it. The patterings of panic soon follow: how will my follow-up act for tomorrow night fare? How did my guests tonight respond to the suggestion of a donation in lieu of payment? Will it be enough to fund my menu tomorrow? I want to ask Julia but she looks so happy being twirled and whisked around by Hugo. I think we all have a bit of disco in us. You can be as tasteful as you like by day, but what's life without the froth and splendour of sharing your silliest dance postures, moving to the beat and just letting it all go?

Suddenly I wonder: what if all this – and by all this I mean Frankie – is my imagination? I look over at his portrait. Matthias Drewe, whatever else you may be, you are one hell of an artist. You have captured him so completely, looking straight on, sporting chef's gear with the markings of work, his kitchen behind him and Frankie in his prime, dazzlingly handsome Frankie, pure in his love of creating magnificent meals even though the rest of his world sounds as though it was slightly shambolic. But then, I'm hardly one to judge.

A hand is offered to me. I turn to see Serge with his arm extended – but behind him stands Frankie, looking luminous.

'May I?' Serge obviously takes his dancing seriously; puddles of perspiration gather in the many crevices of his well-worn face.

Frankie echoes him, dazzling me once more with the way he looks into me, like he can see each meal I have created, knows every boy I have kissed, heard every road-trip song I have sung and witnessed every tear I have shed. I have never been looked at like that by a man before. Does a ghost still classify as a man?

I take Serge's hand and he leads me into a twirl and dip. 'More Than a Woman' plays.

Frankie hangs his head above my dipped one. 'I think it went splendidly.'

'You do?'

'Yes,' Serge says, lifting me back up and manoeuvring himself into a foxtrot position, mainly to show off to Mum. 'I do this, dancing is my thing. Girls used to line up for a twirl with Serge.'

It's true, Serge can dance with amazing panache, the lion of the restaurant's tiny cramped dance space. But my eyes remain on Frankie, who moves behind Serge.

'You have been more than a woman to get Fortune back,' Serge tells me as he slows for a moment to take a breath and sway me gently. 'You should tell owner to extend lease. We will be here for long time.'

'I don't know who that is, I just deal with the real estate guy.'

'Frankie didn't leave a will.'

'Oh, that's rubbish, I did!' Frankie stops his dance move to argue. 'Anyway, you were talking to him earlier.'

My stomach drops.

'I think I know who owner is,' Serge states loud and proud.

I watch Frankie carefully. 'The bald guy who kept asking me questions? Paul?'

'Not him,' says Serge. 'Paul works in magazines, was food editor, is still pain in bum. No, owner is the young handsome guy, Charlie.'

'You mean Charlie the food critic?'

'He's a *food critic*?' Frankie looks appalled.

'Yes, is Frankie's son.'

Serge spins me, amplifying the whirling feeling I have of rugs being pulled from under my feet. Frankie said he had a son, but the dancing green eyes, the sweet smile, the attraction – *that's* Frankie's son?

And it is in this moment I realise that I *did* find Charlie attractive. I also realise I have a crush on Frankie, and this does not work on any level.

Frankie squints at me.

'Your son?' I say.

'Not *my* son,' Serge explains patiently. 'Frankie's.'

'The last time I saw him he was eight and bawling as he said goodbye to everyone at the wake,' says Frankie. 'Such a good kid. Turned out quite handsome, don't you think?'

This is pointed. I know it, Frankie knows it, and from the murky depths of my feeling of drowning I nod.

'Is good man,' continues Serge. 'He let you stay.'

'He doesn't own all of it,' Frankie warns me.

'Who else?' I manage to ask quietly enough that Serge doesn't hear as he twirls me again.

'His mother . . . and a friend.'

'Which friend?'

'You'll find out.' Frankie pauses, choosing his next words with great care. 'My friend is the trustee: nothing can happen without him. Charlie's mother keeps trying to convince him to team up with her and vote for a sale. He did once in his twenties but between them they only have a forty-nine per cent share.'

'How do you know that if you haven't left the building?'

'Des, their lawyer, carked it – he filled me in.'

'Was your friend, the trustee, involved in your death?' I mutter.

Frankie shrugs as Serge drops me into a final dip.

'You're pale, Lucy. All is good?' Serge asks. I can feel that the colour has drained from my face as I begin to realise that I am most likely a pawn in a chess game of Frankie's making and I have no idea how to play. I am also exhausted.

'I need to go home.'

'I'll take you,' Julia says firmly, stepping in.

'No. I'll take her,' Mum announces. 'I need to get home and into my nightie.'

Serge leans in on her final word. 'You come back soon?' he pleads, clearly love-struck.

'Maybe,' Mum says with just enough tease. When I was young and she was full throttle with her romances, she used to call it 'the exquisite torture' – the feeling of being left hanging that men seem to adore. Mum is a master at it, but I have never pulled it off. Not with anyone I have truly been attracted to.

'Oh Sara, you are most glorious creature.' Serge kisses Mum's hand, and Mum nods regally.

The party dissipates. Polly announces she has a date with an orthopaedic surgeon next week and she will bring him here. Lana, in her champagne-fuelled exuberance, promises press releases, writers' launches and a potential book deal. Stella holds me tightly and tells me she's proud of me. Sandy hands me a leaflet on animal cruelty and a solemn nod. Hugo arranges to meet me for coffee back here in the morning to discuss the menu and bookings. Julia shows me a wad of cash – tonight's donations – then takes it away to deposit in the bank in the morning, aside from just enough for produce for tomorrow night.

Serge bows and begins to sing a slow, melancholy song in an ancient language that chokes him up; he forgets the words, gets embarrassed, kisses Mum and me once more and then heads on his way.

And then there's Frankie. Standing majestically in his dining room watching me as I leave.

Outside, I turn and spot Old Bill across the road. He stands dead still looking at Mum. Mum mirrors him; it's a stand-off of sorts. Finally Mum breaks the silence.

'Hello, Bill.'

'Sara.'

They stand and watch each other once more; a silent conversation is exchanged between them though they remain expressionless and still.

Finally, Mum says, 'Goodnight.'

Bill bows to her, then turns and walks away.

'Come on. I'm stuffed.' She grabs my hand and leads me off in the opposite direction.

'What was that?'

'Just someone I used to know back in the day.' She flicks her hair and picks up her pace, which is not fast due to her arthritis-induced limp. 'I shouldn't have let Serge twirl me around so much – my hip's giving me gip and your pork's given me wind.'

On cue, a loud bout of flatulence follows and all the romance of the evening is slapped out of existence.

'And as for you . . .' Mum rarely pries, because she doesn't want to deal with any of the heavy lifting involved with getting involved, so this is new.

'You think it went okay?' I ask.

'Better than okay. But what's going on with you and that man?'

Did *everyone* watch my conversation with Charlie?

'Nothing, I only just met him.'

'Well, that's not how you were looking at him. But another chef, *really*?'

'He's not a chef,' I answer too quickly. 'He's a food critic.'

'So why was he wearing chef's garb and following you around all night, looking wherever you looked?'

I open my mouth to reply, but then I take a moment to digest her words. Only my mother . . .

'Mum, that's not Charlie.' I stop walking and study her. 'You could see him? The other chef?'

'I'm not sure what the mystery is. He was there. I saw him,' she states matter-of-factly.

155

'And you didn't recognise him?'

Mum looks blank. 'I wasn't wearing my glasses, and he kept his distance from me. Looked like a spunk, though. And you kept looking at him too – all the time you were dancing with Serge, your eyes were on him.'

'Mum, it's Frankie.'

Mum searches my face and then lets out a laugh. 'Frankie Summers, of course it is.' She leaves me to travel back in her own mind, smiling at the thought of him.

'Mum, he's been dead for thirty-three years.'

'Yes,' she says faintly, her mind far away.

'So, what you were seeing was a ghost.'

Mum comes back to me. 'Yes. The same one you were seeing.'

I nod slowly, relieved that someone else has seen him. Perplexed that that someone is my mother.

'You're in love with a ghost,' she announces gently. And as she utters the words, I know them to be absolutely true.

Salad Niçoise

Ingredients

350 grams mixed green and yellow beans, stalks removed

salt

12 small new/chat potatoes

half a baguette

12 small black olives, stones removed, 3–4 chopped, the rest
  left whole

3 ripe mixed-colour tomatoes, (heirloom if possible),
  roughly chopped

2 lettuces (romaine or iceberg work well), chopped into 2-centimetre
  chunks (discard outer leaves); I include a bit of the stem

4 outstanding fresh free-range eggs

For the tuna and anchovy sauce

1 large bunch fresh basil

6 anchovy fillets

juice of 1 lemon

4 tablespoons extra-virgin olive oil

2 × 200 gram (2.5 centimetres thick) tuna steaks, from sustainable sources (ask your fishmonger)

salt and pepper

1 tablespoon red wine vinegar

1 heaped teaspoon wholegrain mustard

1 teaspoon runny honey (optional)

1 lemon – squeeze just prior to serving

Method

Place the beans in a saucepan of boiling water with a pinch of
salt, then cover with the lid. Turn off heat after 30 seconds to
a minute. Scrape and boil the new potatoes, till just soft. Leave
in water, then cut in half when assembling salad.

Slice the baguette into 2-centimetre chunks and place them on a hot griddle pan, turning when lightly browned. Remove from heat and allow to cool.

Pick and reserve 10 baby sprigs of basil.

To make the sauce, rip off the rest of the basil leaves and whiz them in a processor with the anchovies, lemon juice, oil and a splash of water. Pour about half of the dressing onto a serving platter and set aside. I like to add a few chopped black olives on top of this.

Rub a bit of the remaining dressing into the tuna with clean hands. Season with salt and pepper and set aside.

Pour the rest of the dressing into a big bowl with the vinegar, mustard and honey (if using), then mix together until combined.

Boil the eggs for 5 minutes in rapidly boiling water. Drain and rinse under cold water for 3 minutes. Peel *carefully* (the yolks should still be runny).

Drain the cooked beans and add them to the bowl with the dressing. Add the olives and tomatoes and toss the salad together.

Place the tuna on the heated griddle pan and cook for 1–2 minutes on each side, or until blushing in the middle.

Tear the toast into croutons and arrange over a large board with the lettuce. Scatter the dressed beans, potatoes, olives and tomatoes over the top.

Tear each tuna steak in half and add to the board. Squeeze lemon over.

Scatter over the reserved basil, and top with quartered eggs – which will ooze.

Don't spend too long photographing before consuming.

31

Frankie, 1982

I FIND HIM SQUATTING OUTSIDE THE TOILETS, FOCUSING ON THE contraption that's all the rage: a square with multiple cubes in different colours and movable sides. He was on at me to take him to buy one with his pocket money last time he visited, and now he sits in his own dimension working it patiently, his tool to ward off the bevy of mourners who offer him their sympathies in the awkward way adults stiffly speak of death to kids. The quick dismissal of grief in the hope of offering them better times ahead, I suppose: 'I'm sorry your dad's dead, but what say you come and use our new pool next Saturday? We have a diving board to boot!' That kind of thing. No wonder the poor kid has tried to escape.

'You've got three sides done? Bet you wouldn't have stayed up all night working on it if I hadn't carked it.'

I don't expect him to hear. All I want is to throw my arms around him, pick him up, tickle him till he shrieks – and tell him it's okay.

Instead he looks gravely at me. 'Yes, I would. Mum says I'm as stubborn as you.'

I nod, a lump clumping in my throat at the knowledge that I won't be with him, that I was a lousy father when I was, heaves in my chest. 'You're a great kid. I'm sorry I wasn't a better dad.'

Charlie lowers his eyes again and shrugs. 'I still liked you.'

'I liked you too, kiddo. And that's saying something, because you know how I feel about kids as a rule. But you – you're an extra good one and you're going to do well.'

'Why'd you go?' He bites his lip, which has started to quiver.

'I didn't want to. It wasn't my plan, but who knows, maybe it will be better this way.'

Neither of us believes this. I hold his cheeks in my hands and kiss his sweet head. 'You take care of Mum. Tell her she's too nice to be alone. And I'm sorry.'

And I *am* sorry, achingly sorry that the love Helen felt for me wasn't reciprocated, and that I hurt her, when all she did was help me. I am ashamed.

'Will you come back again?' he asks hopefully. 'Come and see me and sleep over? You never did that.'

'I know.'

Margo Weiss approaches, taking her turn to console Charlie, and he can no longer see me. At least I got to say some kind of goodbye.

32

Lucy

AS SOON AS I FALL INTO SLEEP I'M FILLED WITH IMAGES OF Frankie, Charlie and the evening. The guests all speak in words I can't understand, utterances and languages and whispers always just beyond my grasp.

I'm delivering endless meals that evaporate before they're eaten. Dishes with secret recipes I cannot locate as I search through a gallery of paintings, knowing that it's all in a code I have no idea how to crack.

I awake to the still black, and not even Mum's snore is audible.

It's 3.25am, of course. I shift sides, recollecting the dream and trying to piece it back together and make sense of the night and what I will have to do once the light appears.

By 4am I am back searching through his recipes with my bedside light on and tepid tea growing cold on my bedside table.

Just focus on the food, the meals, the restaurant, your own Fortune. This agreement with myself soon morphs. Has he set me up? Is he just using me? And then: could Charlie see him too? Are there rules with relations and ghosts? Oh Lucy, just think about food, I reprimand myself.

Coq au vin literally translates as 'cock with wine'; that's almost funny. In its early years the recipe was a rustic one – of French peasants, making use of an old cock who is past his prime but still flavoursome when cooked correctly, slowly, in a good dry burgundy, though I have also experimented with pinot noir, champagne and brandy. Frankie's recipe is old school, of course, with a burgundy he would no doubt have enjoyed a glass or two of as he cooked.

The cock of the walk, how appropriate. How Frankie. Also the perfect idea for Sunday night's dinner. I can source the chicken at the market this morning. The trick – aside from using top-quality fresh produce – is time. And I see that Frankie's recipe allows the two days I like too. One to let the stock sit – and the stock must be made with chicken that has been seared. And one after the coq au vin is cooked so it can sit and settle in its own flavours.

There is a long list of dates scrawled around this recipe: this dish is a favourite of his. The amount of bacon has been crossed out and increased twice. He certainly likes a fair whack of it. And sautéing the mushrooms in the bacon lard intensifies all the flavours. It's a comforting yet muscular dish. Not for wimps. It's unabashedly rustic and it will be just the thing for anyone needing a paternal hug in a bowl . . . as I could do with now.

Frankie, the old cock, and Charlie, the young one. It's so difficult to see this when they appear to be around the same age. Imagine seeing your parent at the age you are now. I was already ten when Mum was thirty-five. It was around then she fell for Graham, who was our introduction to the ashram and the instigator of our move up north. It didn't last, of course, but she never expected it to. She was still getting over George. Yes, my mother, it seems, has worked her way through the alphabet of men. I wonder if she will pick back up after her hefty hiatus with an S for Serge? Oh lord, there's such a long way to Z.

George I liked. He fixed things. He fixed my bike and usually carried tools and wore work shorts. He bought Mum flowers and straightened our letterbox. One day he was on his way over for dinner and to fix the taps onto my dance shoes. I had helped Mum bake a lemon meringue pie. Grandma had written out the recipe – the only time Mum had ever asked for one, and Grandma was as pleased as punch. It took all day and a few failed attempts, one involving too much sugar, one with a soggy pastry. But we got there.

It was the first time I had ever whisked eggs. The pie came out looking beautiful. Mum spent an age getting ready and wore a new dress. She announced that she and George were getting serious. I was happy to hear this. I dressed up too and practised a tap routine to show him after he'd attached them.

We waited. And waited. It got later and later, and it was past dark when finally Mum put on her nightie and cried. She wanted to chuck the pie, but I saved it and sat up and ate a fair bit of it. The next morning I took a piece in to Mum with her tea.

The phone rang. It was Ruth, the friend who had introduced Mum to George. I heard murmurs, and then Mum went back to bed with wet eyes. She told me George had been crossing the road outside the hardware shop, where he had bought some nails for my taps, and a speeding truck mowed him down. That was the end of poor George. For the remainder of my childhood I thought it was my fault. I gave up tap. Mum hates lemon meringue pie. I make it as my tribute to what they might have had.

When I think about it, the ghost of that guilt has followed me everywhere, particularly into my relationships with men; after seeing what happened the one time Mum seemed really vulnerable, I got that it seldom bodes well. My relationships have lacked the drama of Mum's, bar the recent theatrics of Leith, but they have also lacked a true feeling of ease, of trust in my own lemon meringue pie.

I wonder: how does Charlie remember his dad? Is it anything like the way I see him?

I'm at Fortune unpacking the produce, placing the chooks on the bench, when Frankie reappears. He looks over the ingredients.

'Coq au vin. Good.' He attempts his usual bravado, but I can see he's off. Chastened. Solemn. Nervous.

'That was your son last night. Charlie.'

'Yes . . .' He starts another sentence but stops before anything decipherable is out of his mouth. A lot like my dreams.

'Had you seen him since . . . Does he see . . .' I too trail off.

I grab a stockpot. Frankie wanders around, picks up the recipe book, looks at his notes and the list of dates.

'Are you using burgundy? And extra bacon?'

'Yes, and yes,' I reply.

'No, and no,' Frankie offers in return.

I'm lost.

Frankie sits up on the kitchen bench. 'No, I have not seen him since . . . well, since my wake, which was here. I saw him and he me, but since then, no. And last night I stood in front of him as he ate his soup and he seemed to sense something, but no, he didn't see me. Do you think he's handsome?'

'Yes.'

Frankie moves the mushrooms around, sorting them into piles. 'Good.'

He won't look at me. I start to chop into the chicken, sectioning it to sear. 'Why is it good?' I ask without looking at him.

'Well, it makes sense, doesn't it?' He sniffs the bacon. 'You are giving this two days?'

Now I look at him. 'Frankie, I have made coq au vin before. It may not have been the religious experience you put on offer, but it wasn't bad. Why is it good?'

Frankie looks up, looks down, looks everywhere but at me. 'Well, it's obvious, isn't it?'

He may be a ghost, but at this moment he is such a man!

'No, Frankie, it's not *obvious*. Nothing is obvious – not why I felt like I was being used last night so you could assemble the cast of characters for your whodunnit; not what you really want from me or the restaurant; not what you think of what I did; and especially, particularly and totally not why you think it's good that I think your son is handsome. Forgive me for sleep-deprived stupidity, but none of it is *obvious*!'

Frankie looks at me fondly for a flash. 'You can trust me, Lucille.'

'Why – because you're the oracle on the afterlife?'

'You don't get it, do you?'

Dear god, he drives me nuts. What made me think I was in love with him? I can't even get a straight answer out of him.

'I don't do riddles, Frankie. If you were alive now I don't even know if we'd be friends. You're a drunk, womanising, ill-tempered—'

'Gambling, arrogant arsehole. Have you been talking to Helen, perchance?'

Which one was she? 'Who is Helen?'

'Charlie's mother.'

'Frankie, I've barely spoken to Charlie, how would I know his mother?'

'I was being facetious. I'm sorry.' He sighs. 'I *was* all those things. I don't know if we would be friends either, because if I was alive chances are I would be too busy trying to shag you to be your friend.'

Before I can say, 'You would?' – because his admission is, of course, partly what I want to hear – I am saved by Hugo, who walks in with croissants and several newspapers.

'Cavalry's here, no autographs, please. How are we this bright, beautiful, cheerful morning?'

Frankie throws his hands in the air in frustration and disappears.

'Have you read any of the reviews?' Hugo asks.

'I'm too terrified.'

Hugo moves to the ancient coffee press with a bag of freshly ground beans. 'We're going to need a proper espresso machine that wasn't invented before the wheel,' he remarks.

'When we can afford it.'

'Which will be when?'

'We opened last night, Huges, how can I tell?'

'I can tell you. It will be soon.' He holds up his phone theatrically. 'We are booked solid for a fortnight. Now, please, miss, may we buy a machine?'

'Can I start paying my staff first?'

Hugo executes a perfect eye roll. 'If you insist. When are you going to start letting yourself enjoy this?'

'After you're all paid and I know if I can extend the lease.'

'Boring,' Hugo chimes. 'Why don't you trust a bit more?'

Of course Frankie reappears at this moment. 'Yes, trust, Lucille!'

'I do trust. I wouldn't have taken the risk of signing a lease and opening if I didn't,' I argue.

'Good, well, don't start being a scaredy cat now. Here, listen.' Hugo turns to the lifestyle section and restaurant reviews. He adjusts his position and rustles the paper with a flourish.

'I'm impressed you bought actual newspapers for this,' I say, fighting my nerves.

'What else is he going to read it off – his hand? Get on with it!' Frankie storms.

Serge enters with a copy of the paper. 'Yes, read review, read it!'

Hugo obeys.

'By opening her new Fortune, Ms Muir, formerly of Circa, has invited us through a portal back to the standard and quality once enjoyed at Francis Summers' Fortune during the golden years of his reign.

'The ambience has not changed, though the restaurant has been streamlined into something more feminine yet equally engaging and inviting.

'There were moments during the opening-night festivities when I almost expected to see the greatly missed flamboyant Summers stride into the room to inspect our enjoyment. Ms Muir's appearance may have been more demure and fleeting, but there is no mistaking the fearless passion of her food, which does her predecessor proud.

'From French onion soup with a flavour as golden as the gilded bowls that contained it, to a timeless gruyère soufflé prepared with a delicacy and lightness of touch most of us only dream of, to a more modern take on the niçoise offering itself as the go-to dish of aspiring food photographers and a challenge to those of us bound by convention. Then on to another more modern take on pork belly, succulent inside and crisped to a sublime crackle outside, along with scallops as fresh as a kiss from the sea. There is love in the food, from its conception through to its execution and its welcomed consumption. The evening's tour de force was without question Chef Muir's deconstructed meringue with accompanying pistachio crumble and raspberry cream. In a way the dish perfectly embodies what she has done in creating her new Fortune: that is, beckoned us back to a golden, abundant time but stamped her own identity lovingly and firmly on its entrance. Fortune is for now a three-month experiment. Fortunately it takes reservations. I strongly recommend you make a booking soon and take someone you love. Sometimes all that glitters is indeed gold.

'*Reviewed by Martha Coleman.*'

Frankie beams at me. I swallow a lump in my throat. He, Hugo and Serge break into applause and wolf whistles.

Serge announces proudly, 'I have read them all. They all good. Even Ewan's wife, though she asks for gluten-free and more attention be paid to OH&S regulations.'

On cue, Ewan taps on the door.

Serge waves his hands. 'We not done yet. I have tools but no finished, it's only eight am.'

'That's okay, I just came to check in and lend a hand. I don't start work till nine. And Katherine wanted me to give you her suggestions ASAP.' He hands me a hefty printout of notes that include diagrams and arrows. I marvel at the effort she's put into her report card.

'Thanks, Ewan.'

'Really good grub, by the way.'

Hugo scrolls through his iPad. 'Oh, the mirth, Leith wrote one too. He was obviously still deeply stoned.'

Ugh, just when things are going smoothly, Leith gets a mention.

Frankie is incredulous. 'Who does he review for? He's supposed to be a chef, for god's sake!'

'Is it on the Circa webpage?' I ask Hugo.

'Yep, there, and then he posted it under Martha's review. He's such a dick.'

'Read it.' My stomach knots.

Hugo clears his throat and delivers an unnervingly accurate impersonation of Leith. '*I don't get all the fuss. Muir is a nontalent who is hiding behind another man, albeit a dead one. The place is crap and the food is what you'd have in some rundown French town populated by inbred villagers. I didn't taste it, but I can tell she is going down, fluffy meringue and all. Take your ancient granny or, better still, go and get a life.*'

Hugo stops reading. 'This, coming from the man who has never created anything on his own. We need to get Uncle Harvey on to him; it's libel.'

'Just leave it,' I say. 'It does him more harm than us.'

Ewan remains thoughtful. 'This is the man who owns Circa? Katherine won't like him giving a bad name to emerging reviewers.'

Hugo pounces on this notion, fuelling Ewan. 'She'll be outraged.'

'I better get over there and check out their plumbing situation. I'll be back for your inspection by three.'

Serge salutes him as he leaves. 'We be ready.'

As Serge works his way through Ewan's list of required repairs, Henry arrives with my order and Hugo sets about packing away the deliveries.

Frankie corners me in the cool room. '*You* are a tour de force, Lucille.'

'You made it happen. I didn't mean to be all . . . weird before.'

'I like you weird. I like you every way you are.'

My heart begins to pound, and he does the diving-into-my-soul-through-our-eyes thing again and all I want is to explore the universe we could create together. Or even just feel the touch of his hand. Or trace my fingers along his lips.

'Lucille?'

I blush back to life – with the ghost.

'Sorry, I was . . .'

'I am so proud of you. Forget what Leith says. You are not standing behind anyone. That's clear.'

'Thanks.' My mind is a blank; I want to kiss him, possibly more than once, probably more than once. I scramble for a subject change. 'What's next with—'

'They will be back, those men. They seem to think there is a secret in my book of recipes.'

'Is there?'

Frankie laughs. 'Only how to make a decent soup, as you now know. And . . .'

'And?'

'There is a list of dates.'

'From when you made each dish, right?'

'Yes, but there are also some that denote when I made a few investments . . . and when I got out of them after receiving a tip-off that might have been considered shady.'

He pauses for effect. 'However, I suggested to certain people that the recipe book had more links to the deals than it really does, to provide me with a backup, if the need arose.'

'So you could use it for blackmail?' Here we go, I'm being pulled into a web of extortion and dodgy deals. So much for the kissing thing, though I still want to a bit . . . a lot. Oh, concentrate, Lucy!

'So I could be safe. As it is, it's a clandestine connection only I could decipher – it wouldn't stand up in a court of law. But the crooks who were involved wouldn't know that.'

'And what is Paul in all this?'

'He's a no one, really. A performing seal who did favours for them, mainly to try to help them squeeze me out of the game, make me lose my standing so no one would believe what I said.'

'That they were shonky?'

'Yes, and that they had their hands firmly in the pockets of the local council and a few parliamentarians; there was insider trading.'

'But would that be enough reason to kill you?'

'These men built careers on their reputations. Their greatest fear is to lose face.'

Suddenly Frankie's face changes, softens, a look of love and loss passing over it. I look in the direction of his gaze and see Charlie chatting with Serge, helping him carry a safety railing.

Charlie looks up at me and smiles brightly. How could I have missed that he is Frankie's son? By the light of day they could be twins, with the same twinkling eyes and magnetic grins, though Frankie's certainly has an extra edge of naughtiness.

'Serge called me,' Charlie says as Frankie and I approach. 'I offered to give a hand with your OH&S list. Most of it is what the owner should provide anyway.' He looks at me quizzically.

'You're Frankie's son,' pours out of my mouth, and he looks relieved not to have to explain.

'I am. Not that I knew him. Not well, anyway.'

'Oh, yes you did, Charlie, you saw what was best in me,' Frankie appeals to him.

Charlie tilts his head towards his father. 'I can still picture him, when I'm here. I guess it's his spiritual footprint or something. He was a crazy guy.'

'Spiritual what? That's all you can say about me?'

I try to help. 'You must miss him. He *was* your dad.'

Charlie shrugs. 'He wasn't around much. Always here in the kitchen; this was his home. I think he was funny.'

'I was fucking hysterical! Tell him, Serge!'

'Funny and moody,' reflects Serge.

'So, you're the owner, my landlord?' I say over Frankie's pouts and groans.

'One of them. There's also my mum. You'll meet her soon, I'm bringing her here for dinner. And a silent partner. Mum says it's one of Dad's old girlfriends, but we don't know which one because he had so many . . . mostly at the same time.'

Serge laughs. I look at Frankie, who won't meet my gaze. 'I have a mother with a similar track record.'

Serge stops laughing. 'Your mother is angel. She coming back soon?'

'You never know with Mum, Serge, she's a bit of a heart-breaker.'

'I should be so lucky.' Serge kisses his knuckles and offers them up to Mum by way of the sunny October sky.

'Well, menu plans beckon. Thanks for helping, though.' I shake Charlie's hand again. 'Oh, and did your girlfriend get off okay to uni?'

'You're fishing,' accuses Frankie.

'I wouldn't know and she's not my girlfriend . . . not any more,' Charlie replies, unruffled.

'Oh, so you take after your dad?' I look at Frankie as I ask this.

'Hardly.' Charlie half laughs. 'Dad and I are different in every way possible, particularly when it comes to relationships. My mum made sure of that.'

'Oh save me, what has she done? Read you *The Female Eunuch* at bedtime and taught you how to crochet clitorises?'

'I think that's a good thing,' I offer Charlie with a smile.

'Can't you see through it, Lucille? It's just another approach. I should know, I tried this one too – the *All men are misogynists except for me, I believe in women's rights* palaver. Any man with a shred of decency knows women are better than us, it's not rocket science.'

'Maybe . . .' Charlie blushes.

'I'd better get . . .' I point to the kitchen and fade out, with Frankie storming after me.

'What was that?'

'I have to get moving.'

'That's an understatement,' Hugo chimes in. 'Julia and I have booked you in to be waxed and tinted on your lunch break at two.'

'I don't take lunch breaks, and I don't need—' Hugo's look stops my sentence in its tracks.

Now it's Frankie's turn to muse over me. 'I like a bit of hair in the nether . . . it's womanly.'

'Oh my god, I am not having this discussion, I am *not* hirsute.'

'No, but you are *overgrown*. Spring's here and Julia tells me you plait your leg hair as a pastime.' Hugo attempts to relay this as gently as possible.

Frankie finds much merriment in this.

Before I can reply, Charlie re-appears with a hammer. 'I know you're going to be under the pump, but would you like to catch a movie or something sometime? Just casual?'

A movie . . . a movie . . . a film . . . a date?

'She'd love to,' answers Hugo on my behalf.

Frankie groans. 'A movie? That's the best you can offer? Oh, ye gods . . .'

'Lucy?' Charlie's smile requests a reply.

'Sure. Great. Yay.' Oh fuck, I am abominable at this at the best of times, but being asked out by the son of the ghost for whom I am falling offers itself as a uniquely difficult predicament. I wish I could tell Julia.

'It's good business sense,' adds Hugo. 'Him being your landlord and all. Besides, you can't say no, he's holding a hammer. Charlie, I've forwarded you Lucy's details. She will be free on Monday. That fine with you?'

'Super.' Charlie waves and heads back out to the yard.

'Now aren't you glad you're getting waxed?' Hugo offers matter-of-factly.

Frankie groans again.

Coq au Vin

Ingredients
5 tablespoons plain flour
salt and pepper
1 × 2-kilogram organic chicken, jointed into eight pieces
olive oil
200 grams smoked streaky bacon or pancetta, cubed
1 small onion, peeled with 2 cloves inserted
2 carrots, peeled, halved lengthwise, and chopped
2 leeks, trimmed, washed and roughly chopped
150 grams small shallots, peeled but left whole
2 garlic cloves, bruised
2 sprigs fresh rosemary
3 sprigs fresh thyme
2 bay leaves
100 millilitres cognac
1 bottle red wine, a nice one from Burgundy
100 millilitres chicken stock (preferably homemade a day or so
    before, or use store-bought if desperate)
250 grams small button mushrooms, peeled and thickly sliced;
    50 grams reserved, to serve
ground black pepper, to taste

Method
Place the flour into a bowl (or sometimes I use a plastic bag) with
some salt and pepper, then toss the chicken pieces in the flour.
Shake off the excess, transfer the chicken to a plate and repeat
the process.

Heat 4 tablespoons of oil in a large deep pan (Le Creuset works
well) and fry the chicken joints until they are golden-brown. (Do
this in batches if your pan is not large enough, adding extra oil

as necessary.) Add the bacon or pancetta and stir until lightly browned and crispy. Using tongs, remove all the meat to a plate.

Now place the leeks, shallots and garlic in the pan and fry gently for about 5 minutes. Next, add the vegetables, mushrooms and herbs to the pan with a splash more oil, then cook for 5 minutes, stirring once or twice. Pour in the cognac and bubble up to the boil and reduce, scraping the pan to deglaze, for 2–3 minutes. Pour in the wine and bring to the boil.

Return the chicken and bacon or pancetta to the pan, ensuring all the chicken is immersed in liquid, and cook, uncovered, until the wine has reduced by one-third. Pour in the stock, give the pan a good shake to allow the contents to settle, and return to a simmer, season with black pepper and cook, covered, for 1 hour at low heat until the chicken is tender. Remove from the heat, and allow to stand before placing in the fridge overnight or up to 2 days.

Before serving, remove thyme sprigs, heat another 4 tablespoons of oil in a large frying pan and, when hot, fry the reserved mushrooms for 8 minutes, seasoning well and stirring frequently until nicely browned. Remove. Reheat stew and add freshly browned mushrooms and chopped parsley as you serve. Heat a baguette, add quality salted butter, roll up sleeves and get to work.

33

Frankie

NOTHING CAN REPLACE OR COMPARE WITH THE SWEET simplicity of a rack of lamb. Whoever first tried to cook it deserves, in my humble opinion, to be canonised – Saint Lamb Chop – and the same applies to the soul who decided to pair it with mint sauce. One of the happiest partnerships of all time.

Sweet, succulent lamb cutlets sitting pertly together, perfectly roasted, and in my day gathered in a circle and adorned with virgin white top hats, filled with a fruit and rosemary mince – there is a dish of royal worth.

The rack likes to enter a scorching oven and then have the temperature lowered so she may slowly open herself to the wealth of tender flavours she bestows upon our palates. It is imperative that she be rested after her roasting. Usually at this time I finish off the spuds, parboiled then roasted in duck fat, bringing the heat to a lofty height to ensure crispiness triumphs.

There are so many accompaniments for the classic roast because lamb is companionable with so many chums. Peas, though, remain a favourite of mine, as do the Middle Eastern spices and char-grilled aubergine and tomato relish. She is the queen of the dining world. Most of us feel the giddy hope of home when we read lamb on a menu.

If I ever doubted the existence of karma in my living years I renounce my arrogant ignorance now. She exists, all right – and what a grand bitch she is. Placing me back here to try to sort my mess, yes. But to put Lucille in the middle of it – the woman who has turned my beliefs about the fairer sex inside out and upside down – provides the ultimate in spiritual slaps.

I have never wanted to share with another the way I do with her. I have never longed to taste and touch the way I want to taste her lips, touch her cheek, slip my arms around her waist. Lust, I am familiar with, but not this, this longing for her happiness above my own. This listening for her at the door from the moment she leaves at night. This terror that she will grow bored of me, see me as a fraud, or not like my recipes, the only gift I have for her. And I would do anything to keep her here with me and me with her, but I know this cannot happen. The very favour I have asked of her is the one that will send me on my way to either oblivion or some grand mince pie in the sky.

How did I miss this while I was alive? This meeting of minds, this all-consuming desire? Wondering what it would be like to hold her all night. To care for her when she's ill. To protect her from pain. Why has this urge always failed me before? My desire to show off for her is almost overwhelming, I am a whisper short of performing a back flip whenever I hear her say 'yes'. I love the way her mind works, her connections of ingredients, her imagination, the alchemy she creates as she re-imagines my dishes in ways that are far beyond what I could have ever brought to them. I want her to thrive. I want her to blossom with me. Yet now comes the cruellest irony and the big lesson for my till-now-missing humility: my son's attraction to her, and probably hers to him.

He is a handsome man and a good one too; I can smell his decency a mile off. I am both proud and jealous of it. Decency, I was short on. He inherited it from his mother. And she raised him well. He is calm and good and alive and single and lonely. The least I can do is help them on their way to a tremendous future.

If only I were here again. She and I, together in the kitchen. That would be something. I hunger for her sighs, listen for her laugh, imagine what her hair would feel like falling on my face as she kisses me . . . It's no good. My son deserves the happiness I robbed both him and myself of for all those years. I guess this is fatherly sacrifice. And if I were alive today I would be old enough to be her father. Oh, what a motherfucking horrible situation. Is it possible fate has made a balls-up?

34

Lucy

'WHAT IS IT?' FRANKIE ASKS, HIS NOSE IN THE AIR. HE HAS BEEN in an appalling mood since Charlie left. Ranting and stamping. Planning the menu with him advising, clarifying, challenging and correcting has been no picnic.

I've decided on a weekly menu with one vegetarian/vegan option. I can thank the images on Sandy's leaflet for the extra work. That said, I have always been careful when I source my meat and seafood, and I am pleased about the increase in awareness of ethical meat and seafood consumption.

Frankie was a mass of eye rolls when I went to get waxed; sometimes I wonder if he likes me at all beyond wanting me to help him. So different to the Frankie of this morning. He would have been a nightmare to work with in his day, and the more I hear of him, the more he sounds no better than Leith in terms of womanising, the only difference being that Frankie was more open about it, proud even. I guess it was the seventies, the era of open relationships. Did any of them work or was it just a clever slogan for masking the carnage of heartbreak people caused each other? Still, I guess he never lied. He is mercurial, bordering on impossible. How ever did Helen cope?

'It's burrata,' I inform him.

He eyes sceptically the snowy ball of cheesy dew. Perhaps this will improve his mood. I'm alone in the kitchen for a moment, the calm before the storm of my second night. Serge is out having a fag, Hugo has taken some of the Matthias Drewe pictures to the framer, and Julia is at home for the night, needing some downtime with Ken and Attica, her feet in blisters from her Trojan efforts last night.

Just Frankie, me and the ball of burrata. 'It's mozzarella mixed with cream encased in a skin of mozzarella. It's like edible heaven. Watch.' I take a ball that has just reached room temperature, marry it with a fresh peach and some freshly torn mint. I push the fork into the burrata and watch the creamy mixture burst through. I add just enough peach and just enough mint to the fork and hold it out for him, a perfect bite.

He takes the fork, examines the combination, closes his eyes and smells, then takes a pinch of the burrata between his fingers, feeling the creamy silken texture. Oh, how I wish he could taste it.

He looks back to me, his foul mood lifting, for now. 'I understand.'

'I wish you could try it.'

Frankie stares at me for a long beat. 'I do too,' he says before shifting gears. 'So, you'll match this with the lamb?'

'That's the idea.' A good one at that. 'I wondered . . . with your pea, asparagus and lemon risotto?'

'Yes, a worthy entrée.'

'Except . . .' How do you tell a master chef your risotto is dodgy? I guess the truth is what's called for. 'I, um . . . it's not my strong suit.'

'Oh?' He thumbs the burrata a little more.

'I'm embarrassed to say it, but it's kind of stodgy.'

'A culinary confession of the highest kind: stodgy risotto. I get it. You're not adding enough wine and you're rushing—'

I start to argue but he raises his hand, then leads me to the stove. 'Show me,' he says simply.

Reluctantly I begin. He talks me through each stage, and part of me wants to smack him for putting me back in a remedial cooking class, but the other part, particularly the part that pulls off a joyously light risotto, wants to jump for joy with gratitude for the masterclass. Finally, my fear of a dish many parents make on a weekday has been overcome.

There's also something soothing about Frankie when he gives directions, like a backup that helps me breathe. It bodes well for the beginning of my second night, which will undoubtedly attract more ghosts for us both.

35

Frankie, 1979

BILL SITS OPPOSITE ME, HIS WIG BESIDE HIM ON THE TABLE, HIS white cravat of the law stained with merlot. Another long lunch for the boys has been enjoyed. There is no service tonight, it's just him and me. Cigars and port. A lunch with Bill is always long, and usually involves duck and a throbbing skull for the next three days.

He tops up his port, old tawny, Taylor's, top notch. As are all things with Bill. Something is on his mind. Bill is a master of words; my great respect for him is that he seldom wastes them.

'There's trouble ahead, Frankie.'

'There's always trouble ahead, Bill. That's what life is, one confounding bloody racket, one big messy bouillabaisse.' I attempt to laugh it off but I see his concern and his determination to relay it to me.

'I mean a tempest.'

I nod and wait. What is he on about? Helen is at home with Charlie, lovers are around, my parents let me in the house for five minutes before we began to yell and they disowned me again, crème brûlée for tomorrow is chilling, boeuf bourguignon is sitting, God is in his heaven and all is right with the world.

'The Gold City deal.'

Bill had convinced me to stick a wad of money I didn't have into some sure-fire property-development deal, high-rises on the Gold Coast or some rot. It's not my area, but I trust Bill, though not some of the cronies he has been known to hang out with – politicians and lawyers, all as crooked as snakes.

This is a cause for alarm. I am on thin ice, thinner than usual. I need that money or I will lose Fortune. I have borrowed against it once too often to get myself out of jams. I am steering clear of the racing track and the coke, but even with these fat-cutting measures I am sinking into a pile of hot shit with some men you wouldn't invite to your Aunt Ruby's for tea and scones.

'How bad?'

'Nothing yet. I got a nudge from one of the other building companies.'

'What do we do?'

Bill performs some kind of silent ethical arithmetic. 'I will buy out your share. Now.'

'So, what, leave you in the shit? Hardly.'

Bill has decided. 'I got you into this. I know you're flying by the seat of your pants and they have one unholy split in them already.'

'How will you get out of it?'

Bill laughs. 'I won't. If I make a move they'll be onto me for insider trading, I'd be disbarred in a heartbeat. But you, I can help.'

'Bill—'

'Say thank you and shut up. I've organised for the money to be wired to you from a different account. Use it to keep your-self afloat, Frankie. Not up your nose or getting women down your pants.'

Like I said, he has a way with words.

'There's something else.' Bill tops up my port and his once more. 'I'm going to be a father.'

'More cigars, that's brilliant news! Sheila must be beside herself. You dirty bastard, they don't usually let you in the bedroom after that many years of marriage – so I've heard.'

His look stops me in my tracks. 'Oh, it's not . . . Bugger.' I have to admit, I – the Libertine of Woolloomooloo – am stunned. Bill is an honourable man. He adores his wife; they haven't been able to have any kiddies, which is bad luck because I can tell they would be doting parents. I can imagine Bill coaching the kids' footy team, collecting fallen teeth and helping with homework.

'Someone else, Bill – a oncer?'

Bill laughs. 'A gentleman never does anything just once.'

I can see he's torn. 'She's a younger woman. I met her here, funnily enough. Dazzling smile. We just . . . it just . . . happened.'

Of course. The cards fall into place. The young beauty who sits next to him on occasion. I have to laugh at my own species; humans use that line to justify an assortment of bad behaviours, the get-out-of-jail-free card for all manner of strife – 'I didn't mean to shove my nob up his arse, sir, it just happened.' Oh shit, buggery bum, this is not going to go well for Bill. I sense the Titanic of marital breakdowns.

'I love her.'

'No, you don't!' I grapple for a way out for him. 'You're cunt-struck by her, is all. You love Sheila. You and Sheila fit, peas in a pod, barbecues on Sundays. Bill, this is a schoolboy crush, a fleeting moment with a bit of a twist. Pay her off. Does she even want the kid?'

Bill looks incensed. 'It's not like that. It's been . . . we've been together for over a year. She's never asked for anything. It's me. I want to be with her.'

'Oh, lord love a duck. Is she in love with you?'

Bill doesn't answer.

'Does she want the kid?'

Bill nods.

'Fuck-sticks. Does she want to be with you?'

Now Bill begins to sob. Poor bastard, he's been undone by love. Of course, poor old Sheila is probably at home wailing into her pillow, wondering why her husband has gone cold. Lord save me from the pathetic mess of true love, it never does run smooth; actually more of a backed-up bog if you ask me. Give me St Honore and a pretty girl for a night any day.

'What will you do, Bill?'

'She says she wants to go away – not with me, but to raise the kid. I'd marry her. She says no, I should stay with Sheila, forget it.'

'Perhaps she's right?'

Not according to the judge. I see it in him as he drinks himself into oblivion. He has decided to punish himself, he will take himself down.

36

Frankie

WITHIN A MONTH THE PROPERTY DEAL HAD COLLAPSED. IT WAS all over the papers; Bill's involvement was much more extensive than I'd imagined, running into mines and sheep farms as well as property. Things fell apart for him quickly after that. He was accused of partiality to the soup he'd got involved with and was disbarred. He told Sheila about the young lass he'd knocked up and she kicked him out. He went to find his young love and of course she'd already moved away. Shows you how thin the veneer of our paltry existence is. Soon after, Bill took it as a mission to drink his way through his cellar. He gave everything he owned to Sheila and headed out west in search of the lass. He never found her, though he stayed away for years. When he came back I was on my own post-death big dipper. He began to guard the premises. I never forgot how he'd saved me financially. I made sure he was remembered; one of the last things I did before he took off was to cook his favourite meal and go over my will. Admittedly it was written on the back of a milk carton, but it was signed and dated. And he honoured it completely.

They say you can't save another soul – each of us in the afterworld will tell you that that is bullshit. Humans save each other all the time. The trick is not to kill yourself in the process.

37

Lucy

SECOND NIGHTS ARE NOTORIOUSLY DIFFICULT, AND NOT JUST IN the restaurant industry. There's been many an actor who has sailed through her first night only to flounder on the second; novelists and pop stars who skyrocket to fame with their initial offering and fall from grace with their follow-up act. Then there's relationships: after a mesmerising first date the couple discovers on their second that there is little to say and the person they have been raving about to their friends is not the one who sits opposite them now.

The second night is the scales-falling-from-the-eyes night. Can the restaurant live up to the excitement of the first night? On the second, there is a sense of solemnity, and the real work begins. This is a business and it provides a service. Will it be consistent? And the biggest question of all: will the food be as good or was it a fluke?

Did I fluke it last night?

I didn't tell Frankie that Mum could see him. I know I have to, but I guess a part of me wants to preserve the bubble of us. Once I burst that with the news, Frankie will be all over it with questions, he'll summon Mum in and everything will change. It's also partly because I am avoiding Mum, and partly because I'm not sure if what she said is true. 'In love' is a commitment, and he is a ghost, and I have a date with his son. Also, I am a few weeks out of a marriage, and he is a ghost I have only just met. Mum has always been impulsive. I, on the other hand, have the procrastination aspect of my psyche down pat when it comes to matters of the heart. I just can't think about it, because in no world does the possibility of Frankie and me turn out to be anything good, sustainable or real. Perhaps it's a work crush. What if Leith was just a little bit right in his stoned review – what if I *am* looking for another man to hide behind, albeit one who can see through himself? And have I mentioned that I am going on a date with his son? Charlie is real and helps fix things and asked me out on a date that may involve both of us eating food. Oh god, what am I going to do?

I wish Julia was coming in. I need her sanity right now. As it is we have Polly, who jumped at the chance to help when Hugo called her. While studying medicine, Polly worked behind the bar at a ritzy cocktail lounge; she took to mixing cocktails as though they were crucial chemistry experiments, and soon began to create her own range of 'elixirs'. I am sure in a past life – if we have such things – she was a witch. As well as her curiosity about altered states, or perhaps because of it, she can drink anyone under the table. She serves brilliantly and is unflappable. She also simply ignores anyone she considers to be too drunk or too rude to serve; I am hoping the number of them is limited tonight, though it's a full house.

Things begin their journey south when Serge takes control of the music. He replaces it with his iPod, onto which his niece has downloaded all of his favourite songs.

Things in the kitchen, however, are heating up. Guests are in, I'm serving cream of mushroom soup with traditional garlic bread. The soundtrack to *Xanadu* plays. The sun has set. Polly has already taken herself off table five: the drunk argumentative guy with the beautiful wife is back. Polly informs me she will not serve him after he grabbed her bum – grinning at his wife as he did so – while she was opening his wine. Hugo has taken over but is not having a field day either, mainly on account of the barrage of homophobic remarks the man is making, spoken barely under his breath. Awful Paul is also back, with some more leery old men, though Polly is managing them. They're here to find out more about the recipe book, I know.

As Olivia sings 'Xanadu', I hear Frankie storming about, swearing that he cannot listen to it again. I hear a fumble, followed by a loud crackle and flash like a whiplash in a lightning storm, followed by a thunderous thud.

Everything goes dark.

I hear patterings, scramblings and Frankie yelling out, 'Fuck!'

I race out to the dining room. I can make out his outline as my guests mutter and question and Hugo races around lighting candles.

'I was trying to change the bloody tape player,' Frankie mutters. 'There was a song I wanted to play you, and your guests deserve to hear something other than "Xanadu". I was watching Serge fiddle with it all day, and I figured that if he could work it, I could too. I guess I gave it an extra charge.'

I am torn between asking him what song he was going to play for me and where I will find the fuse box. I opt for the latter.

'It's out above the bins. Get Bill to show you. He's around.'

I take one of the candles and head out, accompanied by Polly.

Bill is indeed standing on guard and points to the fuse box as soon as he sees me. I have a look, flick on a few switches. Nothing happens. Polly takes over . . . nothing.

'Here.' Bill hands his flagon over and has a go. 'She's buggered,' he says a few moments later. 'Needs a sparky.'

'Noooo!' I wail. 'Are you sure?'

'Your oven's gas,' he replies. 'Give 'em a candlelight supper.'

'Yes, good call,' Polly backs Bill up as I immediately visualise the contents of the cool room, rapidly spoiling.

With Hugo at the helm, candles are lit and the dining room soon looks beautiful in its amber glow. In the kitchen, serve-by-feel occurs. Thank god it's risotto.

Hugo charms the diners and refills their wine.

I turn back to the risotto, and I feel him, closer than ever before. They say when one of your senses is taken away the others are heightened; maybe that's what is happening. But right now, his smell, his warmth are almost overwhelming, and for a moment I am sure I can feel his chin on my shoulder.

'I'm sorry, Lucille.'

'Something was bound to happen,' I stammer. 'Second night. I just hope it won't cost a fortune or take too long to fix. If it's overnight I'm going to lose all the frozen goods and the stuff in the cool room, the chicken, the duck – it will wipe me out.'

'That won't happen.'

'You don't know that.'

'Have faith.'

'What was the song?'

'Doesn't matter, the moment's gone. If that's what happens when I touch electricals, I don't like to think what would happen if I touched *you*.'

'Would you like to, though?' The words escape from my mouth before I have the chance to rein them in.

'I have nothing to offer you but short fuses. Charlie is—'

'Forget it.' I'm glad it's dark so he can't see my regret-filled face.

'He's my son.'

'Frankie, I am not pass-the-parcel,' I erupt.

'What about Ewan, he is handy and helpful. He will know electrician, yes?' Serge asks me, looking mystified by my last comment.

'Serge, you're a genius!'

Ewan, Katherine and their friend Phil the electrician arrive twenty-five minutes later.

They get right onto it as I serve up my lamb racks in the dark; most of the candles are in the dining room. Fortunately I usually go by smell when judging when to take them from the oven. Frankie is the same, though we don't exchange words now, because we're at odds with each other and because Katherine is holding court and 'assisting' me. She, like Frankie, is unconvinced about the burrata, until I make her try some; soon she's plunging her way into the creamy goo and topping it with peach and mint. 'Not bad' is the verdict.

Ewan and Phil reappear. 'What happened?' asks Phil, looking concerned.

'Just some extra voltage when I tried to change tracks on the iPod.'

'That wouldn't be it.' He moves in closer. 'Your electrics have had a massive voltage surge, akin to a major electrical storm.'

'Major,' echoes Ewan, looking impressed and grave.

'I'm going to need some more tools and a backup generator,' Phil goes on. 'I'm calling for extra help. We'll be here for at least a few hours.'

Apparently Frankie's touch created an electrical ground-zero situation. What was I thinking?

38

Frankie

RUMOUR HAS IT THAT EWAN MACCOLL WROTE 'THE FIRST TIME Ever I Saw Your Face' for his lover Peggy Seegar in 1959 when they were apart – primarily because he was married to someone else. He later married Peggy, but that song, it says it all: the hope, the thunderbolts that strike when you realise you are absolutely, irreducibly, irredeemably, irrefutably in love.

Being with her in the kitchen, watching her work and laugh and hope. Why has it taken me until now, until I am stuck in the wasteland of no time, to feel this feeling?

I am in love with the girl my son wants to date. With a living, breathing woman who will want what I can never give her.

And yet.

And yet.

It's no bloody wonder I blew a fuse.

39

Lucy

I'M HEADING AWAY FROM THE BATHROOM WHEN I AM GRABBED by a man, his face lit demonically by a light that he holds under his chin, like I did when we used to tell ghost stories on the commune as kids.

I give one of those silent yelps, the ones I do in my nightmares when I'm searching for my big roaring scream to set things straight but no sound emerges.

I try to make sense of the bizarrely lit features. It is one of our guests, the bully from last night with the beautiful wife.

'Boo! Sorry, didn't mean to scare you.'

My voice finally arrives. 'Right. What are you doing back here?'

'Just popped out for a smoke. Another great meal, thanks.'

He seems genuine, but there's a hint of malice in his tone and I wish Frankie was here. Where is he?

'Thanks for your patronage,' I say evenly, quite a feat under the circumstances. 'Two nights in a row is keen.'

He stares at me almost flirtatiously. Oh, where is Frankie? 'You have no idea.'

'I'm sorry about the lights,' I say. 'It's almost fixed.'

The man shrugs nonchalantly. 'My wife is cooing that it's romantic, but whatever.'

Okay, it's official: I dislike this guy. A lot. Frankie? 'She's very beautiful. Your wife.'

Another shrug.

'I have to get back to the kitchen. The bathrooms are that way.'

'I know.' He flicks his light from the torch on his iPhone around the space. 'The pictures, where are they?'

'Sorry?'

'The paintings I did for Frankie.'

The penny drops. 'You're Matthias Drewe?'

He sighs in frustration. Clearly I am an imbecile to be asking this question.

'The pictures are at the framer.'

'You have all of them?'

'I wouldn't know. I think there's about five. The owners want them to remain with the restaurant.'

'They're worth a fortune, you know.'

'I wouldn't know,' I repeat. Oh, please go. 'I hear you worked for Frankie, a long time ago.'

'He was an arsehole.'

On cue, Frankie appears. 'I missed you too, sunshine.'

Relief engulfs me.

'What did you say?' Matthias Drewe sounds pissed off.

'Me? Nothing. I have to go and prep your dessert. Enjoy your night.'

'You don't mind if I use the staff loo.' It's a statement, not a question.

I step away as he heads into the lav. Frankie stands by the bathroom door.

'Off you go,' he says to me, 'get back to the kitchen, the soufflés are due out.'

'Don't do anything stupid,' I warn.

'I can't even use the tape player, what can I possibly do here?' He blinks innocently.

The lights come back on just as I am pulling the last of the soufflés from the oven. There's a mixture of applause and exclamations of dismay from the dining room – clearly some of the diners prefer the candlelit ambience. Katherine heads out with her notebook at the ready.

'Glad we'll get a closer look at those.' Paul has entered the kitchen and gives me another Cheshire cat grin. Of course this is all happening on the second night. 'Excuse my appearance in the kitchen. Old habits die hard – I *was* a food critic.' He really is smarmy.

'And they allowed you in here, back then?'

'Frankie did.'

I find this hard to believe.

Paul's eye travels to the red recipe book open nearby. As he makes a move I step in front of it. 'Paul, you must go and sit down, these have to go out immediately.'

'I don't remember Frankie making . . . coffee, if I'm not mistaken?'

'What an excellent nose you have.'

'All the better to smell you with, my dear.' His comment is spoken with the cadence of a joke but an edge of sinister remains.

I force myself to laugh. 'Shoo, go back out and sit. This is my grandmother's recipe and she would be annoyed if she knew you were holding me up.'

'I wouldn't dream of it. I just wanted to offer you my congratulations and ask if I could have a glance over that little book. I thought you said the owner had it.'

'He brought it with him today when he popped in,' I lie.

Paul looks perplexed, but quickly covers it with a benevolent smile and heads out.

The coffee soufflés are carried out by Hugo, Polly and myself, and the mocha-whiskey-cream sauce that accompanies them is poured at the table.

I note that Matthias has not returned to his table, and that Frankie is absent too. I decide to pour the beautiful wife's sauce into her soufflé.

'Oh, maybe I should wait,' she protests.

'Soufflés don't wait, that's what makes them special.' I finish pouring. 'Please, you'll offend me if you don't try.'

The beauty nods and tastes. The woman obviously likes desserts, which makes me like her.

'Oh, that's heavenly.'

'Thank you. I'm Lucy. I think we met briefly last night?'

'Yes, I'm Vivianne. Another stunning night. And I loved the lights-out.'

'We aim to please. Your husband is the artist of our paintings.'

'Yes.'

'You're an artist too?'

Vivianne holds her breath for just a moment. 'Art historian. More Matthias's administrator these days. Did he ask you about the exhibition?'

'Sorry?'

'Silly man, that's why I sent him out to find you. He has an exhibition next month and we – well, *I* – wondered if we might borrow a few of his works. It's a retrospective and there are a few spaces. It's just up in Woollahra at the Knox Gallery. Just for three weeks?'

'Um . . . I can ask the owner. Er, owners.'

'Would you? Great, thank you. Also, we would love to book out Fortune and have you cater his opening-night party. Would you be interested?'

'Definitely.' Vivianne elevates further in my esteem. A dessert-lover who's booking out the restaurant: what's not to like?

'Super. He has such a strong bond with this place; he and the owner were very close when Mattie was a little boy.'

I want to say, *Yes, the little rat sabotaged, stole from and used Frankie*. Instead I opt for: 'Interesting. Please enjoy the soufflé.'

And I head back to the kitchen in serious need of a drink.

It's another fifteen minutes before Matthias re-emerges, whingeing to Hugo that he has been locked in the loo. I think he got off lightly.

All is well in the dining room and diners linger over last drinks and conversations. It seems the candlelight provided an intimacy intensifier of sorts. But I . . . I am done with this day. We finish the clean-up and present Katherine, Ewan and Phil with our eternal thanks, a bottle of champagne, and VIP admission for the next month.

Hugo announces that he's heading out on a date – one of the waiters from Circa he has been flirting with, sleeping with, or doing something with. He also tells me that Leith has had to shut his doors for the next five days while plumbing repairs are carried out, following Ewan's thorough investigation for his council report. Leith will be spitting chips. Katherine has sent him a reading list of suggested authors so he can work on his review-writing skills, and added him to an email list for a rehab centre so he can address his cannabis dependency. Perhaps there is a God.

Serge, who spent much of the night assisting with the electrical dramas, reappears with a poem scrawled on a page from one of Ewan's OH&S manuals. He hands it to me with an earnest ceremonial flourish.

'Serge, couldn't you have helped me wash up and *then* written a poem?'

'The muse, Lucy, the muse has struck.' He thumps his fist against his chest. 'Not for many decades has the muse been with me.'

'Oh, lord love a duck, he's a goner. Poetry is a bad sign,' Frankie appraises.

I look at Frankie, who is wearing a kaftan once more and looks like he could be off to a poetry reading himself.

'Serge gets crushes. Well, less crushes, more fixations. When he's like this you just need to yell a lot and boss him around with specifics or he'll spend all his time writing sonnets.'

'All that over my mum?'

'We are all fools for love, Lucy,' Serge laments.

'But Serge, you don't even know Mum. You met her a few times in the seventies and then again last night. You don't know what she's really like.'

'My soul recognises hers.'

'I don't think so. You haven't seen her watch TV stoned for eight hours straight, or snore so loudly it wakes the neighbour's baby, or pluck her chin hairs, which she inherited from Grandad – they are thick hairs, Serge. It isn't all Barbra-and-Barry duets; Mum is a selfish woman who will squeeze the life force from you at every possible opportunity.'

'Oh, how I long for that!' Serge swoons.

'It's no use,' Frankie declares. 'He's lost.'

'How long will it last?'

'Forever!' Serge states with finality.

'A few months, probably, though he once spent a year carrying a torch for a lady who sold him a suit.'

'Why don't you just ask her out?' I suggest. 'Or go visit her at home? That will cure it.'

Serge looks suddenly terrified. I whip the poem off him and write Mum's address and number on the back. 'She's always home.'

Serge studies the paper, now the holy grail. He mumbles thanks and then heads out, looking dazed.

'He won't go there straight away,' Frankie assures me. 'He's too shy. It'll take him a week to call. He might post something to her, though.'

'What, like his ear?'

'More poems. You'll have to ban them while he's at work or he'll burn everything. He's quite a nice poet, mind you. Too soppy for me. I like Ted Hughes.'

'You would.' I place the last of the food in the cool room then turn to Frankie. 'Polly's waiting for me.'

'A night on the town, hey?'

'Just a few drinks to unwind.'

'Sounds a fine plan, and well earned. You've survived your second night relatively unscathed.'

'Other than electrical outages, psycho artists, crooked food editors and now a sous chef in love with my mother – yep, smooth sailing.'

'Smooth sailing's overrated.'

'How would you know, you never had it.'

'Touché, Lucille.'

We hover around each other, the electricity swirling in the air between us once more intensifying to a near crackle.

'Well . . . goodnight.'

'Goodnight, Lucille.'

He watches as I lock him in and leave. Watching me with an intense curious stare. There's a force field growing between us. I feel a continual urge to remain in his close vicinity. But there is a life outside Fortune where Polly waits. We head up Cowper Wharf Roadway, arm in arm.

'Who were you talking to in there?' she asks me.

'Oh, just the ghost who lives there.'

'Cool.'

We keep walking. You have to love Polly, she sees the world so differently; her experiences working in palliative care and being an anaesthetist mean nearly anything goes.

'I talk to my mum still.' Polly's mum died when she was fifteen, setting her on her journey to both save lives and try to get the gist of what lies beyond death.

'Does she talk back?'

'All the time.'

We laugh and wander on, passing the navy vessels sleeping in their monolithic grey steeliness on the water and the young naval officers with their white caps knocking on or off or heading to clubs in the Cross.

Up the hill onto Wylde Street, which makes us both breathe deeply into our lungs, there's a warm softness to the salty air that promises summer. The night is filled with a multitude of stars.

'Oh god, you'd miss this, wouldn't you, if you weren't here anymore?' It's an aloud thought but Polly agrees. How does Frankie get through, no timeline, no sunrises, no this, just a peep from the doorstep, just him in the restaurant cooking meals people have already eaten, or watching me prepare food he can't eat? It must be torture. No wonder he wants it all solved. I felt guilty walking out tonight; I know he'll be waiting for me to come back. Why can't the rules of the afterlife include the occasional walk up to Potts Point? No one could see him. Who sets these rules anyway?

I point up at a twinkling cluster. 'You know that's the great lamington constellation?'

Polly nods. 'You so need a drink.'

•

We're on our second martini in the little Italian bar we love when the world begins to feel right again.

'So, how's separated life?'

'Better than the alternative.' We toast to that. Polly was always polite to Leith but there was no love lost between them. He was also too terrified to try to crack onto her. Polly is as loyal as she is stunning. Right now, Leith feels light years away.

'I like my new life. It has to work, doesn't it?'

'It *is* working. Really, it's about frequency – you have to keep yours high.'

Polly, an insomniac, when not experimenting with chemical combinations, is also a student of quantum physics. She often lends me books and sends YouTube clips dealing with different aspects of it . . . all of which I get a page or a minute into before my eyes glaze over. I like the broad-brush concepts, but the actual science of it is confounding to a girl who just scraped through Unit 2 Biology.

'Do you believe people can come back from the dead?' I ask her.

'Sure, we resuscitate people every day.'

'But after they've been dead a while?'

'Like zombies?'

'More like . . . ghosts.'

Polly bites into her olive, orders another round from the gorgeous young Italian waiter who has been watching her longingly, and continues, all without missing a beat. 'I'm not anti it. Would I call them ghosts? No. I don't know what I'd call them, but I can see there could be a collective of atoms and molecules that constitutes a being of types caught between before and after – between dimensions, if you like.'

'Right. A ghost.'

'The thing you have to remember, Lucy, is that time isn't just long, it's also wide.'

I finish the rest of my martini in an attempt to help that statement make some sort of sense.

'One of the most basic findings in quantum physics is that one particle can, with momentum, go into two slots . . . we can be in two places at once.'

'So, you can be dead and not dead?'

'Sure, ask any fool with a broken heart. The conundrum is, how do we measure it? Wavelength is inversely proportional to a particle's dimension. But when I shine a light on particles to measure them, I am to all intents altering them . . . just how much, who can say?'

'Is this a scientific way of asking, "If a tree falls in the woods . . ."?' I'm lost.

'Kind of, yes. All times, all things, all beings, all fashions, all arguments, all births, deaths, marriages, natural disasters, political triumphs, fights with your ex, orgasms with your lover – all of them co-exist. It's our way of measuring it – time – that falls short. Light inevitably alters the speed of particles. That's the wave–particle duality . . . the uncertainty principle.'

'I could apply the uncertainty principle to most of my life.'

'We all can. You just need to expand your thinking.'

'But if they all co-exist, how could the me of today co-exist in a reality I never had in my waking life?'

'Because reality isn't exclusive to waking hours. Actually, reality as we think of it doesn't exist, not solely, not with the monopoly we credit it with.'

'Oh god, I bet you did well at first-year philosophy.'

'We all did, it's the one subject you can't fail; it was the arts subject all the would-be med students took. But quantum physics is about the *how*, not the *why*. Now, tell me about the fucking fantastic date you have with the hot guy.'

More martinis arrive.

'I don't know anything about him, really. He's a food critic, he's Frankie's son, he's my landlord, he came and helped with the council inspection, he's—'

'Keen.'

'I don't know. He was on a date with Miss Almost Underage when I met him; he's not going to be interested in someone who's got wrinkles. He probably just wants to talk about the restaurant, let me down lightly that they won't extend the lease.'

'So, your positive affirmations are working out well, then.'

'You don't believe in those.'

'I didn't, but I do believe in neuroscience, and you activate the same neurons thinking forward as back, so why not make up something good about going forward?'

Somehow when Polly says things like that they make sense. When I turned thirteen my mother gave me a copy of Louise Hay's *You Can Heal Your Life*, which I promptly put on a shelf and never read. My grandparents gave me a copy of the *Royal Family Photo Album* that same year, which, also unread, went straight on the shelf beside it. What I'd been hoping for was a new bike. So much for that affirmation.

Talking about Charlie makes me squirm, because there's an elephant in the room – a ghost in the restaurant – that refuses to be addressed. I can't seem to think of Charlie without thinking of Frankie, which then makes me feel like a character in a French farce.

'Do you miss Leith?' Thank goodness Polly has interrupted my thoughts.

'I haven't had the time or inclination to think about him,' I reply with honesty.

'Bit of a dud move by Maia. She hasn't been to yoga since they hooked up.'

'Leith has that effect on women. I dropped my bundle when I was first with him.'

'Cheers to that.'

We drink . . . and we drink . . .

Later, ramble trumps insight as we make our way through a very nice bottle of pinot. I love martinis and I love red wine. Sadly, neither loves me, and the combination of the two on top of stress and sleep deprivation leads to me not noting that my teeth feel furry or that my vision has gone into the soft-focus lens of an eighties Jessica Lange film.

'No relationships work out,' I declare morbidly into my half-empty wine glass. I crunch into a crostini wrapped in prosciutto, and spill half on my lap.

'Christ, why are you being so negative?' Polly tops up my glass. She seems way more sober than me though she has consumed as much.

'Okay, how many really happy, faithful couples do you know?'

'Do we have to do this?'

'Shhh, yes. You know how many I know? One. My grandparents. And maybe Julia and Ken, but that's *it*. Out of all the people I know, they're the only ones I could rate . . . ever.'

'Luce, you grew up on a commune, what do you expect?'

'Are your parents happy?'

'Shit no. Well, Mum's dead, as you know, but when she was alive they were a disaster. They stayed together because of us, and because Dad was too stingy to fork out for a divorce.'

'See? And your sister is divorced. You're single. I mean, come on, seriously, it's a wasteland of wounded hearts and grazed souls and then you die and get trapped in a world where you can't swallow.'

'Swallow what?'

'Food.'

'I know lots of great couples.'

'Who?'

'I've met heaps through work.'

'But that's when people are sick or dying, they're all on their best behaviour.'

'Or maybe the truth is coming through.'

'But one of them is about to cark it, what's the use?'

'The use is that the love you make is equal to the love you take.'

'Don't quote the Beatles at me when I'm pissed.'

'There are couples whose love makes me believe in the goodness of life. The ones who are there caring and tending and holding no matter what's happened. And it's not just overnight; it can go for weeks, months, sometimes on and off for years – that can't be an act.'

'They've realised what they had too late, though, haven't they?' I argue. 'They're working to a deadline.'

'Babe, we all are. Take the hot guy to a movie. Takes the heat off too much dinner conversation, especially if you're as bleak as you are now.'

'I'm not bleak. A movie makes it a real date.'

'As opposed to a budget-planning session?'

'I'm not ready.'

'You were over Leith two years before you left him.'

'I need to be by myself to get it together before I'll be ready to meet anyone else.'

'You have been by yourself for a long time while you've been married. Besides, I don't subscribe to that dogma. You meet people when you meet them. If there's a connection and you're single, you should go there.'

'I never want to have my heart broken again.'

'I'm not sure that's completely up to you.'

'What about you and the surgeon?'

'He's hot, but I think he just wants to have some fun. He talks about himself in the third person, usually the sign of a dickwad.'

'Have you ever been really, deeply, importantly in love?'

'Not yet. But I will be.' Polly says this with such certainty, there could be no doubt of its truth. But my eyes are beginning to close . . .

The rest is a blurry cab ride and proclamations of eternal friendship and really getting to the core of existence, whatever that means.

By the time I get to bed with my burgundy-stained teeth, the room is spinning. I drink half a glass of water and sleep with one foot on the floor, a trick my first boss taught me to try to stop head-spins. My last thoughts before the relief of drunken oblivion finally claims me are of Frankie. Frankie, and what was that song . . . ?

40

Frankie

WOMEN MARCHING OFF INTO THE NIGHT WITH THAT RHYTHM are usually either on a mission to tell off an ex, have revenge sex, offload to a chum, spend a fortune on a frock or get stuck into a cocktail – or a combination of all of them.

I wish I could have gone with her.

41

Lucy

MY ALARM, WHICH I SOMEHOW HAD THE SENSE TO GET POLLY to set on my phone before disembarking the cab, sounds just a few hours later, and I wake to bird droppings in my mouth, a pounding heart, and black dogs howling in my brain. The memory of this type of hangover is what stops me from drinking too much on most occasions.

Not last night, though. I am ill: clammy, queasy, one-step-from-heaving ill. My focus is still blurry, which means I am possibly still drunk. I hope to god I am sober enough to drive, I think as I load up the ute with the esky and ice, sucking on some and thankful that the new day is still in darkness, though dawn is creeping in incrementally as I drive westward to the markets.

It is a truth universally acknowledged that a woman in possession of a hangover as severe and as foul as mine should not be at the Sydney markets on the morning of the annual cherry auction to mark the new season. Sadly this truth is amplified by the harsh reality of the markets, which are early this year, with the general public running about in the full grip of cherry mania. This long tradition sees many of the cherry growers make their way to market to see their fortunes rise or fall depending on the quality of crop and its sales. The first day of the cherry sales is like the Oscars of the fruit and veg world. Travelling celebrity chefs, food writers with newly released books, morning-television personalities and weather men all converge on this day of days. By the time I arrive, the markets are packed, but fortunately my usual stall-holders have kept some top picks aside for me, in particular some stunning artichokes.

And then come the cherries. A photographer passes and asks me to pose for a quick pic with Peter, one of my favourite growers. Through the thick lens of sunglasses I attempt a smile and find myself having to swallow hard to prevent a projectile vomit. Then I see them at the centre of the crowd: Leith looking shiny and fresh, Maia beside him, announcing their new restaurant, *their* new restaurant that has apparently been in the planning stages for the past nine months but kept 'under wraps until now'. A project in Pyrmont – Square One, a little brother to Circa. Cameras flash. I approach them, hoping that if I do throw up it will land on Leith's face. He sees me but his camera smile remains fixed.

'Nine months, Leith? You two were pregnant and I had no idea?'

'You didn't tell me about your Fortune,' he counters.

'I didn't get a chance to. That was one hour in the planning and you were Tweeting about it within three.'

'Same thing,' he says with a chuckle designed to make us look like we're best friends.

Maia looks apologetic. My stomach rumbles.

'You look pretty green around the gills and you reek of alcohol.' Leith's still smiling.

'That's rich coming from the glutton of hash brownies.'

Maia excuses herself and darts off.

The smiling stops. Thank fuck.

'See, you've upset her.'

'Just tell me why you cried so loud about me leaving, making me go on that holiday with you and waxing lyrical about reunions, if you were planning this all along?'

There's no answer from Leith, and a giant human-sized cherry walks up and hands me a sample bag of fruit. My stomach churns.

'I have to get the rest of my stuff,' I say.

'Yeah, well, I'm pretty busy.'

'Really? I heard you were having a bit of a break from Circa while they fix the plumbing?'

Leith waves to some oncoming press. 'You're going down without me to prop you up. Look at yourself, you're a joke.'

Leith stalks off towards his next opportunity for self-promotion. Forty-eight hours seems to have transported him squarely into the rage phase. I can only hope his new restaurant keeps him busy. And it's surely only a matter of time until he's hosting a reality TV show.

•

By the time I pull up at Fortune I am a mass of cold sweat and dehydrated remorse. Bill, who is sunning himself outside the restaurant, watches me disembark and struggle with the esky.

'You look rough.' This is something coming from Bill, who seldom lets his flagon of sherry out of his sight. I must look bad, because he helps me unload, though he still won't venture inside.

Frankie awaits. Inspects me.

'You need to lie down in a dark room and then drink my remedy.'

By this stage I am struggling to speak. I manage a nod. I unpack the produce.

'What for tonight?'

'Cherries, artichoke,' is all I can manage before fleeing to the loo to throw up. When I return, Frankie takes over.

'Beef carpaccio with artichoke hearts, pulled pork pithivier with a side of steamed greens, and cherries jubilee . . . no, wait, cherry cobbler with vanilla-bean crème fraîche ice-cream to climax. Yes?'

I manage another nod.

'Drink three glasses of warm water with Panadol, eat a salted cracker, and then call Serge and tell him to come early and make the Frankie Revival Brew. Then go and lie under table eight. There's a blanket in the linens next to the napery that Julia washed.'

I am too hungover to do anything but obey. What was I thinking getting shitfaced with Polly on a work night? I get drunk once a year, never on a work night. Oh, my head.

Two hours later I re-emerge and Serge oversees me as I consume a concoction that is the colour of Worcestershire sauce and has the consistency of custard. Within it I taste egg, chilli, lemon, anchovy and bacon. I swallow the last of it, Serge and Frankie both nodding at me as I do.

'Oh god—'

'No, don't throw it up! Hold it down. Come on, woman, take charge of that digestive tract!' Frankie urges.

I clench my jaw and hold on.

'Breathe, chef.' Serge conducts with his flowing hands, and through the swelling nausea I notice he has had a haircut and a shave.

The revival brew and my insides settle, and miraculously within an hour I am less of a waste of space. Even so, Serge comes into his own. Frankie stands beside him, telling him what to do as Serge, after a five-second delay, speaks Frankie's instructions aloud to himself, remembering back.

'Fold it in slowly.'

'I must fold it in slowly.'

I stick to nodding and reminding him of amounts and times while slowly sipping another concoction involving a lot of garlic that is part two of Frankie's regime.

'I bet you don't miss hangovers,' I mutter to Frankie when Serge is in the cool room.

'I do, actually. I had too many of them in the end, of course, that's what happens – you drink to cure the hangover rather than enjoy the wine – but a rip-roaring hangover at an appropriate time is a gift.'

'I don't understand you at all.'

'It's like a bushfire: it rages through and clears the cobwebs, it increases humility, it can re-set you.'

'I'm not sure if it's reset me. Leith was there this morning, first day of cherry sales. He's opening another restaurant, with Maia, was planning it for nearly a year.'

Frankie's nonplussed. 'What of it? He can't touch you now.'

I realise that this is true. I'm the one who left. I want to reclaim my old Eames chair that was Grandad's from our old apartment, and I am owed some compensation for Circa, but not today.

'Get what's owing to you and keep clear. Thank your lucky stars, I say.'

I nod as Julia enters. 'You're early.'

'Just as well, you're a mess. Good night?'

'Polly and martinis. How bad do I look?'

'You look a lot better than you did,' Frankie, pleased with his efforts, notes.

'On a scale of one to ten?' says Julia. 'Minus three. You must have needed to let off some steam.'

'I had a lot going on in my head.'

'I know, honey. And now?'

'More like the test pattern on TV.'

'Good.' Frankie is impressed.

'That makes it an excellent time,' announces Julia.

'For what?' I ask.

'An intervention.'

'Jules, it takes more than one person to make it an intervention. And it was just one night.'

'It's not about you getting plastered last night, though don't make a habit of it.'

'So?'

'Sara called me. She says you're avoiding her and that's why you went out.'

'Oh god.'

'*Are* you avoiding her? More than usual, I mean. She says you know why.'

'Do *you* know why?' I counter.

'Because of her romance with Ewan?'

Frankie roars with laughter at this point, and Serge reappears.

'Ewan?' I ask.

'Apparently he likes the older ladies. Poor Katherine.'

'*What?*'

Julia nods confidently. 'He sent her a poem, put it under her door last night. She said he wrote it in iambic pentameter . . . mostly.'

'What? No, that was Serge! *Serge* is infatuated with Mum, not Ewan!'

Frankie's chuckles reverberate through the kitchen and my head.

Serge looks grief-stricken and jealous. 'Sara is making love with Ewan?'

'No one is making love with my mother! Serge, did you sign your poem?'

'I didn't think there was need, of course is from me.'

'You wrote it on a page from Ewan's manual.'

'Brilliant work,' cackles Frankie.

'She hasn't decided to reciprocate on the poem, has she? She's not chasing after Ewan, is she?' I ask Julia as a horrible vision enters my mind.

'No, she said he doesn't have enough facial hair for her. Serge, you're back in the running, but only if it doesn't interfere with your work here.'

Serge bows. 'Nothing can come between me and her.'

'You mean Mum?'

'No, her – the restaurant. Fortune, you, Frankie – I am yours first.'

'Just keep it that way.' Julia uses the same stern schoolmistress voice she uses on me, to excellent effect.

'Now, as for you,' she continues, staring me down. 'Your mum says you can't avoid her or the truth and you both know it. I'm guessing that means the fact that she thinks she's on every man's wish list?'

I nod, but I know very well what she really means. I try not to look at Frankie.

'Anyway, she's coming in to lend a hand later.'

'Huh?'

'Like you're in any condition to refuse help. She can polish glasses or something.'

Serge begins to whistle.

'Now, you need to go and fix yourself up and get to work.'

'Right behind you, tiger.' Frankie winks. I wink back.

'What was that?' Julia frowns. 'Who are you winking at?'

'My destiny.' The other good thing about hangovers is that they simplify your words and clarify your thoughts.

Cherry Cobbler

Ingredients

4 cups fresh cherries, picked over, rinsed, quality-tested and
    drained well
2 tablespoons cornflour
⅔ cup plus an extra 2 tablespoons sugar – raw is good
2 tablespoons fresh lemon juice (about ½ a lemon)
1 cup plain flour
1 teaspoon baking powder
½ teaspoon salt
85 grams cold butter, coarsely chopped
½ teaspoon lemon zest and ½ teaspoon chopped fresh rosemary

Method

Preheat the oven to 170°C.

Working over a bowl that's deep enough to contain cherry
spray, pit the cherries, discarding the pits and reserving the cherries
and any juice. Next, add the cornflour, ⅔ cup of sugar and lemon
juice and stir gently until combined.

In a small bowl, combine the remaining 2 tablespoons sugar,
flour, baking powder, salt and butter. Blend the mixture with
your fingertips until it resembles breadcrumbs. Now stir in ¼ cup
boiling water, stirring with a wooden spoon until the batter is
just combined.

In a quality baking dish, heat the cherry mixture until it reaches
a bubbly-jubbly boil. Remove from heat. Once the bubbles have
stilled, smear heaped tablespoons of the batter over the cherries.
Now sprinkle the lemon zest and rosemary over the top. Bake
the cobbler in the middle of the oven for 45–50 minutes, or until
the top is golden.

Serve the cobbler with quality vanilla-bean ice-cream. Prepare
to desire seconds.

42

Frankie, 1982

A DOG OF A HANGOVER, BARKING WITH THE SHARP-TOOTHED howl of vitriolic demons. A burning through my sorry eyes as Paul and his employers come into focus.

The remnants of a night that began three days ago and blurred into betting losses, and whores sprinkled with nose candy, begin to descend.

I hear the click-clacking of their heels along the street. One wishing her client-for-the-night a happy birthday and luck getting back to Watsons Bay without his wallet. Another petal of memory floats down to me: Jim calling the ladies of the night and then demanding a discount because he'd done so much coke he couldn't keep it up.

'Morning, gents,' I attempt as a basin of vomit erupts from my gut and lands on my well-stained sheets.

Simon the judge, Bill's pal, was there too, I recall. His specialty is performing cunnilingus in front of his mates, instructing them as he goes. He considers it a community service of sorts. Though poor Vera looked like she'd rather be researching her family tree than being used as a model for the elite of Sydney's legal and political circles' oral pursuits. I hope she charged him enough.

No one is looking all that excited to see me this morning. And yet the last few days have been a lockdown of orgiastic indulgences.

'You need to sign it, Frankie.'

'What's that, Clive?'

Old Bill warned me about these blokes before he took off. Told me to stand clear. I didn't. Over two years have passed and there's no sign of his return. Rumour has it he's taken to living on the streets. There's no need for it, but that's what he did. Always with a bottle in hand. My addictions have my life pointing in a similar direction.

Idiot.

'The contract for the restaurant.'

'Fuck off.'

'You're eighty grand in the red, Frank.'

'Still not as much shit as you'll be in when you get home, Jim. Will you tell your wife about the threesome with the girls before or after you blow out the candles on your cake? Many happy returns, by the way,' I say.

'You're sunk, Frank. No one will sell to you at the markets, we will make each night at the restaurant like walking through a graveyard.'

'Why do you want it so bad, fellas?' I ask. 'It's just a little place.'

'It's affecting all the other spots around town. You know that.'

'That will happen wherever I go, because most of the chefs around here couldn't tell the difference between a brûlée and a blowfly.'

'But you won't be working anywhere else. You'll be on garden leave. Unless you fancy opening a fish-and-chippy in Ulladulla?' Jim offers.

'And Clive's wife fancies opening up a frock shop, so we need the space,' Simon reasons.

'Oh, I see. A dress shop. Why didn't you say? I like Tracy.'

There are four of them now gathered around my spew-sodden sheets. I am naked, which reduces one's powers of negotiation.

'I like her style,' I add.

Clive nods, proud despite the fact that he has spent the night sodomising a fellow barrister named Keith.

'I especially liked her wraparound skirt, I think it was blue and green . . . it looked spectacular flung up around her ears when I fucked her on my kitchen bench last week and she howled with gratitude that someone who knew how to fuck her up the correct orifice had made her come. Really, Clive, you would have done well to take notes during Simon's lecture earlier, though of course he considers himself the king of cunni because his dick is smaller than a virgin's Tampax.'

The first blow is always the worst. After that there's a bizarre sense of spiritual liberation in having the bejesus thrashed out of you. They opt not to kill me; at this point in time, their levels of corruption are already creating murmurs around town, so me turning up dead so soon after being seen with them would cause a stir. But they want me gone. Of that I have no doubt.

Wallop, thrash, kick and hit; fortunately none of them is any bloody good at a decent fight and they are without their heavy-weights. Plus they too are worse for wear following three days of carnal indulgences. But my ongoing presence in their lives is a thorn in their collective side, about as welcome as a book of poetry at a footy grand final.

The great crime I have committed is not extending my rampant appetites to their well-coiffed wives, but rather my true talent: my cooking. My cooking has given my restaurant a name that cannot be bought, bartered or stolen by the joints they collectively own. My culinary presence has lifted the bar, when all they want is to maintain a mediocre monopoly. They have offered to buy me out and re-employ me for outrageous amounts of money, but the thought of saying *yes, boss* to any of them is beyond the pale.

A further – and, if I'm honest, perhaps greater – cause of their angst is the fact that my ramshackle little terrace is all too close to the major development they have been planning at the now-derelict wharf. No longer operating as the woolshed it began as, and with no world wars to deploy troops to, the huge cavernous beauty lies in a state of disrepair. Their plans, which with their connections are sure to be passed through state government, will ripple around the attached neighbourhood. Tracy's dress shop, of course, will be one of many at the entrance level of their monolithic casino.

The other residents in the street will have to be bought off. But my friends' connections with both local council and state politics can bring this into play. Not to mention a relocation of the local public housing residents, who will no doubt be carted off to unfamiliar streets with no infrastructure in one of the godforsaken housing estates they are dropping the poor into out west. I will not be party to this.

I remain a haemorrhoid in their daily existence, the personal pile of their collective aspirations.

Later, one of them must have panicked, fearing that they had beaten me to death. Serge appears, blankets me up and takes me up to St Vincent's. I am released in time to cook dinner that night, albeit feeling mighty sorry for myself and minus two teeth.

I am surprised I have remained this long. I push everything to its extreme, more out of curiosity than a death wish, but the fact that I have made it past my thirtieth birthday is a pleasant surprise to me. Don't get me wrong, I have no desire to end. I love life. The problem is I love it so much I have squashed mine out of existence.

43

Lucy

THE EVENING PASSES WITHOUT INCIDENT. I CAN'T SAY I REACH giddy heights, but between getting the meals out and the desire not to let Mum catch me chatting to Frankie, my full focus is happily absorbed by the dinner.

If anything, it has made me more grateful for the ramshackle team I have gathered around me. Even Mum does well with her bit, which is admittedly simple: polish a few glasses, chop herbs and sprinkle them while Serge proclaims her a genius.

I think a lot of people get involved with restaurants because they provide a sense of family. Families and food are interchangeable in many ways. The meals you share are what define your relationships. Working with a group of folk who, for whatever reason, feel that food is important enough to be prepared and served well connects you to a sense of tribe.

Serge, who recites recipes as he prepares them and sings to his cakes to ensure they rise. Hugo, who understands the grace of cohesive service, intuiting people's palates and requests, the child of a family in which mealtimes are connected with serving and loving. Julia, who loves to eat with people she loves, even if she's not big on sharing desserts. And Mum, who, while enjoying an erratic relationship with both food and mealtimes over the years, likes to be waited upon and is certainly good on the tooth when it comes to sweets. And then there's Frankie, he with the palate of the Messiah and a devotion to meals akin to Mother Teresa's care for the poor. Meals and their creation are inextricably knitted into his DNA. It is how he loves and how he serves, and it is what he cannot let go of, and possibly why he cannot leave.

I feel a thud in my gut. I don't want him to go away, ever. Over these past days, hours, whatever the amount of time, which I know is limited, the meals I have shared, created, served and consumed beside Frankie have taken my love of food, of cookery, to a whole new level. Having him with me is like being home. And my joy of this is intrinsically connected to his presence, in my head, if not my world.

The rub, of course, lies in my upcoming date with Charlie and the fact Frankie ebbs and flows into wanting to match me up with him. Yet for all my power of will I cannot see him, do not feel him, as any kind of father figure in my world. He is increasingly becoming the inspiration for it.

I watched *Harvey* with James Stewart when I was a kid, and loved it, and I also tap-danced to 'Me and My Shadow'. I get the attraction of the lonely soul pairing with the non-existent one – even if it's a bunny – and that when the lesson is learned the imaginary friend departs. If I were writing this as a fairy tale the lesson would be the restaurant becoming a success and me learning to have a healthy relationship with a lovely young man like Charlie, rather than a power-hungry git like Leith. And then I would marry Charlie and we would open a franchise and call it Frankie's and we would live happily ever after. The problem is I hate franchises, and hanging with Frankie is my favourite part of the day. These, of course, are hungover ramblings and I would do well to stop them in their tracks. I am not ready for a relation-ship with anyone, mortal or otherwise. And yet . . .

Sunday passes in a whirl, the coq au vin is a hit, and before many more hours it is Monday, the date of my date with Charlie.

I head into the restaurant to do some prep for tomorrow, check supplies, see Frankie.

He is not in a great mood. 'Menu plans?'

'We did them already.'

Frankie groans. 'For tonight, I mean . . . with Charlie.'

'Oh, um . . . I think we're just going somewhere for a bite and a movie.'

'You're seeing a film on a date. Christ, is he really my son?'

'What's wrong with that?'

'It's intimacy avoidance.'

'And you want intimacy escalation?'

He doesn't answer me. I notice he does this a lot. He acts almost as if he hasn't heard and then raises a totally unrelated and yet compelling topic; the master method of distraction. Too clever by half.

'The peaches from the little village near St Paul de Vence are like no other if you seek the ultimate peach crostata with sabayon.'

'Frankie, do you want me to go out with Charlie?'

'I was there a few days after I befriended Bjorn; he had directed me there with the address of a relative I could stay with written in his beautiful hand on a scrap from his sketch pad. I still have it somewhere. Perhaps it's in the recipe book. Shall we look? I think it's important you see it.'

'The address?'

'The handwriting.'

'Do you want me to go to dinner with Charlie tonight?'

This time he deigns to hear me. 'Do I want you to have a life that continues outside these walls, is that what you're asking? Dear girl, you must do whatever brings you pleasure, though I don't imagine two hours shut up in a dark room with someone you don't know watching rubbish on a screen is overly enticing.'

'Oh, you're a real romantic.'

'I've had my share of grab-and-tickle in a cinema. And yes, before you ask, I do like films. *ET* is a masterpiece.'

Where is this man from? I feel the churning of anger blocking my throat, and when I speak my voice is wafer-thin and sour. 'I think it's nice that we're becoming friends. He *is* your son.'

'Friends, lovers, spouses,' he says with the cadence of a taunting singsong. 'Knock yourself out – and then come back and help me figure out who killed me.'

'You really don't care?' I challenge.

He snaps. 'Lucille, you're not asking me for my son's hand in marriage, are you?'

I hate him at this moment. Fury rushes up and I want to slap him. I want to feel my hand against his cheek, my skin on his. Oh god, he is maddening. 'Maybe we'll have one of those dates that lasts twelve hours ... or even twelve years.'

'Just as long as at the end of it you come back and do your job and keep your promise.' He's back to being the epitome of composure.

'That's it?'

'Were you hoping for another reply, Lucille?'

I bang pantry items as I restock and hurriedly finish making my puff pastry. He sits on the bench watching, not speaking for a change.

We are both determined to out-sulk each other.

Frankie suggests an alternative for my pastry, which I ignore. Why am I so mad?

I finish up, expecting some parting smartarse comment, but nope, not a word. I wipe down the benches. Nothing. Grab my bag. Nada. Switch off the lights and close the door. Zilch.

44

Frankie

CHRIST ALMIGHTY, THIS IS THE MOTHER OF COMPLEX RELATION-ships; we may as well be on stage at the Acropolis.

What she doesn't hear because she's too determined to be in a mood is me calling after her.

'Just as long as at the end of it you come back to me.'

45

Lucy

PREPARING FOR NON-DATE DATES IS FUN . . . RIGHT? SO WHY has all mirth so fully deserted me? Having an intimate, intense relationship with a ghost is not without its shortcomings. One being that there is no hope he will text or call or email an apology, or turn up and say, 'Wait, I'm an idiot, a fool, of course you shouldn't go out with my son . . . I'm in love with you.' And then what? How would we even consummate it? The notion of kissing a ghost, sex with a ghost is not really appealing; but that's the problem – he feels so real to me that part of me is furious with him for not grabbing me and kissing me. This is impossible.

In my outrage I drive up to Paddington and venture into Scanlan Theodore, my favourite clothes shop in the world. Of course I can't afford anything, but I figure just a look won't hurt – I can consider it visual retail therapy. Oh, what fools we all are when it comes to what we desire. Once inside I'm confronted anew by the cool allure of this shop's concrete floors, the perfect spacing of each of its beautifully crafted pieces, the huge change rooms . . . not that I will be going into any of them. And then I see her – the dress of my dreams, the dress that belongs on the date I wish I was going on. Perhaps it will bridge the gap between my two worlds.

I haven't bought a new article of clothing in an age. There is a bond for my next apartment to save for, plus the paintings to pick up from the framer – though Matthias Drewe has offered to foot the bill so he can use them in his upcoming retrospective . . . I touch the resplendent silk, and like the cleverest magician the feel of the fabric melts away all stress and strain. I decide it would be silly not to try it on – the soft coffee belted dress coos at me as I whisk her into the change room. Jay, the assistant (who is at art school and is always reaching new levels of understanding and orgasmic ecstasy with her sexy jewellery-designing boyfriend), helps me. I finish zipping, walk out, look in the main mirror and see, aside from exhaustion and frizzy hair, a happier me than I have been in years. It has been such a long time since I have liked who I am. Sometimes a new signature frock can help you with your own evolution. Is it possible that the right man can too? I know that the right meal can not only transport you back into your past but give you a taste of the life you are dreaming of ahead.

With dress in bag I arrive home and commence a makeover of sorts. It has been too long since I have taken the time to let conditioner soak into my hair, applied a face mask and used an eyelash curler. Somehow, no matter how hard I try to smooth myself out, I always appear slightly ruffled. I'm a kinetic person, I guess – there's always some hair flying away, a button not staying put. But not tonight.

Mum inspects me before I head out. 'Could do with some more bling.'

'That's fine, Mum.'

'Where are you going?'

'The Japanese in Potts Point.'

I can see she is trying hard not to say what is about to come out of her mouth. 'You can't ring it if there's no doorbell, Luce.'

'Mum, we're just getting to know each other.'

'You're going along to try to get more information on Frankie. That's who your new dress is for. Not poor old Charlie.'

'You don't know Charlie, nor do I. That's why I'm—'

'It's like the guru used to say: you can run from your destiny but you can't hide.'

'What does that even mean?'

Mum bites into a brownie and considers. 'No use fooling yourself.'

'Please don't say the heart is a lonely hunter.'

'I wasn't going to. You know you're an intimacy-phobe. But you're backing the wrong horse going out with Charlie. Don't use him.'

Oh, how I hate my mother being right.

'Mum, one of the horses is a ghost.'

'Who's bringing you back to life. Don't be such a square.'

'Goodnight, Mum.' I kiss my mad mother and head out.

•

The restaurant is opposite the fountain on Macleay Street. It's the perfect place to take someone you don't know well, because the sushi bar offers a wealth of distraction. The food is also masterfully prepared and very, very good.

Charlie is waiting for me. He looks lovely, his soft brown curls falling perfectly, framing his masculinely angelic face. He stands to greet me, kisses my cheek. He's wearing a well-tailored blazer with t-shirt and jeans, and his leather shoes have a shine. As I take in the smell of very expensive cologne I realise I am searching for the roast dinner of Frankie's scent. In his own right, though, Charlie is truly lovely.

'I thought we'd sit at the bar, in case we run out of things to talk about.'

Humour too; I like him.

'You look beautiful,' he adds.

Like him even more.

Sake is an age-old answer to first-date jitters. I know it's best served cold, but on occasions when anxiety rides high, the comfort of its ricey boozy warmth is a true soft landing. We order some, and then we order more . . .

'Thank you for not taking me to Circa.'

'Well, that would just be rude. You know Leith's opening up another—'

'I know.'

'Are you two still friends?' Charlie treads lightly with his question and accompanies it with a hopeful nod.

'That's one name for it.'

'I know Maia . . .'

'I thought I knew her too. Wrong, obviously.'

Charlie laughs. 'Yes, it's weird, she always said she wasn't going to have kids.'

'I'm sorry?'

'We went to uni together, and I used to date one of her friends. You were talking about her pregnancy, weren't you?'

A blow to my chest as I down the remainder of my ceramic thimble cup. 'Sure. Yeah. Big news . . .'

There's a pause filled with Charlie's evident desire to backtrack.

'Didn't Leith tell you?'

'I saw them at the cherry launch . . . How pregnant is she?'

'Three months, they're telling people. You've been separated how long?' Charlie pours more sake. He looks concerned.

I waft my hand around in the air in an effort to pluck out a number. 'A while . . . a, um . . . yeah . . . a bit. Shall we order?'

We get to work while I take a few moments to add up badly. I am guessing Leith didn't know when he tried for the awful

Seal Rocks holiday, but his bizarre appearance at Mum's and his deathly silence since the opening of Fortune now make more sense.

It's a strange feeling to realise your husband is having a baby with someone else. We had decided against kids, the restaurant was our baby. And don't get me wrong, I don't want him back. I guess the main feeling is stupidity. How did I not click about the affair with Maia and not pick it at the markets? I even said that line about pregnancy, for god's sake. I'm an idiot. That poor woman is going to be tied to him for life. I make a mental note to contact Hugo's uncle and get cracking with the divorce. I want my Eames chair, the rest of my clothes—

'Do you like eel?'

Charlie draws me back with an expert eye to the menu. I shepherd my eyes to the world of miso and sashimi though my mind spins to calendar dates and pregnancy tests. Had she planned it?

'The crab is excellent,' Charlie says.

'Yes, love crab . . .'

Is that why she decided to stay on – she knew she was pregnant? Why didn't she tell me? How could she, though? I still don't hate her, but him – ugh.

'Oysters?'

Charlie now has my full attention – I do not trust a man who doesn't eat oysters or drink on occasion. 'You like oysters?'

'Completely committed to them, and the ones here have that—'

'Wasabi infusion. I know, it's my favourite.'

Lovely man, lovely single-living-cute-likes-oysters man sitting next to me. Come on, Lucy, get with the program, you should be thanking your lucky stars.

'Did you grow up around here?' he asks.

Except I can't. I can't play the first-date game. I don't know if it's Leith, or Frankie, but the thought of getting to know the universe of another person, and allowing them into mine – the hits and misses of my flawed self – makes me want to lie down and pull life's doona over my head. Oh god, Mum's right again, I am an intimacy-phobe and that's why I'm crushing on a ghost. Get it together, Lucy, answer the man.

'I grew up on the south coast with my grandparents and up north near Casino, mostly on a commune.'

'Wow. How was that?'

'Colourful.' That's what I say when I don't want to go there; come on, Lucy, dig deep. 'I mean it was fun and free, but a lot of it wasn't great, and the food was shocking.'

Charlie laughs.

'What about you?'

'A lot more sedate than you, aside from Dad. I grew up in Cremorne with Mum. We ate risotto once a week – that was my culinary highlight – and hot chips after school.'

'Did your mum re-partner?'

'Yeah. Dave, very calm, opposite of Dad.'

'Are they still together?'

'They would be but Dave died last year.'

'I'm sorry. You were close?'

'I guess. I liked him because he was everything Dad wasn't: he was patient and around and called Mum on the way home from work to see if she needed anything.'

'He sounds nice. I'm sorry . . .'

'Mum's doing well, she's back at work.'

'Good. What does she do?'

'She lectures in economics.' He smiles. 'She's great, you'll have to meet her. I'm like her. I mean . . . I don't mean . . . you know what I mean.'

'I do. Maybe you have your dad's love of food, though?'

Stop fishing for more info on Frankie, Lucy.

'Dad thought food writers and critics were the Antichrist. He was a bit of an arsehole and he suicided because he couldn't deal with his life.'

Ouch.

'What do you mean?'

'Dad thought he was a rock star and wanted every day to be glorious and huge and applauding of his brilliance. Anything normal like children or homework or hanging out bored him . . . or relationships. I think he realised he'd have to settle down at some stage and decided against it. He went for the big finish instead.'

'You definitely think he suicided?'

Charlie gives me a strange look. 'He hanged himself. He left a note.'

Stop asking questions, Lucy.

'Could he have been set up?'

Whoops.

'By who? The thing you need to know about Dad is that when you scratch the surface he wasn't that interesting. There was a lot of hot air and candour but nothing much underneath – just a load of movement and clashing pans. You've probably romanticised him because of Fortune.'

'Maybe, but . . . I just have a hunch that he didn't really want to leave you and he'd tell you that if he could.'

Charlie sends me another strange look. 'Thanks.'

'Blame the sake and my pseudo-psychic mother. But . . . did you like him when he was alive?' I am doing it again; stop talking about Frankie.

Pain surfaces. 'I idolised him.'

'You never wanted to make the restaurant yours?'

Charlie shifts uncomfortably; this cannot have been the conversation he was hoping for. 'Mum would have hated that, she badly wants to sell it but the conditions of the will won't let her. She says it's Dad being impossible still – trying to make us all remain around him.'

'Is that a bad thing?'

'It is if you've gone and if you were crap while you were here.'

'Did anyone hate him? Like really, really hate him?' Oh, ye gods, I suck at sleuthing and Charlie is getting suss.

'He wasn't popular with a few of the other restaurant owners, and he fell out with Paul Levine after a bad review, and he had a room of disgruntled ex-girlfriends, and Mum wasn't speaking to him when he died. And why are we still talking about my dead dad exactly?'

I try to laugh it off. 'Sorry – it's just being in there all the time, there's a strong sense of him.'

'I know, I could even smell him the other night. But can he not be here on our date as well, please?'

'Of course. Sorry.' We toast sake thimbles again and canvass an array of first-date topics, though we come back to restaurants and food quite a bit. He's really lovely and I would give anything to desire his kiss.

The food continues to arrive until we are sated, and then we walk up to Oxford Street side by side, cones of Messina gelato in hand. It's pretty much a perfect date.

We watch a new-release action film that avoids any controversy of politics or intimacy. I'm comfortable with him but all the time I'm . . . bugger it, I'm staring down at his hands and thinking how like Frankie's they are, the tilt of his head, the laugh, the walk all so very Frankie.

He's calmer than Frankie, more measured, gentler – probably kinder. If I'd met him first rather than his dad would it be different? I keep hearing Mum's voice in my head, and though I can fool myself about many things, this one I will not do. He's such a nice guy it wouldn't be right.

The film ends, the popcorn's been had, Charlie walks me back to my ute and the silence of the end of a date descends.

'That was lovely, such a great night, thank you,' I say.

'Pleasure. There's that new Korean place in Redfern, would you like to try that next week maybe? It's meant to be edgy.'

'Edgy Korean . . . hmm.'

I look at him smiling openly down at me. He's lovely. He draws me into him.

Here is the moment. I search his eyes and for a microsecond they are Frankie's and I painfully want my lips to touch his lips. I draw my breath and move my lips to his cheek.

'Thank you. Spending time with you is great.'

Oh god, was ever a more awkward sentence uttered so clumsily?

Charlie, ever the gentleman, holds my arms. 'You and Leith . . . that must be hard. You wanted to reconcile with him?'

'Oh god, no. But, um, thanks.'

Another awkward pause. Should I say something else, the I-have-feelings-for-your-dead-dad speech perhaps?

'I'm bringing Mum into the restaurant,' says Charlie.

'Great!'

'I'm not sure, she hasn't been there since Dad died, but I want her to try your food.'

Don't say anything else, Lucy. Shut up and get in the car.

'You are really lovely, Charlie. Your dad would be proud of you.'

Fuck.

Charlie nods, looking confused. 'Thanks.'

'Well, 'night, then.' I load myself into the ute and start it, leaving him waving by the kerb.

And I drive straight back to Fortune.

Wasabi-Infused Oysters

Ingredients
a dozen oysters
1–2 teaspoons high-quality wasabi paste
a pinch of white pepper
a dash of white vinegar
a splash of mirrin

Method
Shuck the oysters in a pan of water on a low heat, allowing them to open before finishing them off with an oyster shucking knife (be careful not to be in a hurry or a bad temper).

As the oysters warm and open, mix the remaining ingredients in a separate bowl.

Using a chef's syringe, gently inject each oyster with the wasabi filling. Only use a small amount in each, about the size of a 5-cent coin.

Serve immediately with a glass of very dry bubbles and sparkling conversation.

46

Frankie, 1982

I AM SITTING DOWN TO EAT LUNCH WHEN IT HAPPENS. MY MEAT supplier, Merv, has sourced me the most succulent veal cutlets, fresh from the Casino abattoir, humanely raised and fed solely on their mother's teat, the softest pink in colour, the smell of milk in their flesh. It's autumn and mushroom season, fresh chanterelles from Bowral picked by maidens with flowing locks and wide grins, delivered by their leader, the fearless April who refuses to wear a bra or remove her wellingtons. Veal and chanterelles make the most romantic union: mix the mushrooms in a creamy white-wine sauce, serve with a side of Brussels sprouts cooked to tender perfection, and you have the Mozart of dinners.

Last night I barely slept. A full moon shone in my eyes and I allowed her to be my sole mistress; as she grinned at me in her luminous excellence I had a rare feeling of peace. I may as well have been in a bloody confessional box: in her insistent light I started to realise that I want a life with love, not just all this shag and scatter. I tried to shake it off, telling myself I was thinking like a premenstrual hippy, but it persisted: live a better life, Frank – make it count.

I have always known that my life needed to make an impact, via food. It needed to elevate and in its own small way celebrate civilisation, but I was so hungry, I never stopped for the fifteen-minute wait to allow myself to feel sated – for fear I wouldn't, I guess. Anyway, I know all too well the perils of the epiphany, but last night's had the quiet, gentle satisfaction of a truly loving kiss – not too heavy, full of warmth and home. I dozed off near 5am, and for the first time in an age, woke without a filthy hangover.

I made coffee, patted the neighbour's dog, went to the markets early, picked up the paper and came in even before Serge. I have prepared for the night ahead and made my lunch, and now I sit with the paper and a glass of chablis. I have taken three bites and am contemplating this divine combination with reverence when an arm grabs my throat, a bag covers my head and everything goes black.

The bastards could at least have let me finish my veal. And they could at least have looked me in the eye. Cowards.

Veal Steak with White Wine and Chanterelles

Ingredients

8 × 1-centimetre-thick slices of boned veal loin, carefully trimmed
salt and freshly ground black pepper
plain flour, for dusting
2 tablespoons butter
250 grams fresh Australian chanterelles, wiped clean, trimmed
    and delicately sliced
2 tablespoons full-bodied white wine, or madeira if you must
¾ cup heavy cream
1 scant tablespoon chopped parsley

Method

Season the veal lightly with salt and pepper, and dust with flour.

In a large well-loved frying pan, melt the butter over medium heat. Cook the veal for 2 minutes on each side or until brown.

Warm a platter and have it at the ready.

Lower the heat, then add the chanterelles, cover and simmer for 4 minutes. Remove the veal from the pan and set aside on the warmed platter.

Continue to tenderly cook the chanterelles until the liquid takes its leave – don't allow them to dry out though! Add the wine and bring to the boil. Cook briefly, taste to check flavour. Lovingly whisk in the cream, then simmer for 4–6 minutes, until the sauce is thick and velvety.

Season to taste with white pepper and salt, and spoon the chanterelles over the veal. Sprinkle with parsley.

Serve hot with boiled new potatoes, crusty bread to mop up the juices, a glass of fine chablis and an excellent article to read.

47

Lucy

THE PROBLEM WITH JAPANESE FOOD IS THAT, NO MATTER HOW brilliant it is – and I believe it to be one of the highest cuisines – I always feel hungry again a few hours later. Its delicacy is part of its attraction, I know, but sometimes you just need – or at this time what *I* really need – is a steak, a giant T-bone to get my teeth into. Oh, who am I fooling, it's most likely sexual frustration. Charlie and the near kiss, the conundrum of Frankie.

Old Bill stands on guard and tips his non-existent hat to me, bows and disappears into the night.

I turn on the lights and expect Frankie to be waiting for me. But there's no one there.

I call out – nothing. Panic darts into my chest. Has he taken permanent leave, thrown in the towel because of my petulance? Does he even get a say in how long he is a ghost? Has his karma been worked through, or does he think his job is done, or . . . where *is* he?

I grab a T-bone and set it on the grill, pour a glass of shiraz.

What if I never see him again? What if I really did make him up? I remind myself that Mum has seen him, so therefore he exists, in a post-life way.

What if he is gone – gone-ghost-gone? I would regret that our last conversation was such a dud. Perhaps he's still sulking, watching me grill my steak. I sauté some spinach to accompany it, make a quick béarnaise sauce.

'Frankie?'

Surely he will tell me I need to add more cream?

'Frankie?'

During one of my counselling periods with Leith – we saw four different therapists over our five years of marriage – we were given an exercise. The therapist asked: what if this was the last time you were ever going to see the other person, this was going to be your last goodbye. What would you say to them? We had to write down our answers and then face each other on our therapist's ample red velvet couch, hold hands, look each other in the eye and 'speak from the heart'. I am ashamed to say I lied. I said all the things you say so the other person can go on in peace with a spring in their step – 'Thank you, you have changed my life, I have loved every second with you, yadah, yadah, yadah' – but I really wanted to say, *I feel like I'm choking, I hate that you never go down, I wish you peace and I used to like our sex and thank you for the great times but you have trampled on my heart, you have never really seen me, and though I wish you well I am glad to see the back of you.*

I think Leith lied too. He was fucking Sabrina the teenage kitchen hand at the time.

But if I never saw Frankie again? If I never saw him again it would be the worst thing ever. How can someone come into your life and penetrate your being so completely? In our short time together he has inspired and uplifted me in a way I have never experienced before. His determination to see me thrive, his humour, his sense of fun, even his moods . . . I have never craved another's presence like I do his. If I never got to see him again I'd be bereft that I didn't get to thank him, truly thank him for cheering me on and for being himself in all his hairy, sexy, politically incorrect, hysterical, bossy loveliness. Oh god, *where is he?*

'Why do women never eat on first dates?'

He's back on the kitchen bench, book in hand. I am so relieved to see him I burst into tears.

'See, that's what too long without a decent feed will do to you, Lucille. Must you weep? Your steak's ready, and yes, you need a dash more cream in your béarnaise.'

'Thank you,' I blubber.

'What for? Saving your sauce from wateriness? Well, yes, that warrants gratitude, I suppose. No need to get worked up about it, though, cherub.'

I bawl again and blabber, 'Thank you for coming here and helping me and for . . .' I start again.

'Lucille, for want of a better expression I live here, and you are helping me. For god's sake, woman, did you watch a film about cancer or Christmas holidays with the in-laws or something? What's got into you?'

'I couldn't kiss Charlie.'

Though he tries to hide it I see relief cross his face.

'Why not? He's a very handsome, very decent young man.'

'He's the same age as you.'

'I was never decent. I wish now I was.'

I leap in – what have I got to lose? 'I couldn't kiss Charlie because every time my hand touched his or he tilted his head or linked my arm I wanted it to be you.'

'Ah . . .'

'I want to kiss *you.*'

We stand looking at each other for what feels like an eternity. Oh, please say something, Frankie, tell me you want that too. Tell me anything.

'Your steak's going to be overdone.'

Not that. I turn off the heat and prepare my plate. I sit. I pour another glass of wine.

Frankie gets up and grabs another wine glass. 'I think I need one too.'

I pour him a glass. He sits smelling and savouring and as he looks into it he mutters, 'That would be very nice.'

'The wine? Yes, it is.'

'To kiss you.'

'Oh.' My heart pounds and he reaches for my hands, nearly touching me. I feel the warmth of him, I want to kiss him so badly I am about to explode. His hands hover over mine, and he looks to me with a question. I nod. Slowly he places them onto mine and for a millisecond we're engulfed in each other. Somehow I feel his body almost completely within mine and then – zap, we're thrown across the room.

Wine spills.

'Frankie?'

He's down on the floor, but after a moment he shakes himself and gets up. 'We might need to work on that.'

'Did you feel it, though, before the shock?'

He grins boldly. 'For the sweetest second I felt every curve of you.'

'Can we do it again?'

'I think, dear lady, we will have to pace ourselves . . . I feel quite faint.'

I am beside myself with the joy of feeling him. 'That was amazing.'

Our eyes meet and without him speaking I hear him say, 'Yes.'

•

Later, alone in my bed, I can't sleep. A safari of thoughts and possibilities stampedes across my mind. We touched. He likes me. We can do it again, and again, and maybe if we practise we will be able to do it for longer, and . . . oh, how I'd love him to be lying here, musing next to me. There must be a way, there has to be a way.

48

Frankie

WHAT IF I RUIN HER LIFE? I HAVE SWORN TO MYSELF I WILL HELP her and be a good father to Charlie, but that moment with her is worth a few lifetimes of this in-between world. To quote the Bard, 'She makes hungry where most she satisfies.'

I never want to leave her side, but what's in it for her? Dear god, I want to kiss her all over, lay her down on a bed, savour every inch of her incandescent skin, feel her warmth within, hold her, hold her . . . what if I am ruining her life? What if this obliterates us both? Is this why I'm stuck here – to be punished until I feel more overwhelmed than a girl scout on a detoured cookie hunt? I long to taste her. This feels different. Besides the obvious, her joy is what I seek, her pleasure beyond my own. Her silken skin, her rosy lips; to have her rest peacefully beside me, to watch her sleep and to hold her as she wakes. What has become of me? Surely a gathering of my exes has devised this devious plot. The joke, dear women, is on me. Just don't hurt her.

49

Lucy

I WAKE TO THE DISTINCTIVE SCENT OF A MAN'S AFTERSHAVE. But not just any man's aftershave. I totter barefoot into the kitchen, and there stands Serge making pancakes for my mother, who, it seems, is still in bed. Serge wears one of my grandmother's aprons. He whistles as he works.

'You like pancakes, princess?'

'Princess?'

'Yes, this morning you are radiant. This morning everything radiant. You are princess and your mother, she is queen.'

My stomach grumbles, not from hunger.

'And the queen's still asleep?'

Serge nods. I see he's brought over a load of groceries and stocked up Mum's fridge.

'What we doing today?' he asks, as if this situation is nothing out of the ordinary.

'Um, just, you know, the usual. I'd better get to the markets actually.'

'You want me to come?'

'Sergio?' My mother's best minx tone beckons from the bedroom. 'I'm ready for some pancakes.'

Serge smiles at me, embarrassed.

'You'd better stay and wait on your "queen". Besides, I'm meeting Julia there. I'll see you at work.'

I make a very quick exit and check in on Mum, who sits in bed in a paisley robe rubbing hand cream luxuriously into her palms.

'How was your date?' she asks expectantly.

'How was *yours*?'

Mum shrugs, quite pleased with herself. 'Not bad, actually. I fancied some pancakes, so Serge offered to come over and cook—'

I hold up my hands. 'Please don't give me details.'

'They don't call him Serge the Stallion for nothing.'

'Mum! He's my sous chef. Please don't say another word.'

'Suit yourself.' She stops rubbing her hands and studies me for a moment. 'You look different.'

This throws me but I try not to show it. 'How?'

Mum gives me a knowing look, then shrugs again.

I jump into the shower and then head to the markets, resolving to start looking for a flat. As sweet as Serge is, the thought of witnessing him and Mum re-enact *9½ Weeks* is more than I can handle.

'You need a place near work,' Julia announces as she bags a heap of Brussels sprouts. 'So, you think they—'

'I'm assuming so, yes,' I interrupt. I can't bring myself to say or even hear the words.

'That is possibly the least attractive image I've had all year.'

'Try being related to it.'

We walk on. The instant I smell peaches I think of Frankie's recipe, and of him wandering around the market in France.

'So, how was it? Charlie?'

'Good.'

'Good?'

'Good,' I repeat.

Julia takes me in and sighs. 'You're not into him.'

'It's complicated.'

'He's gay?'

'No, he's lovely. It's just that I . . .'

'Lucy, this had better not be about Leith.'

'I promise you it's not.'

'Good. Then, what? He's too perfect?'

'He's lovely,' I repeat lamely. 'It's just that he reminds me too much of his father.' There, I've said it. Relief engulfs me.

Julia raises an eyebrow. 'His father? His *dead* father who would be, what, *sixty-three* by now had he not killed himself a few decades ago? *That* father?'

'Possibly.'

'What are you talking about? You know you're sounding slightly unhinged again, right? I get it: it's been a big month and now your mother is sexing the sous chef and that would send the best of us over the edge – Jesus, make sure he gives his hands an extra clean before he touches anything in the kitchen, won't you.'

I decide I will not be sidetracked by Serge's hand-sanitising habits, I have to tell her now. 'Frankie was murdered. He's—'

'Murdered! Did Charlie tell you that?'

'No . . . he did.'

Julia takes the peach I am smelling and puts it down. 'What is going on with you?'

Deep breath, Lucy, and spill . . . now.

'He's a ghost. Frankie's a ghost and he's at Fortune and I can see him and he can see me and we talk and I am in love with him.'

'Fine, why didn't you say?'

I wait for the tirade I know is coming. 'Jules?'

'Next time just tell me to mind my own business,' she says with her sour-lemon double-blink.

'I'm not joking. He's at the restaurant. That smell you like – it's him.'

Julia studies my face for a punchline. She starts seven sentences, but then goes with a slow shake of her head.

'Jules, I'm telling you the truth. Cross my heart.'

She paces the peach aisle. Stops. 'How long?'

'Since the first day we went to clean the restaurant.'

'A ghost?'

I nod.

Julia exhales a slow, deep breath. 'Okay.'

'Okay you believe me, or okay you're going to commit me?'

'I have five words for you: *The Ghost and Mrs Muir*.' She does a quick wince at my blank expression, then forges on. 'Classic film, nineteen forty-seven, based on the book by Josephine Leslie, written under the nom de plume R.A. Dick because as a female writer she wouldn't have been taken seriously. The film starred Rex oh-so-hot Harrison and Gene Tierney, set in England, filmed on the Monterey Peninsula in California. You need to see this film.' Julia freezes, wheezes then yelps. 'Wait, her name was Lucy too – or Lucia. You're the fucking ghost and Mrs Muir!'

'What happened in the film, did they get together?'

Julia stares at me, incredulous. 'He's a ghost!'

'But did they?'

'He helps her, he leaves her to it, she eventually dies and then he comes to take her to wherever dead people go.'

'That's it?'

'No, there's this cad she falls for, and he breaks her heart.'

'Great. So much to look forward to.'

Julia hands me back the peach. 'We are going home to relieve the babysitter and then you are going to take me step by step through what's happened. And yes, I am angry with you.'

'What for?'

'I expect to be kept in the loop with your love life, living or otherwise. That's what best friends are for, particularly sleep-deprived new-mother, married best friends.' She puts her arm around me.

'Mum's seen him too.'

''Course she has. Has her boyfriend?'

'No, but he can smell him, like you. Frankie wants me to help him find his killer.'

'Why'd he choose you, why not Charlie?'

'I was there, I guess, at the right time. I think he used to be a man-slut.'

'A dead, murdered, man-slut. Honey, you never choose the easy road, do you?'

She takes my arm and leads me to the ute. I am only slightly worried she's going to have me scheduled, but her love of old films is working in my favour.

50

Frankie

THEY DINE SIDE BY SIDE, THE LIVING AND THE DEAD. IF WE BUT knew how each passes through the other I would have my answer and could find my way to her in the fullness of life. For now all I can do is encourage her, be there. It won't be enough; in time she will weary of being confined with me within these walls, she will hunger for the exchange of life experience and to make love with someone who has breath.

But today she is happy, and thoughts of finding my killer fade beside the desire to just be with her for as long as she will stay.

51

Lucy

I KNOW SOMETHING IS WEIRD AS SOON AS I PULL UP. THE PAST few days have been spent avoiding Mum and Serge's bedroom antics, being probed by Julia and grabbing whatever time I can with Frankie. I feel the flush of love and all I want is to be with him in the kitchen.

The door is ajar – we've been robbed, is my first thought. I walk in and see that the restaurant is full of roses; stunning roses of all colours, everywhere.

I call out to Frankie, who replies, 'Kitchen! Now!'

I walk through, and there is Old Bill being held against the wall by a well-dressed thug while Paul Levine scours Frankie's little red book.

Frankie paces.

'Can I help you?' escapes from my lips.

'Always so polite. You could have taught Frankie a thing or two about manners.' Paul waves the book in front of me.

'What does he want?' I ask Frankie. 'And why is Bill here?'

'Bill was doing me a favour. They snuck up on him. They think it contains a code.'

'What code?' I ask.

'You know the code?' Paul looks up from the book.

'You cannot be here. I'm calling the police.'

'How do you know about the code, Lucy?' Paul feigns casual interest.

'Tell him you know where it is,' Frankie implores.

'I know where it is,' I say carefully. 'What's it for?'

Frankie and Paul both hesitate, and in the brief silence Old Bill pipes up. 'It's for the safe that has the contracts and all the information on the shonky property deal.'

'Thanks, Bill,' I say as Bill grunts and nods.

'Let him go.' Paul nods at the thug, who releases Bill.

'Bit ripe, mate. Seen a shower lately?'

'Not recently.' Bill smiles and breathes heavily on the thug, who is immediately repelled.

'Where's the code, Lucy?'

'Where is it?' I repeat.

'Tell him it's on the back of my portrait.'

'It's with the framer,' I say.

'What?' asks Paul.

'The portrait Matthias Drewe did of Frankie, it's on the back of that.'

'Which framer?'

'I'm not sure. Somewhere in Paddington. You'll have to ask Matthias. Mind you, they're changing the backing, so maybe it will be erased.'

'Oh, clever woman.' Frankie claps his hands. 'Send them on a wild goose chase!'

'Is that what you were looking for when you killed Frankie?' I ask Paul.

Everything stops.

'Frankie topped himself, we all know that.'

'No, he didn't. He was murdered.'

Old Bill starts to rock to and fro on the spot.

'Did you kill him to get the code, just so you could develop your properties, the casino or whatever other crooked deal you were involved with? Or did you kill him because he could see through you, and his presence eclipsed yours?'

'Lucille, be careful,' Frankie, who now stands beside me, urges.

The thug walks very close to me.

'Lay a finger on her and I'll deck you.' Old Bill straightens up. He really does smell vile, but I couldn't be more grateful.

'So will I.' Hugo appears as if from nowhere.

There's a beat of awful intensity. No one moves.

'Sorry,' the thug offers by way of apology.

We all take a breath, albeit a shallow one.

'Who's getting married – why all the flowers?' Hugo asks.

'No idea,' I reply.

'They're not from me.' Paul attempts humour and fails.

More silence.

'That's a very nice suit, by the way,' Hugo says to the thug. He does this when he's very nervous, uses compliments as an ice-breaker, but I fear this one may land him a broken arm.

But the thug looks pleased. 'Armani. A man needs a good suit.'

'Only one person is responsible for Francis Summers' death, and that's him,' Paul directs at me.

'I don't believe you.'

'Get the book back, Lucille,' Frankie insists. 'I won't have that twit re-creating my recipes.'

I put out my hand. 'Give it back, Paul.'

Paul performs another flick through the pages.

'Now.'

'I'll be calling Matthias Drewe,' he says as he hands it back.

'Tea, anyone?' Hugo breezes over to the kettle, then looks back to the thug. 'How do you take yours?'

'White with one, ta.'

Paul turns to his offsider. 'Mark, we're leaving.'

Mark smiles apologetically at Hugo, then at me. 'Lovely restaurant. I'll bring the missus.'

They take their leave.

'I'm off too.' Bill nods at me.

'I'll say,' quips Hugo. 'Why don't you let me perform a miracle makeover on you, Bill?'

'Get out of it.' Bill is unimpressed, though he chuckles.

'What exactly was going on?' Hugo asks the question on my lips.

'Bill was helping me,' says Frankie. 'Weren't you, Bill?'

'What's with the avalanche of roses?' Hugo adds.

'I don't know,' I say again.

'Charlie?' Hugo suggests.

This is too much for Frankie, who booms, 'They're from me, woman! I got Bill to do me a favour. I asked him to fill the restaurant with roses. He went a bit literal, but there you have it.'

'They're from Bill,' I announce to Hugo, beaming.

Hugo takes this in, nodding slowly and raising his eyebrows before walking off into the dining room.

I turn to the old man. 'Thanks, Bill.'

'I dreamt that Frankie said you needed flowers, roses. Lots of them.'

'A dream or a conversation?' I query.

Bill performs a long low whistle. 'So you see him too, and you're not even on the turps.'

'Can you see him here, now?' I ask.

'Can you?' he counters.

I nod. And so does he.

'What was that all about with Paul?' I ask them both.

Bill answers. 'No matter. That code, they'll be out of luck when they find it.'

'Why?'

'I got there first, years ago, emptied the safe, the one in his storage unit. They would have destroyed this town.'

'That's right,' affirms Frankie, looking fondly at his old friend. 'Paul didn't kill me – he wanted the code and he didn't know Bill had cleared the safe. The killer has to be someone who knew what we'd done. Paul was merely ensuring his tracks were still covered, and trying to steal my recipes.'

'How did you get hold of the contracts?' I ask.

'A long lunch here, they were pissed, I ducked in at the right moment with a distraction . . . Bill grabbed them.'

'So, it's someone who was at that lunch?'

'They didn't click for days, didn't realise that what they'd left behind was the original and without it they'd be – how to say this delicately? – fucked.'

I look from Frankie to Bill. 'Bill, has anyone else been snooping here over the years?'

'Plenty of them. Most of the ones at the table on your opening night, but I don't think they knew the code.'

'What about Victor?' Frankie's face is alight with excitement. 'He had a temper.'

'He had a massive heart attack on the tennis court and dropped down dead a decade ago.'

'Oh, too bad . . . funny, he's never stopped by for dinner.'

'And Frankie, by then it was all over anyway. The state government passed legislation for the development – they kept quiet about the casino – but there was a major outcry from the locals and they had to back down.'

'So killing me, if it was for those contracts, was a waste?'

'Yes and no. The contracts had specifics about the casino, and they implicate a handful of men who wouldn't want to be named.'

I do a double-take at Bill, the man who has barely given me more than a grunt for the past weeks.

'Any use taking it to the press now?' I ask.

Bill shakes his head. 'Better we keep it up our sleeves.'

'Have you two spent much time together?' I ask suddenly, thinking of the thirty years or so that have passed with Bill spending most of his days outside the restaurant.

Frankie smiles. 'This is the first time I've got him inside. He was terrified of the sight of me for the first ten years, but we're getting there now.'

'How did you get in, Bill?'

Bill holds up a key.

'How did you get that?' I ask as Bill and Frankie exchange looks. 'Did you steal it from me?'

Bill puts his hands in the air. 'Not guilty, your honour.'

'Don't be ridiculous, woman. Bill is the silent owner of the place!'

I look to Bill, who nods. 'You're the one who owns fifty-one per cent?'

'It was the least I could do,' says Frankie. 'Besides, I knew he'd keep this place safe. He took a bullet for me more than once. He lost everything because he's one of the few humans walking this planet with integrity. Yes, he may look like a homeless bum in need of a wash, but he's a bloody saint.'

Finally I find my voice. 'Bill, why didn't you sell?'

'I promised Frankie I wouldn't. I broke one vow, a long time ago, and it didn't work out too well. I'm not breaking another.'

'But you could have lived here!'

'I do,' he states plainly. 'This is the way I like it. Now, I have to get down to the TAB before my girl runs.' He bows and heads out.

I look at Frankie. 'Wow.'

'Is that all you can say?'

'Considering I thought I was walking into my death, I don't think I'm doing too badly.'

'What about the roses?' Frankie looks like a schoolboy, hopeful, terrified and completely vulnerable.

'I love them.'

'Good.'

'Thank you.' I burst into the giddy grin of a six-year-old on a pony.

Hugo strolls back into the kitchen with a rose between his teeth and presents it to me. 'We're booked out again. And Charlie is bringing his mother. Polly is coming in to help.'

'Good grief.' Frankie pales, as do I. I haven't been in touch with Charlie since our date. How do I tell him I'm seeing someone else, his dear old dad? And what's he going to think of all the roses? Why is it that everything happens at once?

No sooner have I had that thought than my phone rings. Maia.

'Are you going to answer it?' Hugo and Frankie ask in tandem.

With my phone in one hand I grab the spatchcock I have selected for tonight's menu and head for the cool room.

'No more hiding, Lucille,' says Frankie. 'For either of us. Face your demons.'

I shut the door in his face, hover another moment and then answer.

Pancakes

Ingredients
3 eggs, lightly whisked
1½ cups milk
1 teaspoon vanilla essence
2 tablespoons melted butter
1½–2 cups plain flour (depending on weather and egg size)
pinch of salt
extra butter for frying, of course

Method
In a bowl, mix together the eggs, milk, vanilla and melted butter. I use a whisk. Sift the flour and salt into a separate bowl. Making a well in the centre, add the egg/milk mixture. Use a favourite, non-smelly wooden spoon to gradually persuade the flour into the centre.

Beat with the whisk until smooth and silky, then pour back into the bowl and stand the batter for 1 hour.

Heat a small well-greased flat, heavy pan (cast iron is best) over medium heat. I give the greased pan a quick wipe with paper towel to absorb excess grease. Pour in 2–3 tablespoons of the batter and swirl the pan to coat it evenly. When small bubbles appear and batter begins to set, shake the pan and then flip the pancake over to cook the other side. You may call upon the assistance of a spatula if your flipping isn't up to scratch. Remove from the pan and repeat until all the batter is gone, creating a stack.

Plate and add toppings as basic or as ridiculous as you like. Arrange on a tray with tea, juice and papers, carry it into your lover's room . . . and close the door.

52

Frankie

A ROSE BY ANY OTHER NAME . . . A GIRL BY ANY OTHER NAME . . . no. It's only her; everyone else seems a droopy gerbera in comparison. She's 'Clair de Lune' played by a maestro and picnic hampers of hope. No one else could ever have been Lucille. And whoever my killer is, it's only him . . . or her . . . but who is it?

If only I had been paying attention. It was a blur before I realised, and then a noose. Was there more than one set of footsteps? Hard, heavy, fast hands. If it was a woman she had organised a fellow to do the heavy lifting, which would indicate a plan. It was so quick. Surely someone cleared the space while the other bound, blinded and gagged me. And I'm no lightweight. Yet I was lifted like a feather.

If it was one of them looking for the code for the safe they would have tried a bit of torture before they topped me. If it was some kind of warning, it certainly went awry. Or a joke that went horribly wrong? Well below the belt.

Who is still living with this on their head? Has time eclipsed their guilt? I was certain that re-igniting Fortune would draw them here. If someone had wanted my actual recipes that badly, surely they would have nicked the book, bribed or blackmailed it out of me. But they murdered me. There had to be some kind of passion involved. Or that's what I like to think anyway.

53

Lucy

I TURN ONTO MILITARY ROAD AND TAKE IN THE FULL GLORIOUS vista of the cliff faces of Vaucluse down to the gentle harbour of Watsons Bay with her rocking boats and her jetty awaiting ferried tourists in pursuit of fish and chips and holiday snaps, the sea baths where game swimmers perform patient laps, and across to the jewel in the crown, the Sydney Harbour Bridge and a glimpse of the top sail of the Opera House. Watsons Bay is a sanctuary from the buzz and pace of the city, a perennial seaside holiday that beckons bare feet, sandcastles and naps under the massive maternal Moreton Bay figs.

We meet at Dunbar House, the location of many a bridal shower and morning tea with fussy aunts. She's there waiting. Looking nervous. When we were friends we would occasionally brunch here after a stroll and a dip in Camp Cove on our day off. Now there is the tension of a first date without any of the joy. I wish for a clever barb, witty but not cruel. All I manage is: 'Well, this is weird.'

Maia nods. She has the authentic dichotomy of green and glowing that early pregnancy often offers. I sit beside her and look at a table of laughing women in their early thirties across from us: a bridal shower in full swing.

'Congratulations on Fortune. It's the buzz of the town.'

'Thanks. And congratulations to you too.'

'Do you mean that?'

'Part of me does. Leith and I were done for such a long time, and with recent events . . . it feels like a lifetime ago.'

There's a pause. Perhaps I should go now? But I need to know. 'Do you love him?'

Maia nods and starts to cry. Before I know it my arm is around her. 'Why didn't you tell me?'

She blubbers, clearly relieved to be making her confession. 'It wasn't planned.'

'The pregnancy or the affair?' I cannot help letting that one slip out.

'Either.'

'How long?'

'About a year.'

Another blow to my gut. 'And how did you . . . doesn't matter.'

'I wanted to tell you so many times, especially because you were so miserable and wanted to leave him.'

'But you know what he's like, Maia.'

'I know. I . . . we're different, you and me. I love him. Really love him.'

'That won't stop him cheating and breaking your heart.'

Maia nods, but I see that look. The look we've all had at one time or another. The look of arrogance saved for the first flush of love. The *I am different because my love will transcend and save this situation and change him* look. God knows I wore it for the first year with Leith. Now I think I'm going to bring Frankie back from the dead like a teenage vampire film with that look.

'Shit. This is shit,' she says.

'It was a really shitty thing to do, Maia. Why did you say you'd leave and work with me?'

'I never did, Lucy,' she protests. 'You jumped on it and then you assumed . . . you never actually asked me.'

'Yes, I did,' I reply. Though there's a knot of doubt . . . I know that was my intention.

'No, you didn't. I loved working with you. I wanted to support you. I didn't know how to broach what was going on, so I kept mute. I thought in time when you and Leith had finally finished properly I could tell you everything and . . .'

'What, we'd all have Sunday barbecues together and share Christmas ham? You fucked my husband behind my back while you spent your days baking mille-feuilles with me. Not to mention planning another restaurant. That is *not* good behaviour.'

Maia bawls again. I pass her a table napkin, which she uses to blow her nose with passion.

'Sorry, it's the hormones.'

Scones with jam and cream are delivered on a three-tier cake platter. Our waitress's sunny smile crumples at the sight of us. She makes a quick exit.

'So, you didn't plan the pregnancy?'

'I wasn't thinking, but . . . I'm thirty-four, there's no way I wouldn't keep it.'

'And what does Leith think?'

'He's so excited about being a father, he said you deprived him of that.'

'*I* deprived him of that? Oh, for god's sake, *we* decided to keep our focus on the restaurant.'

Maia absorbs this, looking slightly stunned. The girls at the bridal shower erupt into laughter and clinking glasses.

Maia eyeballs me. 'Tell me truthfully, were you ever really in love with him? Because I don't think you were. Not like I am.'

Another stab. Life really does have a wonderful way of serving up your greatest fear on a platter and asking if you'd like fries with that. I always had a lurking doubt with Leith, not just about his feelings but also about my own. And what I have felt in the short time I have known Frankie has such a different flavour and depth, and it's not even physical. With Leith it was surging hormones and the seduction of possibility. With Frankie it's kinship. He's on my side. Leith was always my competition, which was sexy in its own way, but part of the heightened state came from not knowing if he really had my back. There's not a doubt Frankie has mine. I trust him.

'Sorry, I have no right to ask you that.' Maia resumes her weep.

'You know what you're in for,' I reply.

Maia nods solemnly.

'And you still choose it?'

'I believe in him.' Ah, there it is, the true rub. She believes in him. I never did.

'Well, I wish you luck. I've backdated the separation to when we stopped sharing a bed, so we'll be divorced in six months.'

Maia looks confused. 'He said you hadn't slept together in twelve.'

And there it is. 'Welcome to the world of Leith.'

We eat scones in silence for a minute.

'Does Leith know you're seeing me?'

She shakes her head. 'He knows you know about the pregnancy. I think he's embarrassed.'

Personal responsibility was never Leith's strong suit. The poor woman is in for a world of pain.

How quickly life moves; once you set things in motion, there is no turning back. I'm responsible for my part in a dead marriage, hanging in because I was too scared to leave, even though I knew very well we would never be able to truly make each other happy. Now I guess we're open competition for each other. Game on.

Though Maia and I are both desperate to get away, we do our best to swallow the fresh warm scones with whipped cream and strawberry jam without seeming like we're rushing to leave. Finally, between the rattling of china cups and Maia's frequent toilet visits, I tell her I have to get prepping for tonight.

Saying goodbye to a friendship, regardless of the circumstances, is never fun.

I get in my ute and head straight to Elizabeth Bay. I know he'll be home, probably listening to Lenny Kravitz and clipping his toenails or applying St Tropez tan mousse to his chiselled face. Maia told me she was visiting her mum in Rose Bay, so I know I will have a private audience.

I let myself in the security door, then head up the stairs and knock. I can hear the strains of Lenny Kravitz as Leith answers.

'"Stand By My Woman" – that's pretty ironic, don't you think?'

'You're the one who left.' Leith needs to warm up.

'What if I'd stayed? Would you have expected me to help raise your baby? Maybe we could have all lived together.'

'You're the one who grew up on a commune,' he quips.

'She loves you.'

'Yeah, I love her too.' We share a dangerous pause as he eyes me up. 'I love both of you.'

'Stop it.'

'Luce—'

'Shut up now and get Grandad's Eames and your chequebook.'

His expression contorts into that of a disgruntled bargain-hunter. 'You can have the chair, it's under the ironing, but there's no way—'

'If you don't, I will do a profile piece for the weekend paper about the dark side of celebrity-chef couples – basically about my heartbreak over your philandering and what an inauthentic arsehole you are. Lana has it ready to go.'

'How much?'

'Ten.'

'Grand? No way.'

'Up to you. We both know you're getting off lightly – I should be getting a hundred grand. And don't say you haven't got it – I know for a fact you have.'

Leith struggles, but after a few moments his vanity wins out (again) and he writes the cheque. I haven't mentioned the idea of an article to Lana but I know she would back me up and I know it would hit Leith where it hurt.

'You seem different, LiLi.' He hovers, handing the cheque to me. 'Stronger, sexier.'

'That's what happens when you get a life and a decent relationship. Try to keep your dick in your pants long enough to find out what it's like to be a father, Leith.'

'It Ain't Over Till It's Over' starts up. It used to be our song. I march in and grab the chair.

'LiLi, it's our song.'

'Was. We are officially done. Good luck, Leith.'

And with as much attitude as a woman holding an armchair can afford, I hold up my head and march down the stairs.

I feel alive.

Scones with Strawberry Jam and Clotted Cream

Ingredients

Scones
plain flour, for dusting
3 cups self-raising flour
80 grams butter, cubed
1–1¼ cups milk

Strawberry Jam
800 grams strawberries, washed and quartered
2 cups sugar
3 tablespoons lemon juice

Clotted Cream
600 millilitres cream (fat content of 45 per cent)
1 tablespoon white sugar

Method

Scones
Preheat oven to 200°C. Lightly dust a flat baking tray with plain flour.

Sift the self-raising flour into a large bowl.

Using your fingertips, rub the butter into the flour until the mixture resembles breadcrumbs.

Make a well in the centre and add 1 cup of milk. Mix until the mixture forms a soft dough, adding more milk if required. This is often weather, humidity and mood dependent. Empty onto a clean, lightly floured surface.

Knead the dough nurturingly but decisively until smooth (don't over-knead, or the scones will be tough).

Pat or roll the dough into a 2-centimetre-thick round. Using a 5-centimetre (diameter) round cutter, cut out 12 rounds. Press the leftover dough together, sprinkle some more flour and cut out the remaining four rounds. Place the scones onto the baking tray, 1 centimetre apart. Scones have to be fenced in. Sprinkle the tops with a little plain flour. Bake for 20–25 minutes or until golden and well risen. Transfer to a wire rack.

Strawberry Jam

In a heavy-based saucepan (cast iron is best), lightly mash the strawberries with a fork or a potato masher, then add the sugar and lemon juice. Place the saucepan on a low heat and stir, stir, stir until every granule of sugar has dissolved and you have liquid in the pan. Now, increase the heat to medium and continue cooking for a further 45 minutes, stirring occasionally. Keep your eye on the jam pan – it can be a tad erratic. The jam will deepen in colour and be ready when it sticks to a wooden spoon or a drop sets on a saucer. Allow to cool.

Clotted Cream

Place the cream in a saucepan. Add the sugar and bring to a full-bodied boil, then reduce heat and simmer gently for 10 minutes.

Pour into a dish so the cream comes 2.5 centimetres up the sides. Place in the fridge to set; a thick skin will form on the top.

To serve, scoop off and discard the skin or donate to a furry friend and spread the cream over the scones and jam.

Assemble and serve with tea and sympathy.

54

Frankie

BUGGER AND SHIT AND BUM AND BLIGHT, MY EX AND MY SON and the love of my life all here on the same night.

The last time I saw Helen – actually, the last time Helen saw me – was on her doorstep in 1982 as she screamed at me for returning 'her son' a bit late. Admittedly it was five hours and we may have been to a race track in the company of a youngish lady who fed him such horribly large amounts of soft drink that by the time I delivered him home the sugar-fuelled hurricane of hyperactivity was about to blow – and did, with a huge vomit into the azalea bushes. He was turning green before our eyes and we both knew that Helen would have a less than enjoyable evening nursing him back to reality. But really, the woman had totally lost her sense of humour by then. She couldn't see how it was funny at all.

And I'm sure she had started dating the accountant by then – all signs of life in her personality had vanished and she kept mentioning the 'peace' of not being with me and the attraction of a 'life with security'. Of course she wanted to sell the restaurant – I broke her heart – but I knew that it would be better for Charlie and for her long term to keep it – or that's what I tell myself. Really it was a way of trying to show them I did love them and I wanted to give them something to hold onto. Perhaps I shouldn't have put those conditions on it; I wouldn't have been abandoned here all these years if I hadn't. But now Lucille will know once and for all what a selfish bastard I was. Such is life. All I want is the bloody domestic giddiness of slow-cooked casseroles and Sunday papers with her – exactly what Helen wanted with me. Poor woman, there is nothing worse than being in love with someone who is not in love with you . . . except being loved by someone whose love you cannot reciprocate.

The menu for the evening sounds perfect. Lucille has outdone herself again: country terrine of veal and chicken, which I told her was Helen's favourite; then duck à l'orange teamed with an Asian influence of black rice with nut-brown butter and bok choy sautéed with sesame seeds, apparently one of Charlie's prefer-ences; and Black Forest gateau to finish. Fuck me, the woman is outstanding. It sounds like a menu that would have you calling out for the Epsom salts, but with Lucille's lightness of touch and her ability to breathe new life into my recipes it will be superb.

She came back today in a giddy mood though with swollen eyes. Her ex got some friend of hers up the duff. What a dick. But she went and claimed her things – well done that woman.

Why couldn't I see the pain I caused while I was here causing it? Because as Old Bill would say, my head was too busy being stuck steadfastly up my own arse.

That friend of Lucille's, Doctor Polly, keeps looking at me with a curious stare; I'm not sure if she can see me or merely senses my chaos.

And then there is Julia. Bless me, what a fine bird that woman is. She came in and read me the riot act. She kept sniffing and following her nose to pretty much every spot I moved to in a bid to escape her lecture. She stopped short when young Hugo walked in, but what she was saying was right on the money. Lucille deserves more than me – someone living, for one thing – and I had better treat her well and be upfront. I am not sure what kind of commitment issues she thinks I have, but she made herself and her views crystal clear. The woman is terrifying. I like her.

And then there's Charlie. The last thing I want to do is break his heart. Lucille is definite that she doesn't feel attracted to him. I long to know who he is, and for him to see me, hear me. How things will fadge I have no idea. Decent-after-death doesn't give you many options.

Blow me if the day's festivities aren't capped off by Sara walking in with Serge in tow. Serge is wetter than an Easter camping trip with the sap of a new romance. Lucille wasn't exaggerating; sounds of saliva exchanges between them reverberate around the dining room. Serge follows Sara, a labrador pup in search of his next treat. Good on him, he's never been lucky in love, not truly – his mad crushes mostly went unrequited. I hope Sara doesn't splinter his heart too savagely. Still, like most of us, the lure of being in someone's arms and being loved is enough to risk it all. The living underestimate just how much touch keeps the world turning. What I wouldn't give to be able to feel Lucille's skin . . .

As soon as Serge is in the cool room Sara strides out and reintroduces herself. She tells me she has seen me all along and that Lucille's psychic abilities, and all other favourable attributes, are inherited from her. She then does her own version of laying down the law. I try to reciprocate by inquiring after her intentions with Serge, but she's not having a bar of it. Lucille certainly gets her feminine beauty from her mother.

'She loves you,' Sara pronounces.

'It's mutual.'

'Well, what's your plan? Are you going to try to come back as a real contender or will you just waft around forever?'

'I don't see what choice I have in the matter.'

'Oh, phooey! You're just scared to move on.'

'I'm trying to solve my murder,' I justify.

'Then what? You leave?'

'I don't know. None of this was planned—'

'Oh, you're such a typical male! You remind me of Malcolm at the commune: he got three women pregnant and scratched his head the entire time, saying, "None of it was planned." Frankie, no plan *is* a plan – claim your destiny.'

'Is that something you have on a fridge magnet?'

'So what if I do? It works for me. And you have a lot to learn about the afterlife.'

'Been there recently, have you, Sara?'

'Why didn't you ever date me when I came here?' she asks suddenly.

'You were taken. Even I have my limits.'

'That's not what the other girls said. It's because you thought I was a flake.'

'You were very young, you belonged to my friend – and yes, you were a bit of a flake.'

'I know. But Lucy's not. Don't hurt her, she's a good kid.'

'What are you suggesting, I disappear?'

'I'm suggesting you find a way to stick around, but as a human. There are ways.' She offers me her best mysterious look.

'Have you told Serge about me?' I ask.

'I'm not sure he'd cope. Your death broke his heart.'

'Are *you* planning to stick around *him*?'

Sara considers. 'Who knows? But get a plan, Frankie. Stop treading water in the afterlife.'

With that she heads into the cool room and closes the door behind her, and from the sounds that erupt I know it's not safe to go in. Sara is a goer all right. I can't believe I'm jealous of Serge's love life – my world view is of endless rooms of turned tables.

55

Lucy

MUM IS STILL HANGING AROUND. BETWEEN HER AND FRANKIE, I feel like I'm cooking before a cast of thousands. And then Charlie enters with his mother. She's so elegant it takes my breath away. Tall, with silver hair cut in a smooth bob, Chanel linen jacket with jeans and a crisp white shirt that I'm sure she never spills things on. Rose-gold cufflinks, diamond studs, considered smile. Charlie looks as cute and sweet and affable as ever. Polly looks him up and down and her voice drops an octave as she purrs the menu.

'Hot,' is all she utters to me as she collects the terrine from the pass.

'He *is* a cutie,' I offer as Frankie rolls his eyes and nods reluctantly.

'Fuck that, the guy's *dynamite*,' Polly says as she heads out.

Frankie looks proud.

I venture out to meet Helen. Frankie, equally keyed up, accompanies me.

'Charlie's told me so much about you,' Helen says.

My nervous giggle titters in direct opposition to her smoothness.

'The recipe for the terrine?'

'Frankie's. Well, it's from his recipe book.'

'It was my favourite. But I think your version of it is even better than his.'

I hear a growl from Frankie.

'Thank you for giving me the opportunity to re-open Fortune,' I say.

'Thank *you* for having the courage to make a go of it. It's in a terrible state of disrepair, I'm afraid.'

Another groan from Frankie.

'The silent owner who holds the majority share won't budge on much.'

I nod.

Charlie nods.

Helen nods.

We look to the terrine for an answer.

Helen eyes me intensely. 'It's really lovely to meet you.'

'And you. Enjoy your meal.'

'Lucy, come and sit with me after service, won't you,' Helen says, a whiff of a command in her request.

'Of course.'

Charlie walks me back to the kitchen, as does Frankie.

'So, how's your week been?' Charlie asks.

Oh, he's lovely. How am I going to . . .

'Good. Busy.'

Charlie stops in front of me and laughs. 'Luce, it's okay, I get it.'

'Get what?'

'The fact that you'd rather ruffle my hair than kiss my neck.'

'Well said, son,' offers Frankie.

I'm beyond flustered, but Charlie seems fine. 'When I met you I felt something, an attraction. I thought you did too, but then after dinner the other night I wasn't sure. But then at the car I was—'

'Charlie, I'm sorry. I'm in a weird place right now.'

Frankie stamps his foot. 'Be honest, within reason. Don't lead him on.'

Charlie raises his hands. 'Let me finish. There's a feeling around you. It's weird, and please don't take this the wrong way, but something about you reminds me of my dad. The nice bits, like his food. And maybe it's because you're fixated on talking about him, but something about you feels more familial than erotic.'

'Oh.' Phew.

'And then I was at Glebe markets on the weekend and I saw Sara had her tarot stand. Serge was standing beside her, so I went over and said hi – and she gave me a reading.'

'Uh-huh . . .'

'She's actually pretty good – not that I go in for any of that – but you know what she said?'

'I can only imagine.'

'She said you can't ring it if there's no doorbell.'

'Yep, that's one of her best lines, that and – small world, wouldn't want to be a hooker.'

Charlie chuckles. 'She's cool.'

'She . . . yes.'

'She's really proud of you.'

I'm taken aback by that. Mum and I have never arrived at the Hallmark status of our relationship. I wasn't aware hearing I had her approval would resonate so deeply.

He smiles his gorgeous smile. Frankie's smile. 'So, can we be friends?'

Relief freestyles through me. 'I'd love that.'

'Because I feel like you're part of our team and I can see that Mum likes you. She wants to talk to you about something.'

'About Frankie?'

'No . . . about the future.'

This stops me in my tracks. And Frankie too. We stare at each other: where is our future?

'Luce?' Charlie brings me back.

'Sorry, I . . .'

'Just one more thing. Is Polly single?'

273

Later, the night takes a slight detour when Serge, who is missing in action with Mum, leaves the cherry reduction bubbling and begins a small industrial fire. Frankie attempts to grab the pan, which I don't see because I'm plating the duck, and its metal handle throws him and the pan across the kitchen. He yells so loudly that Mum comes running in, accompanied by Serge, at whom I scream. Polly and Hugo check in to see the mess. Serge apologises, assuring me we have enough cherries to go again.

Polly examines the mess and says with a smile, 'The main ingredients in the Big Bang? Heat, chaos and movement.'

'Is that your way of asking about Charlie?' I reply, trying to focus on the duck.

'No, it's about the congregation of moving particles I keep seeing around this restaurant – but that might just be the chemicals I still have in my system after last night. But, while I'm here, what's the deal? You know I don't cut lunches.'

'We've agreed to be friends and that's it, and I'd like it if you asked him out – random, heat and movement wise.'

Polly studies me while she grabs some more plates to take out. 'Gotcha.'

Frankie winks at me. Oh god, am I ever going to be able to kiss him, and why am I thinking about that when his ex-wife is eating my duck à l'orange?

The kitchen remains sticky. Serge apologises profusely, and Mum heads home for some down time – which is code for *Midsomer Murders*. And order, in her flimsy guise, is temporarily restored.

'What do you think Helen wants?' I ask Frankie.

'Helen is a practical woman, perhaps she sees you as a link to selling up here.'

'But I'm not—'

'Can you imagine us together, Lucille?'

'She's very beautiful, so elegant.'

'I meant you and me. But yes, Helen is a stunner and a good woman and I am sorry I never truly loved her.' His gaze fixes on me, demanding an answer.

'You and me . . . yes, yes. Well, apart from the obvious.'

'Do you have any idea how much I long to kiss you right now?'

'Is that a bit perverse, considering who's sitting in the dining room?'

'A bit of perversity can be fun.' Frankie waggles his eyebrows at me; sometimes he really is still in 1982.

'You're a shocker.'

'Darling, you have no idea.'

'Are you flirting with me, Chef Summers?'

'Is it getting me anywhere, Chef Muir?'

From my flush of colour it's obvious that it is. I want to touch him. Badly.

I attempt to pour my passion into my chocolate ganache, which seems to work, because the Black Forest gateau is the hit of the evening; personally I think it's the extra kirsch I infuse into the airy chocolate sponge that does the trick.

Later, after doing the post-dinner meet-and-greet, I take a seat with Charlie and Helen. As does Frankie. Hugo appears with a bottle of Bollinger and the good crystal flutes.

'Where's that from?' I ask.

'Me.' Helen holds out her glass. 'I wanted to congratulate you properly. Frankie left this place in an absolute shambles, no one has been able to touch it, but you seem to have the key to its becoming a success.'

'Here's to the secret recipe for second chances,' Charlie adds.

We toast.

'I wouldn't call it a shambles,' I protest. 'Maybe it wasn't at its absolute best.'

'He was in debt when he went, and his drinking had become a problem. He had women all over town wanting to take their revenge on him for breaking their hearts, not to mention how he pulverised mine.'

Frankie looks chastened.

'That must have been terribly hard,' I say. 'I'm sorry.'

'I don't know how much Charlie has told you, but his father was not a nice man. In some ways he did us all a favour by removing himself. He had set himself on a course for disaster.'

The thought appears in my mind before I have time to censor it, and I feel sick: did Helen kill Frankie?

'He had a good heart, though, I understand,' I offer, watching Frankie drowning in his own sea of shame.

Helen considers this. 'He did, but he was selfish and that kept him small.'

'Goddammit, woman, *I'm sorry*!' roars Frankie, his face twisted with remorse and rage. 'Tell her I'm sorry, for Christ's sake.'

'He says he's sorry,' I blurt.

'Excuse me?' Helen looks confused, as does Charlie. Hugo swoops in and tops up our glasses without a word.

'What I mean is,' I fumble, making it up as I go, 'from what I know, which is very little, and is probably the best of him because it's via his recipes, he did have a lot of love and he . . . he must have felt terrible that he did the wrong thing by you, and by Charlie. He must have been ashamed.'

Helen nods. 'I think you may have a romanticised view of him, but thank you. Being here isn't easy, and that's what I wanted to discuss with you.'

Oh no. 'Please don't evict me.'

'Of course not. But I would like to know what your plans are, for the future.'

There it is again. Frankie and I exchange a look. The future, our mutual Achilles heel.

'Um, well, I'm going through a divorce, and I hadn't thought much past the next few months, but—'

'Tell her you must stay here,' Frankie implores. 'You must keep it. No matter what happens to me, Fortune should be yours.'

'But?' Helen presses. 'What about after that?'

'I would like to stay here, I would like to keep Fortune open.'

'That's exactly what we'd hoped you'd say,' says Charlie.

'If we can get the okay from the other party we'd like to keep you here permanently,' Helen explains. 'But more than that, we'd like to become your partners.'

'Say yes, woman,' commands Frankie. 'I'll talk to Bill. Say yes immediately!'

'Yes!' How is it that everything is clicking into such perfect alignment?

'And we're going to give this place the overhaul she deserves,' Helen continues, but everything begins to move in slow motion for me.

'What do you mean?'

'You're a very brave woman and what you have done on a shoe-string is beyond brilliant, but the electrics are shot, the floor needs new boards, the plumbing needs an overhaul. Not to mention a facelift for the outside. I'd like to invest in all of that – we both would. I'd like you to have control over the design. Hopefully we all agree.'

'But I can stay open, right?'

'What we're proposing is that you finish the next two months as agreed, building on the buzz that's already lifting your profile and developing patron loyalty. And then we close for the overhaul and re-open with a major bang before the restaurant reviews for next year's food guides commence.'

I look desperately to Frankie. The thought of even a day of not seeing him is hideous, but this would be weeks, and what if the atmosphere is so radically changed via the wiring or whatever it is that Frankie disappears with the old floorboards?

'How long will it take?'

'About six weeks.'

'Agree to it, Lucille,' Frankie says gently but firmly. 'I'll still be here.'

'You don't know that,' I reply.

Helen and Charlie exchange a look. Charlie ventures gently, 'We kind of do. I've been getting a few quotes, and Ewan from the council has been helping us. If we don't make these changes he can't issue you with a permanent restaurant permit.'

'Say yes, Lucille.' Frankie stares into me unflinchingly.

'The other thought is we back you at another location,' Helen says.

'No, no, it has to be here.'

'Yes, Charlie said you're quite attached. I'd like to help you make this restaurant flourish in a way Frankie never let me when it was his.'

'It's true, I kept her away because I didn't want to expose her to my womanising, but really her head for business is brilliant. I owe this to her.'

'But what if I lose you?' I blurt.

'How can you lose us?' Charlie laughs.

'We'll have contracts drawn up,' says Helen. 'I want a deal that sees you as the major shareholder. Do you have a good lawyer?'

'Yes,' answers Hugo, emptying the Bollie into our glasses. In a whirl of camp excitement he calls for the rest of the restaurant's attention. 'Ladies and gentlemen, a toast to the restoration of Lucy's good Fortune!'

Applause and toasts erupt all round, though I am not sure my diners know what he's on about.

•

Later, Frankie accompanies me as I turn out the last of the lights.

'Wait,' he tells me.

He grabs the handle of a broom and uses it to tap away on the iPod.

'Frankie, you'll break it!'

'I've been practising . . . there . . .' He turns to me with satis-faction, then touches a few candles, which immediately spring alight. 'Dance with me.'

He holds the broom out to me. Air Supply starts up.

'Oh damn, that's not what I had planned. Bloody Serge has been at it again.'

'You mean you didn't want to play me "Lost in Love"?'

We laugh. I take one end of the broom, he the other, and we move as close as we can without touching. He begins to spin me slowly.

'Frankie, the renovations . . . I'm worried they'll hurt you.'

'Darling, death barely hurt me, what are a few renos? I won't leave you.'

'Ever?'

'I will stay here as long as I can. I don't want to be anywhere else, not now, not ever.'

'You don't think there's any way Helen could have been involved in your murder?'

Frankie laughs heartily at this. 'I wouldn't have blamed her if she was, but no, it wasn't Helen. She's a good egg. She's going to be great for your restaurant.'

'*Our* restaurant.'

'She'll be great for Fortune. Now, be quiet and let me dance with you while this sickly song manipulates us.'

I obey and he sways me again.

We're obviously both imagining the same thing, because all too soon we're just millimetres away from each other. My breathing is loud enough for both of us, our eyes lock, our hands almost touch. Our eyes close and our lips come together and we dive into the essence of each other. I feel all his hopes and longings, hurts and dreams, see flashes of his life, taste his meals, feel his laugh vibrate through me, touch through his fingers the lovers of his past, raise baby Charlie up through the air, sense the blackness of a bag descending over his head, hands grasping his throat and then—

Pow!

I'm on the floor, he's on the ceiling, the candles are out and the iPod has exploded.

'I felt you.'

'Me too.'

'More this time,' I say. 'I felt what it is to *be* you.'

Frankie floats down and I raise myself up.

'That commune was a wild place to grow up,' he says, staring at me with the same wonder I feel. 'And your grandparents – your grandmother could really cook. And bloody Leith, I got him too. Lucille, your lip, it's bleeding. Are you all right?'

'I saw the bag, going over my . . . your head.'

'Here.' He passes me a napkin. 'I'm scared you're going to get hurt.'

'I'm okay,' I say, pressing the cloth to my lip. 'I love you.'

He straightens up. I continue to dab, fearing I've gone too far.

'And I love you. I've never said that to anyone before . . . not sober, anyway.'

He loves me! He loves me, he loves me, *he loves me*!

'Lucille?'

'Does it feel weird?'

He shakes his head. 'It feels right.'

We sit for a while in the quiet sanctity of us. Finally, we say our goodnights, he walks me to the door, watching me as he always does. Outside the front window, I stop, turn and look in. He remains watching, smiling. We wave once more before I walk away to the unexpected sight of Mum sitting with Old Bill in the gutter across the street. Bill has one hand around his flagon, and the other holds Mum's hand as he sobs freely. Mum looks chastened.

I wave to them both. Mum gets up and helps Bill to his feet.

'What happened to *Midsomer Murders*?' I ask.

'Bill and I were overdue for a catch-up.'

'Are you okay, Bill? Mum didn't make you cry, did she, reading your tarot?'

Bill blows his nose and then takes a swig from his flagon and shakes his head.

'I'll see you soon,' Mum says sincerely. That's the thing with Mum, she's not short on compassion when it comes to people in need.

They bid farewell, and as Mum and I walk away, I know not to ask. She is sombre, to say the least.

'I spoke to Frankie today,' she says.

'Oh boy.'

'I think he's finally growing up.'

'How can you tell?'

'He just seemed more mature, open.' Trust Mum to say this about a ghost.

'Did he say, was he . . . well, did he . . .' I fade out.

'Spit it out, Lucille.'

'Did he say anything . . . about me?'

'Yes, he's fond of you. I think he wants to stick around for you, but once his lesson is learned he will need to reincarnate or space jump or . . .'

'How many options are there?'

'How many grains of sand are at the bottom of the sea?'

We have this conversation as though we are discussing university choices for when I leave school . . . which we never did.

'I love him, Mum.'

'I know.'

'But it's different to anything else I've felt.'

'Good.'

'I think he's the one.'

'Of course he's the bloody one! You've defied death and reality to find each other, you must have some major karmic journey together.'

'Have you ever loved like that? George, maybe?'

'Didn't have enough time with him, but yes, I have had that real soulmate feeling once and it scared the shit out of me. What happened to your lip?'

'I tried to kiss Frankie.'

Mum smiles at that. 'You should talk to Polly about quantum physics some more, it might help you and your ghost.'

We're both drained, and we drive the short distance home in silence, each listening to the infinite questions from the night above us. I face-plant and sleep, dreaming that I am twirling through space and time with Frankie, and then we are walking through a vineyard and he turns to me and feeds me crêpe Suzette.

Duck à l'Orange

Ingredients

2 × 2.5 kilogram free-range happy ducks, trimmed of excess
    fat inside and out, and with necks and gizzards cut off and
    reserved and chopped into bite-size pieces
1 orange, cut into wedges
2 sprigs thyme
salt and freshly ground black pepper
2 medium carrots, peeled and coarsely chopped
2 celery sticks, coarsely chopped
1 small onion, peeled and coarsely chopped
1 tablespoon Cognac
2 tablespoons Grand Marnier
1½ cups chicken stock
juice of 4 oranges
1 flat tablespoon marmalade
1 heaped teaspoon arrowroot, mixed with a little water
grated rind of 1 orange
2 tablespoons cold unsalted butter

Method

Preheat the oven to 220°C. Insert the orange wedges and thyme
into ducks' cavities. Add some salt and pepper inside and out.
Truss the ducks and, once tied, dab all over with paper towel.

Sit ducks on the wire rack of a roasting pan, breast side up.
Bake for 20 minutes until ducks begin to brown and ooze their
luscious fat. Remove and drain fat into a separate container.

Turn down the heat to 190°C and cook the quackers for
another hour.

While the duckies roast, it's time to make the sauce. Heat the
drained duck fat in a cast-iron saucepan that's up for business.

Add chopped duck neck bones and gizzards and brown. Now add the vegetables until they too are coloured.

Add Cognac and Grand Marnier – and certainly take a sip of either . . . both if it's Christmas. Boil and bubble until the sauce reduces into a thick syrupy goo. Add the chicken stock, orange juice and marmalade. Allow concoction to simmer for 30 minutes and then strain it into a clean pan. Discard solids. Leave it be for 15–20 minutes and then skim off any excess fat.

Cook and reduce (to about ⅓ should do the trick) until the sauce is thick and flavoursome. Now it's time to whisk through the arrowroot, which will thicken the sauce further. Then add the orange rind and butter, and simmer.

When the ducks are done, let them rest for a good 10–15 minutes. Free the ducks of their bondage. If you're game, carve the ducks at the table as theatrically as possible. Serve the warm sauce in a separate gravy boat. Pour on top of the plated duck with a high level of panache.

56

Frankie

I HOPE HER LIP IS OKAY.

Damn, she's a hell of a good kisser.

We have no real sense of time here, but it already feels an eternity and I'm listening for the door, watching for the daylight, waiting for her to come back.

57

Lucy

THE DAYS FOLD INTO EACH OTHER IN A STEADY STREAM OF work, love, inspiration and meals. Patrons gather and enjoy, Frankie talks me through his red book and shares anecdotes about the different recipes. All of them mean something. Many were gathered on his travels as a young man and mastered during his time in Fortune.

My days gain a rhythmic momentum. I find a tiny studio apartment just a few streets up from the restaurant and move my clothes, my chair and the spare bed from Mum's to my new address. It's a bolthole, really, because my true home is at Fortune. The hours I spend with Frankie after the restaurant closes expand and the hours I take before returning the next day shrink.

Serge continues to romance Mum, who laps it up. Bill starts to come inside and join us for staff dinner. I give him some handkerchiefs, which he uses, though he refuses all of our offers of assistance or places to stay. He is resolved in his life, for whatever reason. He okays the plans for the renovations, though like me he is hesitant in the face of everyone else's (including Frankie's) excitement. When Helen and Charlie learn the identity of the silent partner, they both seem relieved, though they are curious as to why he remained so mysterious all these years. His reply is that he couldn't be bothered getting involved.

Charlie took Polly on a date; unlike my chaste time with him, they hit it off immediately and have barely spent a night apart since. Charlie hangs out more and more in the kitchen with Serge and Frankie and me. I think it's because he can sense his dad, but he swears it's because he is finally learning to really cook. And Serge loves to teach. Julia continues to lecture me on the dangers of ghosts and insists on multiple screenings of *The Ghost and Mrs Muir*, which I find depressing and she uses as a cautionary tale. Polly attempts to teach me the inner workings of quantum physics, most of which fly over my head and I am quick to disregard because all I really want is to be with Frankie in the kitchen. I fall asleep most nights clutching my pillow, wishing it was him. Everything is bubbling along, and then, as is the way with life, it explodes into a kaleidoscope of crap.

It begins on the morning of Matthias Drewe's exhibition opening. The catering is all a go. I'm at Fortune extra early, but Old Bill, who usually appears on cue for his morning espresso, is nowhere to be seen. I don't think much of it, because there's so much to do, and the remainder of the day rushes by with deliveries of flowers and special ingredients, and check-ins from Vivianne Drewe and her entourage of PR people. The restaurant is closed for the reception, so everything is slightly out of step and Frankie is agitated; he wants to travel the few streets up to the exhibition location. I leave him ranting over the quality of the bacon and head into the glittering gallery with its state-of-the-art lighting, clientele of massive incomes and impeccable tastes and the master works of Matthias Drewe.

There is no denying his talent; the works from the restaurant, now beautifully framed, show the nascent genius that was to develop in years to come. The exhibition's centrepiece, Frankie's portrait presides over the proceedings and self-congratulatory air kisses of eastern Sydney's elite.

Unfortunately, awful Paul Levine is there and seems unimpressed by my presence. It's been weeks since the calamities of Frankie's personal underbelly saga have been discussed. Frankie and I have both been ignoring it, for fear that solving it would remove him from me.

Paul strides up to me. 'Your friend gave us a bum steer. We got the code but the safe was cleared.'

'Paul,' I reply, 'I have no idea what you're talking about or what you're looking for. But if there are any further issues I'd recommend we take it to the police.'

He doesn't like this and moves on.

The gods and goddesses, after ensuring that all works for sale have achieved red-dot status, take their leave of the gallery and head down to Fortune.

The restaurant is packed as canapés are passed around. Frankie's mood seems to have elevated as he claps his hands, walking among the guests, offering advice and ruling over his deaf crowd. Matthias is completely pissed, which seems to be his preferred state. He lurches into women's cleavages as they giggle with discomfort and step back.

Frankie stands beside me, watching. 'Sometimes talent overrules what is tolerable, but don't believe a bead of it, with him it's all for show.'

I'm walking to the bathroom when Matthias takes me aside. Fortunately Frankie is still there.

'Good job on the nibblies – the devils on horseback were one of the first things Frankie taught me to prepare.'

His hot boozy breath blasts my face as he pins me to the wall, holding my shoulders. 'The portrait of him, I'd like to keep it.'

'Get off her, you little shit!' Frankie yells.

'We need it here.' I attempt to push him away, and fail.

'I'll buy it back off you.'

'It's not for sale, Matthias, we made a deal.'

'I want it.'

'Is this about the code, the contract?'

'I don't give a rat's arse about the contract; that portrait's one of my best works. I'll do you another.'

'That's not what we agreed on.'

'You didn't even know him, what do you care?' He pushes me against the wall. I try to wriggle free but he holds me tightly and in one fell swoop licks me from my collarbone to my forehead.

Frankie lifts a nearby glass water jug and brings it down on Matthias's head. Matthias backs off in fright. I free myself from his hold.

'Tell him you know his secret!' Frankie instructs.

'I know . . .' is all I manage.

'You know what?' Panic rises in Matthias's voice.

I look to Frankie, then I decide to improvise. Turning to Matthias, I say, 'Everything. And so did Frankie.'

Relief and shame cross Matthias's face and he begins to wobble then slowly slumps.

'Say, "what you escaped",' Frankie orders.

'What you escaped, for one thing.' I have no freaking idea what I am talking about but it makes Matthias weep.

'And what you escaped with!' Frankie yells, and I repeat.

Matthias flinches.

After a moment of glaring at the figure on the floor, Frankie takes pity. 'Come now, lad, stop sniffling. You were a silly kid who got in too deep.'

'What happened?' I ask.

58

Frankie, 1982

IT'S OH SO EARLY AND NOT YET LIGHT.

I emerge from the restaurant, a party after a party after a birthday that ended at Fortune. A big black stretch waits up the road a little.

Young Matthias, the thieving talented git, hovers nearby. 'Frankie.'

'What are you doing here? You don't start till nine – come back in four hours.'

'I'm in trouble.'

My ears prick up. He's not the only one; Fortune is within a sneeze of foreclosure. I've started to pour vodka into my morning espresso. 'Big-black-stretch-limo kind of trouble, kid?'

He nods and stifles a whimper.

'What?'

'This guy, he comes here a lot,' says Matthias. 'He's really rich and he likes my art.'

'Where's the trouble?'

'He said that if I . . . you know . . .'

'Illuminate me.'

'If I . . . if I blow him and let him fuck me then he'll pay for me to go to art school in London.'

'That's what scholarships are for,' I say.

'I still need the ticket. He said it would be first class.'

'So, you're whoring yourself. Are you even gay?'

'No. And he's not either.'

'Obviously.'

'He's going to kill me, Frankie, if I don't see it through.'

'Rubbish.'

'No, he's serious. He has shares in a nightclub and he's powerful.'

'He's a paedophile.'

Tears now stream freely down the kid's face. He's a mongrel, but no kid deserves this, not even greedy, conniving ones like Matthias Drewe.

'Piss off and let me deal with it,' I tell him.

'No, he'll kill you, then he'll kill me.'

'I doubt that.' I look towards the black limo. 'If I'm not back at Fortune by nine, call the cops.'

'You don't have to do this for me, I've been a little shit.'

'True, but you're one of my little shits. Now, go home and pack your bags. I'll get Tiffany to book you a ticket and you'll head to Heathrow tonight. You selling your measly body is something I won't have on my conscience. But Matthias, I expect you to make a go of it, work hard, paint well, make a motza. Come home a man. You hear me? Now piss off. Now!'

He scurries into the pre-dawn darkness. I finish my fag and head to the car. I open the back door and get in.

'Surprise,' I say.

We're both surprised. It's John, my old footy mate. Good family man with a finger in every pie. On several boards, member of Rotary, barbecue king.

'Shit, it's you.'

Slow seconds of awkward pass before one of us thinks of something to say.

'Hired a nice car for the occasion, John?'

'What the fuck are you doing here?' he says.

'The kid took a pass – I'm hoping I'll do.' I bat my eyelids.

'Get out.'

'Underage boys, John . . . that's not playing fair.'

'Kid's a faggot, he knows what's what.'

'I don't think so.'

John orders the driver to make a move.

'Why not just go to the Wall, John? They're the ones who are up for it. Where are we headed? Home to Pippa for a glass of rosé?'

'If you tell anyone, you're a dead man.'

'You'll have to add your name to the list. In the meantime, you might want to take your endorsement off the casino proposal.'

'What's that got to do with anything?'

'Be a shame for Pippa to hear about this from the papers. Better I tell her myself – after I give her a going-over, of course.'

John lurches for me. I open the door and roll out. But I know there's punishment to come.

We get Matthias on the flight. It's not till I return to the restaurant that I see that the last of my cash supplies has been taken from my hidey-hole. Little shit. I would have given it to him if he'd only asked.

59

Lucy

MATTHIAS FINISHES HIS STORY WITH A HEFTY SOB. HE ESCAPED on a flight Frankie booked him on to London and stayed overseas for a decade. Frankie, Serge and Charlie now stand beside me, listening.

'He saved my life.'

I agree, he did. 'So why do you hate him?'

'Because he saved me, I owed him. He was dead when I got back, and I didn't get to repay him. I nicked some cash he probably really needed.'

'You're a schmuck,' tumbles out of my mouth.

Matthias sobs and concurs.

'He was dead three months after you left – you must have heard?'

Matthias, clearly filled with both dread and regret, weeps some more. 'Tiffany sent me an aerogramme. I think it was my fault.'

'I kill you!' Suddenly Serge launches himself on Matthias. I think he would have killed him too, but he's stopped by Charlie.

'Was it my fault?' Matthias bawls.

I look to Frankie.

'I'd forgotten all about that,' he says. 'Who knows?'

'Who would know more?' I ask, proud of Frankie's heroics but an undertow of panic is emerging. Is this it? Are we close to solving Frankie's murder? And if so, does that mean . . . what *does* that mean?

No one has an answer, then Serge offers up: 'The person to ask is Bill.'

'Or John – John would know more, if it's him. Is he even alive still?' Charlie asks.

The commotion leads to more drinking and dissecting until finally the last of the guests, including Matthias, who had to be carried out in a stupor, have gone. While Frankie and I walk around clearing the last of the glasses, Serge, Charlie, Polly and Julia debrief over drinks out the back. They are joined by Mum, who claims she has come to see me but immediately gravitates towards Serge. As I walk in to join them there's a thump at the door.

'We're shut!' I call out.

Another bang. I walk to the door, Frankie following me. As I open it, Old Bill's badly beaten and hunched body tumbles over the threshold.

From there the twirling of life out of control intensifies. Rather than wait for an ambulance, Serge, Charlie and Mum help me bundle Bill into my ute. He's still breathing but he's unconscious.

At the emergency department as Old Bill is placed on a gurney I stand at the admissions counter attempting to provide his contact details. I use Fortune for his address.

'Next of kin?' the triage nurse asks.

I'm trying to remember whether Bill told me if his ex-wife is still alive when Mum pipes up.

'She is.' She nods at me.

'Sorry?'

'Bill's your dad.'

I wait for her to wink and tell me this is a ruse to get Bill seen faster, but Mum is stony-faced.

'I had an affair with him. He was married. I was way too young. I loved him but I freaked out and took off when I knew I was having you.'

'Bill . . . Bill . . . Old homeless Bill is my father?'

The nurse has stopped typing and is staring at us.

'I told him I didn't want to be a home-wrecker. I lost track of his whereabouts. I didn't know he'd gone so badly downhill.'

'Did he love you?'

Mum nods and sniffs. A plethora of alternate realities play out instantaneously in my mind's eye: birthdays with Bill, Mum with someone who loved her, me calling Frankie 'uncle' . . .

'I told him love was timing, but really I was just shit scared.'

'Does Bill know?'

Mum nods. 'Says he knew the first time he clapped eyes on you – you have my eyes . . . they're your best feature.'

'Holy shit.'

We are interrupted by a doctor who takes us through. A team begins tests and soon it's announced that Bill has suffered a major heart attack. Years of drinking have also caused extensive damage to his liver, made worse by the kicking he received. His chances of survival are tenuous at best.

I clutch his hand and try to imagine what he looked like once, before he became so defeated by life. Bill, who saved Frankie, who lost his wife and his lover and his career and still kept guard. Bill, who has been more faithful to Frankie than anyone. Bill, who is my dad. He can't die yet.

Hours pass over styrofoam cups of lukewarm tea that we take turns to make in the lifeless kitchenette. Time is lost in intensive-care wards. Nothing screening on waiting-room televisions can be heard or comprehended. All magazines are outdated, your heart pounds anytime a medical-looking person walks through the steely white doors that swish shut before you can get a real look at what's behind them.

He gets through surgery. His condition stabilises. Mum says he's a strong bugger.

When I see him next he's wired to a multitude of machines with screens that pop and ping. We wait till he comes to. To be fair, the bruising aside, he looks better than he has since I met him. He's been cleaned up for surgery, and is being drip-fed fluids and nutrients. This is my father. The man I'd fantasised about for all those years.

Having Grandad as a stand-in dad helped me put thoughts of him on the back shelf, but when I was little and scared in the commune I did what so many other little girls do – I imagined the perfect father: tall, handsome with great teeth, appearing either on a horse, a unicorn – or, as I got older, in a Jag – to take me away from the smell of sandalwood. He would of course be a life-saving surgeon who had been on a special assignment in a Third World country, or a member of the secret service who had kept our nation free from harm, and that was why he wasn't around for all those birthdays and Christmas Days. But now he was back he would whisk me away to Pancakes on The Rocks or whatever restaurant I then deemed to be the pinnacle of glamour. For my eighth birthday it was a French restaurant I'd seen pictures of called Pig Alley; for my thirteenth it was the rotating restaurant at the top of Centrepoint Tower; for my eighteenth it was Rockpool; for my twenty-first, Jean-Georges in New York. I would imagine the conversations, the happy hours filled with talking through my life plans, him assisting me, offering to back my restaurants, urging me to go further, think bigger.

And now he was here. The crumpled old bum who swore at me and asked me for a fag the first time I saw Fortune. In the weirdest of ways he has been safeguarding Fortune for Frankie, but also for me.

Please give me time with him before he goes again. I want to learn who he is beneath the body odour and the clutched flagon.

I squeeze his hand tightly.

Devils on Horseback

Ingredients
12 prunes, pitted – alternatively for a sweeter tooth, use dates
½ cup brandy
12 whole blanched almonds
1 teaspoon chopped rosemary
2 sage leaves, fried in butter till brown, cooled and finely chopped
1 teaspoon orange zest
200 grams bacon or speck, rind removed
1 tablespoon extra-virgin olive oil

Method
Soak the prunes in the brandy for an hour to plump them up. Once they are plumped, strain the liquid from the prunes and set aside. If in need, take a few sips of brandy; keep the rest for later.

Insert one almond into the centre of each prune.

Add the rosemary, sage and orange zest to the plumped prunes and mix to combine.

Cut the bacon pieces so that you have a 6–7-centimetre piece per prune. Wrap each prune in a piece of bacon and secure with a toothpick.

Heat a griddle until hot, drizzle the bacon-wrapped prunes with oil and grill until the bacon has crisped.

Place on a platter with attitude, and serve. Or, for a more angelic approach, substitute the prunes with oysters.

60

Frankie

HOW IS IT WE SO OFTEN MISS THE THING STARING US IN THE face? John. Of course it was John: he was a big man about town; if I had bleated like a Goulburn lamb about his awful appetites, he would have lost everything. A proud man like him couldn't stand for that. Not to mention the further unravelling of his property empire.

Of course it was John.

We got Matthias on the plane; thank god my credit cards were yet to be cancelled.

But then the cupboard was bare.

John stayed away from the restaurant. I figured he was embarrassed, and I had so much other crap to contend with, the memory quickly faded.

Obviously not for him.

61

Lucy

DAWN CRACKS THROUGH THE JACARANDAS AS I WALK BACK INTO Fortune. I want to tell Frankie that Bill is stable, he will be in hospital for at least a month and then rehab. I also want to tell him that Bill is my dad.

I hear Frankie before I see him. 'I think I may have got the quantities wrong.'

He is in the kitchen, hovering over his recipe for sturgeon with duck eggs. He is sitting calmly on the bench, but he's faint – a faded photo from a childhood album. Even his voice sounds as though it's coming from a distant hilltop.

'I know.' He smiles sadly as he lifts up his hands, which are fast becoming translucent. I scream out for him to stop it.

'I'm trying, darling girl. I wonder if there's some recipe that will put this to rights, some missing link.'

'Bill's my father,' I blurt.

'Yes, he is.' Frankie nods, satisfied.

'He told you?'

'He didn't have to. You have his backbone, his jaw line and his intellect.'

'Does that make us weird?' I ask.

He laughs his hearty laugh that's fast moving to unknown lands. 'That's funny, considering, don't you think? He's going to be okay?'

'Yes. What's happening, Frankie?' My exhausted heart pounds with a fresh surge of adrenalin.

'The great mystery is solved. It was John.'

'The guy who tried to get Matthias in the car, your football friend?'

'Football mate, murderer – bit of an anticlimax, really. I bet Bill will know more when he wakes. John is behind Bill's beating – there's no mistake with the timing. Matthias having the exhibition would have stirred him up. He was also in cahoots with Paul, though I didn't twig at the time. He wanted this,' he holds up his little red book, the cause of so much angst. 'To ensure my recipes weren't accompanied by my memoirs.'

'But now? What happens now?'

'Lessons have been learned, all is resolved.'

'But where is John?'

'Bill will help track him down. Go to the police, tell them all you know. It's probably going to be a relief for him.'

I move closer to him. 'But what about you? You can't go.'

'I have no desire to leave you. I'm fighting to stay, but I don't seem to be winning, damn it.' He's growing fainter.

'Frankie, you promised, please, you can't, you just can't . . . there has to be a way. I've waited my whole life for you.'

'And I've waited beyond mine for you, Lucille.'

There must be an answer, a solution, a way to stop this. I cannot lose him. 'What about Polly? The time portals? What about Mum and her spirit stuff?'

'Oh dear, we *are* clutching at straws. I'd sooner spend what little time I have left just with you, and the restaurant and . . . and a meal.'

'Frankie, we have to try.'

Within an hour Mum arrives, with Sandy and a confused-looking Serge in tow.

'Frankie is here?' He grapples with what he's been told.

'Yes, I'm here!' Frankie yells in frustration, though his voice is now little more than a whisper. 'I've always been here.'

'Frankie, you here with me now. I am loyal to you, Frankie. And I find a great love finally. And she has nice friend too.'

'Thanks, Serge,' I say to shut him up before he divulges any more unwanted information about Sandy, who shifts coyly.

Mum and Frankie nod to each other. 'You're virtually incandescent, Frank.'

'Not the first time I've been told that, Sara.'

Julia arrives, and then to cap it off, Charlie, looking like he has just woken up, appears at Polly's side. Polly carries a thick medieval-looking science book that belongs in a Harry Potter film. And her iPad is loaded with a page of formulas.

'Anyone else care to join us?' Frankie throws his hands up in the air.

'What are we doing here?' Charlie asks and then kisses my cheek.

'I told you,' Polly states simply. 'We're helping Lucy with her entity, who was your father.'

'*Is* his father,' Frankie and I correct her simultaneously.

'Is this like an exorcism or something?' Charlie's discomfort is momentarily overshadowed by his curiosity.

'That aroma you like here,' Polly explains. 'That roasting smell – it's your dad. Lucy's in love with him.'

'Oh, is that all?' Charlie laughs. Then stops when no one else follows suit. He performs a double-take at me then re-examines the room with fresh eyes, inhaling deeply as he does. 'Dad?'

'Tell him he has turned out well, and to keep cooking.'

I do. Charlie, mystified, is full of questions, which Polly and Sara answer as I sit willing Frankie to stay.

Julia, who has had a lifelong aversion to all things occult, folds napkins silently.

All too soon, but following herbed omelettes at Frankie's request, we are standing in a circle in the dining room. Charlie and Serge have been given a run-down. Sandy, Polly and Mum, the witches of Woolloomooloo, have consulted the oracle and are agreed on an approach.

'All we need is a ouija board.' Charlie attempts humour again. And it fails.

Frankie and I are instructed to stand facing each other as close as we can without touching. I attempt to breathe in every molecule of him. He's so light now he's like the trail from one of those planes that swoop proposals into the sky on cloudless blue days.

Mum and Sandy stand on either side of Polly, who instructs each of us to think of our favourite memory of Frankie. And for Frankie to revisit his favourite ones.

'They're rushing by,' he whispers.

'And now project a vision of what you want, where you want to be,' Polly calls.

'What? I can't hear you.' Frankie is but an echo.

I can't lose him. I want to go with him. I reach out for him, into him, through him. I hear screeching and screams and wild waves crashing. I feel the rush of his touch, and then—

62

Frankie

APPLE TARTE TATIN AT THE BAR OF BALTHAZAR RESTAURANT IN New York. Sirloin steak I cooked the night Charlie told me he was going to be an astronaut. My mother's golden-syrup pudding. Lucille. Lucille's soufflé, the meringue she dropped and called deconstructed, her hair and her—

Visions flash past so quickly. When I left the first time I wasn't able to enjoy it, to see them, there was too much panic, there was pain and then blackness. But now image after image unravels and I feel my limbs swimming through the quicksilver of time, searching, reaching out for Lucille, to hold her, to stop the fall, to land. Oceans of joy and kisses and chocolate mousse, gliding gravies of sexual highs and lonely mornings, puffed pastries of laughter in the kitchen, falling, falling through silken egg whites. I feel her hand reaching for me, touching mine and momentarily travelling within me. Again we feel all of each other: aches, sighs, the sublimeness of her every crevice, and her warmth, the safe warmth of her life force throbbing within mine, searching, and then the brilliant light, and I am gone.

63

Lucy

THEY STAND OVER ME, THEIR FACES SQUASHED WITH WORRY.
Polly and Charlie crouch down and hold me. I hear Mum telling
Serge to stop panicking – I'm okay.

'Frankie?' I ask.

'He's gone, love.'

Serge again attempts to process this. 'So, he was *here*?'

'His smell has gone,' Charlie laments. It's true; beneath the
scents of omelette and coffee, there's no Frankie.

'Where is he?' I demand.

The three witches look at me blankly. Polly clarifies. 'The
theory, based on quantum physics and the Aboriginal dreamtime,
is that there are spiritual portals where you can appear or reappear
from any time throughout your life.'

'But Frankie was already dead,' I say.

'Exactly, that complicated it. Even if it's worked, there might
be a crossover – he could reappear in someone else's portal, or
his own from another incarnation, or—'

'Or if his karma was really done, he won't reappear at all,'
Mum contributes.

'But where will he be then?' I ask, panic storming me.

'Isn't that the million-dollar question,' Mum muses.

'He's in your food,' Serge answers. 'Every recipe you cook, he's in there, he has been all along.'

This is of little comfort, and the fact that this whole episode is becoming a bit like the end of *The Wizard of Oz* isn't helping. I opt for curling up in a ball and crying. Julia clears the room and cradles me.

All I want is to be with him, even if that destination is nowhere. How can fate be so cruel?

Herbaceous Omelette

Ingredients

3 perfectly fresh free-range eggs, at room temperature
Murray River sea salt (or everyday salt) and freshly ground black
   pepper
3 teaspoons butter
1 tablespoon water
2 tablespoons chopped fresh herbs (chervil, parsley and chives
   or tarragon)
1 teaspoon parmesan (optional)

Method

Break the eggs into a bowl and lightly whisk to combine, add
water, then season with salt and pepper and parmesan, if you dare.

Place half the butter and oil in an omelette pan or a small
frying pan over medium–high heat. When the butter starts to
froth and bubble but not yet brown, add the egg mixture. As the
base begins to cook, use a spatula to draw in the egg from the
sides of the pan so the uncooked egg gets to run beneath.

Keep doing this until the omelette is set but still soft.

Scatter the herbs on top. Shake the pan so the herbs and
omelette settle. Using a spatula, fold over one side of the omelette
by a third towards the centre and turn over again, then carefully
ease onto a plate. Heat the remaining butter in the pan and pour
over the omelette.

Serve with some freshly baked bread, a box of tissues and a
long goodbye.

64

Frankie

WHERE AM I?

65

Lucy

WHEN MY GRANDMOTHER DIED, GRANDAD WANTED TO GO TOO. In fact, he attempted to climb into the coffin beside her at the viewing. I'd heard the statistics: men usually expire quickly if their spouse predeceases them, and everyone from the organ player at the funeral to our neighbour Mr Jones seemed to think that's what would happen in this case too.

Grandad had barely boiled an egg on his own before Grandma's departure. They were each other's everything. A month later he agreed, reluctantly, to come with me on a road trip, stopping off at all the best fishing spots we could find between Manyana and Tweed Heads, via a visit to Mum.

The first few days were excruciating. It was the first time I had ever seen my grandfather cry. What was worse was the silence, his grief that followed. Fortunately, fishing is one of the best pursuits for those of us who like to say less. He eased up little by little.

Somewhere between Port Macquarie and Coffs Harbour he decided to live again. He caught fish, he regained his appetite. He told me he had no regrets. He'd had sixty years with Grandma – and who else has that?

Within a year he was attending the symphony, phoning in to the local radio gardening show to discuss roses, and calling me with requests for meals on the weekends that I would spend with him in his and Grandma's rambling gingerbread cottage on the coast. After one of his Sydney jaunts to the Opera House, we sat over a bouillabaisse at a tiny fish shop in Surry Hills, where he proclaimed the meal to be scrumptious and then informed me that it was a privilege to be alive. I've never forgotten that.

In the weeks that follow Frankie's departure I contemplate jumping off the Gap, but mostly I lie in bed watching old films. Often Julia comes over and snuggles up next to me. Everyone attempts to comfort me in their own way, but it's hard when you've lost someone you're not sure ever really existed. Or who existed only to you.

Then comes the rage. It seems particularly heartless of the universe to take him so quickly – we were only just finding our way into each other. Unlike Grandma and Grandad, there are no decades of shared memories or family to comfort me. Serge insists I continue cooking Frankie's recipes, and Hugo makes sure I continue to develop my own. I told Hugo about what happened, and with his usual grace he likened it to having a relationship that is in the closet, as many of his older gay friends have done. When they lost their partners their grief had to remain hidden. That would be just about intolerable.

In no time Fortune closes for renovations. In that interim I focus all my energy on Old Bill. I visit him most days and we play chess, and now and then he tells me a story about Frankie or his own life. His ex-wife, Sheila, comes to see him one day and he picks up exponentially after that. Mum and Serge are often there, too. When Bill comes out of rehab I find a two-bedroom apartment for us. He is shaky and fragile but happy to be here. After consulting Lana, he takes the contracts from the building/casino misadventure to a well-known journalist, Clare McKay. She is hard core and determined to expose the corruption that seems to still be at play at a state government level. The contracts gain a fair amount of traction when they're delivered to the Independent Commission Against Corruption, and extracts from them appear on the front pages of the Sydney papers. Frankie was right: John is the one who beat Bill to within an inch of his life on the night of Matthias's exhibition. Perhaps the exhibition reignited his passions, but whatever the reason, when he saw Bill he took the opportunity, though it wasn't really Bill he wanted to beat. It was himself.

After the commission begins taking evidence, John confesses to Frankie's murder. It was a 'mistake', apparently – he just wanted to teach Frankie a lesson to ensure Frankie wouldn't speak out about his penchant for young men, but Frankie fought back hard, and when John's muscle man moved the chair, Frankie's neck snapped, and that was that.

The outing of this information seems to bring a strong sense of closure for all of Frankie's nearests, except me. John is sentenced. This makes Bill feel a lot safer and a lot lighter; for him it puts Frankie at rest.

More time passes. Polly and Charlie continue their love affair and in autumn as the leaves fall in Macleay Street and scrunch underfoot, they get engaged. We have a party for them at the restaurant, and I spend the whole night hoping, as I do each morning I open up, that somehow Frankie will reappear.

Sometimes I dream about him, the electric shock of his kiss, or in the edges of awareness when I wake I have some semblance on my lips of a sentence I'd just uttered to him.

In May, Charlie announces he wants to be a chef. He enrols in cookery school and takes up his 'mature' apprenticeship at Fortune. He quickly becomes a blessing in the kitchen and Serge champions him beautifully.

Later that month, Maia and Leith have their baby, a little girl called Rose. I briefly wonder if the universe, with whom I am currently at odds, will finish me off by reincarnating Frankie as Leith's daughter, but so far the coast seems to be clear. After many a consultation with Julia I decide to visit the new bub in hospital and be gracious by wishing her parents well. Maia seems happy to see me. Leith is using the corner of a rattle to get something out from between his teeth. We exchange pleasantries and then he moves off to 'make a call'.

Maia and Leith's new restaurant opens with the requisite fanfare, but Circa loses a hat; Hugo and I raise a glass of champagne over that.

I have a moment of thinking that Leith has changed. He appears besotted with his bundle of pink flesh – 'my Rose', he calls her. And Maia looks exhausted but happy and relaxed. It isn't until I am heading to the elevators and see him making a play for a very young and attractive doctor with an impressive cleavage that I am reminded that change comes rarely and is earned rather than bestowed.

More time passes. Mum agrees to be exclusive with Serge following a failed threesome with Sandy. Bill tells me he's okay with it too. He's just glad to have Mum as a friend. To my great relief he's not interested in dating Sandy; he draws the line at vegetarians.

I awake each morning clutching my pillow wishing it was Frankie, searching for his smell in everything I cook, hearing his voice as I work in the kitchen. Nothing tastes right, though Serge tells me it's all fine.

Bill and I inherit a dog, Beau, an overgrown chocolate lab pup whose family have moved abroad. Bill and Beau become inseparable . . . except when I'm cooking. I have never seen Bill happier.

Fortune is awarded best new restaurant the following March and there's a party and speeches and Charlie is beginning to design his own menus. Nothing feels real. When I was with Leith,

I would disassociate and get lost in my daydreams as a means of escape. But this is different, this is a bone-aching longing for something the rest of the world has moved on from, a secret – the other half of which has vanished.

Bouillabaisse

Ingredients

½ cup olive oil

2 brown onions, finely chopped

4 garlic cloves, peeled and thinly sliced, plus 1 extra, halved, for rubbing

1 fennel bulb, sliced finely, tops reserved for garnish

2 sprigs each of thyme and basil

2 fresh bay leaves

1 kilogram vine-ripened tomatoes, skinned and seeded

16 large green prawns, peeled but leave tails on and reserve shells

4 fresh Moreton Bay/Balmain bugs, peeled, shells reserved

pinch of saffron threads

¼ cup Pernod

8 thick slices sourdough

400 grams salmon or trout, cut into 3-centimetre pieces

200 grams snapper fillet, cut into 3-centimetre pieces

12 scallops

300 grams mussels, scrubbed and de-bearded

a handful of coarsely torn flat-leaf parsley

Rouille

1 egg yolk

1 garlic clove, finely chopped

1 teaspoon Dijon mustard

1 teaspoon tomato paste

200 millilitres extra-virgin olive oil

Method

Heat half the olive oil in a large saucepan over medium heat, then add the onion, garlic, fennel and herbs, and sauté for 5–7 minutes or until the onion relents and softens. Pump up the heat, add the prawn and bug shells and saffron, and cook, stirring occasionally, for 5–7 minutes or until mixture blushes to pink. Add the tomatoes and 1 litre of water and simmer gently for 25–30 minutes or until infused. Strain through a sieve into a clean large saucepan, pressing down on the solids to extract as much liquid as possible. The harder you press, the more flavours are revealed. Discard the solids. Add the Pernod (take a quick nip for digestive purposes), season to taste, reserve 2 tablespoons for rouille, and keep covered and cosy in a low-temperature oven.

To make the rouille, place the egg yolk, garlic, mustard and tomato paste in a food processor and process until smooth. With the motor running, add the reserved stock and the oil in a thin stream until incorporated and the rouille is thick. Season to taste, and set aside.

Preheat a chargrill over high heat. Drizzle the bread with the remaining olive oil, season of course, and toast, turning once, for 1–2 minutes or until golden. Rub with the cut side of garlic, set aside and keep warm in the cosy oven.

Return the stock to a low simmer and add the salmon or trout, snapper, scallops, bugs and prawns, and cook, stirring occasionally, for 1–2 minutes or until just cooked through. While this is bubbling, place mussels in 2 centimetres of water in a frying pan over high heat, cover and shake at intervals for 3 minutes, until the majority of shells open. Discard those that don't. Season stew to taste and serve hot, scattered with mussels, parsley, a generous spoon of rouille and the grilled sourdough.

Serve with warm memories.

66

Lucy

EVENTUALLY JULIA DEMANDS THAT I RELINQUISH MY COPY OF *The Ghost and Mrs Muir* and attempts another one-woman intervention about the perils, not to mention the boredom, of spending the next fifty years walking up and down a beach, or in and out of a restaurant, waiting to die in the hope that I will be reunited with Frankie and my ageing process is reversed. She's right and I don't mean to be this self-indulgent.

She also reminds me I'm now in the sunset of my thirties and my fertility is about to fall off a cliff, so if children are something I might be interested in I should freeze my eggs. Or even better, find someone else to impregnate them.

'He's gone, Luce, he's never coming back. You have to move on.'

Anyone who has ever felt heartbreak will tell you how useless this advice is.

I never believed there could be a love like I felt for Frankie. I had hoped for it, but I didn't believe it was real. And then the wonder that he reciprocated it. We weren't done.

I look around and see how blessed I am. He is in everything that I create. He is in me. I just wish he were here. Why isn't he here?

Please come back, Frankie.

I search for him everywhere. I become that woman you see at bus stops, cinemas and airports, that woman you pity – alone but unhappily so. Haunted.

I go through a phase of attending psychic readings, intuitive tarot guidance, chakra clearings – all the things I've spent a life-time dismissing. Most are phoney. A few see the magician in the cards, but he's in my past. None of the clairvoyants see Frankie. One tells me I will meet a young Brazilian man and we might begin a rug-importation business. Seriously, what part of my aura was vibrating with *that*?

I spend several holidays alone in Manyana, walking up and down the beach, replaying all the conversations we shared. It's only when I'm alone that I can still be with us. I imagine him lighting the open fire in the little cottage I rent that's just a few streets from the one my grandparents owned. I think of him sharing the shiraz I've opened, reading me an article from the paper that amuses him. Chiding the television set over the nightly news. Making something decadent for breakfast. The two of us heading back to bed.

And I know that going on in this imaginary life is as destruc-tive as remaining in a bad relationship, but what is there to do? As Emily Dickinson taught me from her lonely life: 'The heart wants what it wants – or else it does not care.'

At Polly and Charlie's housewarming, Lana proposes what she says is the perfect solution to my imaginary love woes. I brace myself to be told to join an online dating site as Julia has been urging me to do, but I am pleasantly surprised when Lana, flushed with enthusiasm, announces her idea.

'Write a cookbook,' she says. 'They're the hottest thing right now. Bugger Leith and his Christmas special, make yours about Fortune and Frankie and your own recipes too. It'll rock.' She downs the rest of her glass of champagne with a panache reserved for the inspired, the fulfilled, and those with a good nose for a great bubbly. She has recently started dating a fetching underwater cinematographer and has spent a lot of time diving in the sea of love. She's glowing.

Polly, sitting with us, proclaims the idea 'totally hot' and then expands: 'Go to all the places Frankie told you about and find your own recipes there. Who knows, you might meet someone – or not . . . Whatever, just go and get out of here for a while. If Frankie shows up, I'll call you.'

'Ha,' I say, but I feel a ripple of distant excitement.

A month later and book deal in place, I'm at the airport bidding Sara, Serge, Julia and Bill farewell. I have the itinerary for the perfect trip: LA, New York, across to London, Paris, the south of France, Barcelona, India, Bali and then home.

As always I search for his face in all the faces I see. The old woman sitting next to me on the plane who sucks on peppermints, snores and wheezes. The man at customs who welcomes me to America while making me feel I could be cuffed and carted away at any time. The sweet servers at the taco stand Frankie wrote about that is now a five-star, celebrity-owned restaurant.

Occasionally I feel I'm close. At sunset on Malibu pier while taking my first bite of a peach and burrata salad. At the Santa Monica seafood markets, while sampling Half Moon Bay oysters. In New York while sitting at the bar in Soho at Frankie's favourite restaurant, Balthazar, eating steak with pommes frites followed by their legendary profiteroles filled with ice-cream, just as good as Frankie told me they would be.

As I search through the Borough markets in London for the perfect prosciutto, or sit in a bistro in St Germaine with a simple roll, brie and glass of red, I imagine what he would say, where we would wander, what we would do. New recipes emerge gently in the mornings on foreign shores and I write them in our red book, beside Frankie's.

The book of recipes fills up. My life takes on more shape as I return and publish, return and cook. I celebrate Polly and Charlie's wedding; at the reception I dance with Helen. I become a godmother once again the following year when Polly gives birth to a baby boy, Louis Francis. Polly begins a dissertation likening childbirth to a new dimension in quantum physics. Bill has gout, followed by pneumonia, but pulls through; Beau remains by his side. Serge proposes to Mum five times before she reluctantly accepts. She asks Bill to give her away, which somehow tickles the perversity in them both.

My new life has a shape that the outward eye would find pleasing: a career I love passionately, a patchwork family of inter-esting souls who gather together frequently, godmother duties for Attica and Lou – I love this little boy, but again I don't think he is Frankie reincarnated, though perhaps that's something I won't know for a time. And if he is, by the time he comes of age I will be the dear old aunt he takes to the opera for Seniors Week.

I write two more cookbooks based on my yearly travels; it seems my main thread to Frankie. I am supposed to say I date, but I don't. Despite the pleas and quizzing from friends, that part of my life remains with Frankie, and no one else is welcome there. My passion is for my food and my recipes now.

Each year I intend to travel a different route, but more often than not I find myself in the same glorious locations Frankie brought to life for me. I hate to admit it to myself, but three years later I am still searching for him. Not overtly now, just in distracted moments.

Following a train trip from Paris to Monaco and summer days swimming in the turquoise waters of the Côte d'Azur, I make my way to the morning markets at St Paul de Vence. I have lunch reservations at La Colombe d'Or, and to fill time I wander between the stalls with their ample trays of berries – raspberries, blackberries, blueberries and gooseberries – on display. I walk up through the stone fruit and happen upon the golden peaches, where I remember Frankie's insistence that they are the best in the world. I will include his recipe for peach crostata in my next book, I think as I amble towards them.

It's then that I hear it.

The booming voice, correcting, challenging and insulting with typical French panache and humour. I can make out just enough of the words – I took a refresher course at Alliance Française but my skills remain rudimentary at best – and from what I understand he is sorting through the fruit looking for six *perfect* peaches. I stand beside him unnoticed and begin my own search through the fruit. I come across what Frankie would have to agree is the perfect peach. I turn and hand it to him. Before our eyes even meet I know it's him. His toasty scent is alive and radiant.

'*Merci*,' he says without looking up.

'You're welcome,' I reply.

He stops. He looks. And looks and looks some more. The rest of the market activity blurs and fades as I look back at him.

Finally, he speaks. 'It's you,' he says in deep resonant French.

I can't speak.

'You found me,' he marvels.

'Yes.' It is the only reply I can manage before I am flooded with tears, both my own and his, and I am lifted into his arms and held with warm, strong flesh and delight. Peaches roll everywhere.

From the tiny bites of French I learn that this market was in one of Frankie's favourite memories, the one he was thinking of when he was zapped. He spent time, though he is unable to measure it, in a place of waiting, determined as he was to come back and find me.

He had had other offers for different bodies. Apparently if you're not looking to incarnate as a newborn and are in possession of extenuating circumstances it gets tricky. One match was for the body of a twenty-five-year-old model who had overdosed and wanted out. I had heard of the demise of the young supermodel several years before. Her lips, her height, her lack of hips had her on billboards worldwide.

'You were offered her?' I ask, stunned. 'The supermodel?'

'Yes, but what would I, what would you and I do? It is still me, but what would you have done? Though to be able to love you as a woman,' he says with that unmistakable twinkle in his eye, 'there may have been some advantages.' Then he smiles his megawatt smile. 'So, I waited, and then – this. No kids, widowed; he wanted to go and find his wife. He offered me this . . . so old, but I took it.'

Frankie indicates his new shell; he's mid-forties, taller than Frankie of old, larger, with a muscular frame, and thick salt and pepper hair going every which way. In short, a complete hunk.

'You know who I am?' he asks expectantly, but I have no idea. 'The man Bjorn in Paris who taught me to live, the artist? His nephew – the one I went fishing with when I stayed here all those years ago – that's my papa! My father is superb, he and his son have never got along better! Wish I could say the same for my mother, she is making me fat, too much mollycoddling, no wonder this guy decided not to stick around, he was harangued to death by his mother. I must still be working off my karma with women. They own a vineyard, it's been in the family for centuries, the same place I stayed so long ago.'

Frankie tells me that Jullian (Frankie's new name, for now) had just had lunch with his mother, a basic *pâté de campagne*, before he said goodbye was about to cross the road and—

'Whooshka!' He indicates his new body. 'But Lucille, it *is* me.' He stares into me with the green twinkling intensity that belongs to Frankie alone.

I know this to be true with every fibre of my being. And the longer I look into his eyes, the more I see through to the man I fell in love with. It is him, finally, with flesh and blood.

'Will it do? I know I'm not as I was . . .' There's that twinkle in his eye again.

I laugh. His ego is firmly in check. Will it do? Will it ever.

Frankie tells me he has only been in his new 'habitat' for a few months, long enough to put on three kilograms and amaze his family and annoy his neighbours with his new zest for life and changed palate. He is causing havoc with the other winemakers. He wanted to come home immediately, but because of the accident he has been banned from travel for six months. He has been trying to learn English, at which he is abysmal. He has been fretting that he would get back and I wouldn't be there. He reminds me he told me to find him in his recipes, and each day he hoped I would come – I point out that I didn't realise he meant literally find him in his recipes.

'What about telephones, what about emails?' I ask.

'You want the grand gesture of our reunion to be that I Tweet you? I ask you to be my friend on the book of faces? Lunacy, Lucille, *non*!'

He starts rambling in a hybrid of French and English, which is fast becoming gibberish. There's only one thing to do. And it has to be done before I explode. I grab his face, and finally, finally, after all the aching and longing and tears, I kiss him, and as our lips meet we merge just as we did that first time in Fortune.

'All okay, then?' He is relieved.

I am ecstatic.

More kissing, our hands tracing each other, and as we walk away he tells me we have to make the crostata immediately. Well, almost immediately.

New recipe ideas begin to fill me. The secret ingredient in all of them is hope.

Together. I see our shadow on the ancient pavement before us – our hands, our hips, our arms touching – and all I can hope is that in many a universe this moment is real, that it is eternal and that we will not be parted again.

Peach Crostata

Ingredients

Pastry
2¾ cups plain flour
½ cup sugar
1½ teaspoons baking powder
½ teaspoon salt
grated zest of 1 lemon
240 grams chilled unsalted butter, chopped
1 whole egg, plus 1 egg yolk
1 teaspoon vanilla extract

Filling
2 cups peeled, pitted and sliced golden fresh juicy peaches
½ cup granulated sugar
2 tablespoons plain flour

Topping
1 egg
1 tablespoon water
coarse sugar to sprinkle

Method
To make the pastry, in a large bowl add the flour, sugar, baking powder, salt and lemon zest, and stir to combine.

Scatter the butter pieces over the flour mixture. Using clean fingertips, ease in the butter until the mixture forms large coarse crumbs the size of blueberries. In a small bowl, whisk and marry the whole egg, egg yolk and vanilla until happily united.

Pour the eggy mixture on top of the flour mixture and stir until the dough is evenly moist and begins to come together. If the mixture seems dry, add 1 teaspoon or so of cold water.

Transfer the dough to a clean floured work surface and divide it into two pieces, one slightly larger than the other. Wrap separately in plastic wrap and refrigerate for at least 45 minutes or overnight.

When you're ready to bake, preheat oven to 180°C.

To make the peachy filling, toss the peach slices, sugar and flour together in a bowl. Set aside to settle and infuse.

On a clean, lightly floured work surface, take charge of your rolling pin and roll out the larger piece of dough into a 30-centimetre round. Position over a tart tin that's slightly smaller than the dough with a removable bottom. Flatten the dough, pressing it gently but knowingly against the bottom and sides of the pan. Trim the edges, leaving a 2-centimetre overhang, which you can fold over against the inside of the rim of the pan like a nice hemline. Pour the peaches into the pastry-lined tart tin, spreading them into an even layer.

Roll out the second piece of dough. Using a knife, cut the round into 10 strips, each 1 centimetre wide.

Arrange half of the strips across the top of the tart, spacing them evenly. Now reverse and place dough strips across the top to form a lattice pattern. If the strips break, perform emergency surgery with a drop of water to patch them together. Press the ends of the strips against the side of the tart shell to seal.

Now to top it off. Whisk together the egg and water in a bowl. Using a pastry brush, gently brush the dough strips with the egg mixture. For some extra sparkle, sprinkle the strips with coarse sugar.

Bake for 45 minutes or until the pastry is golden brown. Transfer to a wire rack, breathe and let crostata cool for 10 minutes before removing the outer ring of the pan and letting the tart cool a tad or completely.

Serve with fresh whipped cream and your own happily ever after.

Acknowledgements

FIRST AND FOREMOST MY DEEPEST THANKS AND GRATITUDE TO Jaki Arthur for being such a champion of my work and for urging and insisting I write this novel. Your fearless ongoing support and your indomitable talents and energy made this adventure possible. Thank you.

Thank you to the wondrous Vanessa Radnidge for loving the manuscript and being such a force of positivity, clarity and grace to work with.

Thank you to my editor, Karen Ward, for your tireless patience and perspicacity.

And the entire Hachette team who have all provided such great encouragement and support.

I would also like to acknowledge the following exceptional people for keeping me sheltered, sated and sane throughout the writing and editing of this book: Antonia Murphy, Emma Jobson, Sarah Smith, Neal Kingston, Kim Lewis, Edwina Hayes, Deb Fryers, Grania Holtsbaum, Dr Robert Hampshire, Ellenor Cox, Joanna Briant, Mel Rogan, Kim O'Brien, Andrew Knight, Gwendolyn Stukely, Jaison, Molly, Coco and Bodhi Morgan, Mark and Stacy Rivett, Sandy Webster, Jacqueline Hughes (Mum), Trudy Johnston and Brad Heydon, Caroline Teague, Marie Burrows, Dr Janice Herbert and Rod Adams, Lulu Fay, Heath Felton, Lorin Adolph and Jonathan Wood.

Finally, this novel was also written in memory of the sublime Tiffany Moulton and the superb James Teague Hampshire, and for the people who love them most.

hachette
AUSTRALIA

If you would like to find out more about Hachette Australia, our authors, upcoming events and new releases you can visit our website, Facebook or follow us on Twitter:

hachette.com.au
twitter.com/HachetteAus
facebook.com/HachetteAustralia

J.D. Barrett is an Australian television writer and script editor with a passion for good food and creating great meals. She has worked on the writing teams for *Love My Way*, *East of Everything*, *Bed of Roses* and *Wonderland*. J.D. lives between Sydney, Byron Bay and Los Angeles. *The Secret Recipe for Second Chances* is her debut novel and she is currently working on her next book.